**"You're safe here," he said. "This is your home now."**

She lifted her face and gazed up at the towering keep. His eyes were drawn unwillingly to her mouth, to those full lips. She took a long breath, just the sound of it an enticement that made no sense. She couldn't be aware she was doing it, driving him mad.

"It's beautiful," she said softly, and her gaze swung back to him. "Proud, and secretive, and so strong."

Her description shocked him with its familiarity. He thought of Castle Wulfere the same way, almost like a woman. *A woman like Lorabelle.*

"You must have missed it all the years that you were gone," she ended.

She could have no idea how deeply true her words were, but he had no desire to discuss it with her.

" 'Tis just a castle," he said, more bluntly than he intended. *And she's just a woman,* he added mentally, his thoughts swerving back to her against his will.

He was lying to himself, of course. She wasn't just a woman. She was like as not his own corner of purgatory, and she confounded him in some deep way that bordered insanity.

Dear Romance Reader,

In July, we launched the Ballad line with four new series, and each month we'll present both new and continuing stories set everywhere from medieval England to the American West—the kind of passionate, romantic stories you love best, written by the most gifted authors. At the back of each book, we'll tell you when you can find subsequent books in the series that have captured your heart.

Debuting this month with a fabulous new series called *The Sword and the Ring,* Suzanne McMinn offers **My Lady Imposter.** The pageantry and adventure of medieval England come vividly to life in the rousing story of one incredible family in an age when men lived and died by the sword and a woman's life might be forever changed by a betrothal ring. Next, Alice Duncan continues *The Dream Maker* series with **Beauty and the Brain,** as an actress hiding her intelligence meets her match in a research assistant who knows everything . . . except about love.

Travel back to Regency England with Joy Reed's romantic *Wishing Well* trilogy. In **Anne's Wish,** a marriage of convenience promises unexpected love—unless a jealous rival comes between the newlyweds. Finally, the third book in Elizabeth Key's charming *Irish Blessing* series reunites childhood companions, but will **Reilly's Pride** stand in the way of a love destined to unite two souls in matrimony?

Kate Duffy
Editorial Director

The Sword and the Ring

# MY LADY IMPOSTER

## Suzanne McMinn

ZEBRA BOOKS
Kensington Publishing Corp.

http://www.zebrabooks.com

*For my parents, Ross and Norma Dye, who passed on to me their passion for books, and for my husband, Gerald, and children, Ross, Weston, and Morgan, who have to live with it!*

ZEBRA BOOKS are published by

Kensington Publishing Corp.
850 Third Avenue
New York, NY 10022

First Printing: May, 2001
10 9 8 7 6 5 4 3 2 1

Printed in the United States of America

# One

England
December, 1349

"I've come for you, my lady."

The knight knelt, head bowed, waiting for her. A white destrier stamped behind him, and beyond, a castle rose out of a swirling mist, glowing as if lit from within the very stone.

She floated, pulled to the knight, who was a stranger—and yet not a stranger at the same time. He lifted his face to gaze up at her as she reached him. He was the most formidably handsome man she had ever seen, and she had waited for him all of her life.

She took his proffered hand, and he rose to gather her against his battle-hewn warrior's body. She tipped her face to meet his and he kissed her, fierce cold and hot together. This coldness and heat raced through her and she felt alive inside, full of something rare and wonderful and completely new.

Something she never thought she'd find, though she'd dreamed. Oh, how she'd dreamed—of this man, of this kiss. Of magic and miracles.

"Wilt thou come with me?" he murmured sweetly against her mouth. "Wilt thou be mine?"

"Saints," Aurelie of Briermeade gasped harshly, the knife clattering to the stone floor of the convent kitchen. She jerked her finger up to her lips and sucked the blood oozing from the wound where she'd sliced herself instead of the bread.

She blinked once, twice, grasping painful reality out of the clinging embrace of sweet fantasy, and remembered that she wasn't alone.

Sister Berenice leaned over a kettle above the fire, intent upon her work. Her worn gray robe drooped down her fragile frame as she stirred the thin cabbage soup that would make their evening meal. It had been just the two of them now for four months, since a few days after Lammas when the pestilence had taken its final victim at the convent, Sister Hildegarde.

*Wilt thou be mine?*

Aurelie squeezed her eyes shut fiercely. She had to stop this hopeless dreaming. She had to stop believing with all her heart and soul that she was destined for some other life, that she didn't have to let the world pass her by because of her poor circumstances.

She had to be practical even though she hated it.

Aurelie opened her eyes and bent to retrieve her knife. Her finger no longer bled though the wound still throbbed, reminding her of her own stupidity.

Knights and white chargers and castles in the mist. When would she ever learn?

*Pound! Pound!*

Startled, she banged her head on the wooden table as she came back up. She grasped the worn, battered edge of it for support as she drew herself to a stand, cocking her ringing ears to listen.

Did the sound come from the convent gate? Could it finally be—

She heard it again. *Pound!*

Fast upon the heels of the renewed sound came a blast of wind that shook the convent's thatched roof. Rain lashed down upon it with abrupt fury. More noise—this time clearly thunder—followed.

A storm! Only a storm.

The accumulated defeat of the past half year pressed down on her, making her chest tight and heavy. She'd merely imagined the sounds of deliverance—much as she'd imagined her knight and his white charger.

She began to slice again. Thunder rolled as the storm continued to rage its arrival. Rain soaked through the thatch, leaking in fat plops through a hole in the roof onto the floor near the table.

Aurelie set down her knife, and retrieved an empty pail to set beneath the leak. She crossed the room toward the fast-spreading puddle.

She heard another sound as the thunder rumbled away into the distance.

*Pound! Pound!*

The pail slipped out of her hand, clattering onto the stone floor. Her head snapped up. Either she was utterly mad, or that pounding really *had* come from the convent gate, after all.

This was not a dream.

"Sister Berenice!"

The older woman startled, her gaze flying to Aurelie.

"Someone's here!" Aurelie rushed to the wooden door of the kitchen and yanked it wide. Outside, the stormy dusk played wildly before her eyes. Rain, wind, and cold slashed inward, wetting the front of her kirtle.

*Pound! Pound! Pound!*

"I'm going to the gate!" Aurelie cried. Retrieving her mantle from a stool near the door, she slipped the thick woolen cloak over her shoulders and quickly tied on her hood.

Sister Berenice dropped to the floor, hands clasped, a prayer of hope on her lips as Aurelie spun around for the door. Outside, the sounds of pounding rose and fell through the howl of wind and the lash of rain. Aurelie ran, uncaring that her mantle and hood were instantly soaked. The mantle flew out behind her in the storm, and her kirtle quickly grew sodden as well, dragging heavily at her stockinged legs as she tore through the rain. She nearly tripped several times as she followed the twisting path between the outbuildings. Wind ripped at her hood until it sailed off her head.

It had been over a month since the merchant had passed by the convent. He had appeared out of nowhere, bedraggled and hungry, filled with tales of the sweep of the pestilence over all England, and of the lawlessness and despair left in its wake. He had sought a night's rest in the convent, and in return had agreed to take their message of need to the abbey at Worcester.

Finally, the help for which they had prayed so long had come!

The fierce pounding continued as Aurelie reached the stout wooden gate. The massive portal vibrated under her touch as she grasped the iron-studded wooden bolt.

She tugged at the bar with cold, fumbling fingers,

relief rushing through her as it released at last. The heavy door flew wide, and her gaze sought eagerly the two men who stood facing her through the storm, the reins of their huge destriers in their hands.

The men were soaked to the skin, their hooded mantles pressed against their heads. Dark eyes glinted back at her from faces dripping with rain. A crack of lightning and a whip of the wind clearly revealed worn leather body defenses beneath their sodden cloaks.

Aurelie stared at the men, breathless and stunned, her drenched, tangled hair sticking to her cheeks. She'd hoped to see servants from the abbey, with provisions—a wagon with food stores, and men to secure the convent until decisions regarding the tiny nunnery's future could be made. But these men looked like knights, poor knights, with naught but their own horses to call their own. As wet and cold and desperate as she.

"We—" The first man shouted, most of his words obliterated by a deafening roll of thunder from the raging pewter sky. "We beg shelter!" he cried again.

Aurelie's heart sagged immediately at the thought of how much food the two men would consume, taking herself and Sister Berenice that much closer to starvation.

*Where was the help from the abbess?*

Not yet having made her vows to the order, Aurelie had never taken part in the work of sheltering travelers at the convent—until the merchant's arrival the month before, when she had assisted Sister Berenice. In the past, when not at study or prayers, Aurelie had been expected to spend her hours toiling in the garden or perfecting her needlework, learning the virtues of work and patience.

Not that she'd achieved much success in either virtue, which had just caused the sisters to shield her even more from the occasional worldly visitors to their secluded convent. She had often secretly watched their comings and goings around the guesthouse. The merchant had been the first man to whom she'd ever been permitted to speak, besides the convent's priest.

But despite her lack of experience with guests, she knew the sisters considered it their duty to take in any who implored a night's lodging—no matter how desperate the convent's food supply. The long, horrible summer had been consumed with the sick and the dying, and the normally abundant convent garden had been too often left untended. They had little to share.

But perhaps, Aurelie dredged up new hope, these knights would agree to take their message of need to the abbess. They could no longer depend on the merchant. Too much time had passed.

"Come!" Aurelie shouted to the men. "Bring your horses to the stable. Hurry!"

She pushed back on the gate, keeping the wind from lashing it shut again and waited as they passed, the sound of their horses' hooves clattering over the stones and mixing with the roar of the storm.

She stepped back from the gate, and the wind blew the massive portal shut with a bang, startling her. Another sheet of lightning ripped overhead, followed by more booms of thunder.

"This way!" Aurelie cried, motioning the men to follow her as she ran, her soggy kirtle clinging stickily to her legs, toward the nearby outbuilding. Her mantle flapped about her shoulders.

The stable was musty and noisy with the torrent of rain pressing down on the thatched roof. Aurelie staggered inside, eager to be out of the elements.

"We have little hay," she apologized as the men led their horses through to the stalls and quickly removed the soaked saddles. The heavy steeds blew moisture out of their noses, shaking their bodies in a convulsion that sent sprays of water scattering around them. "And we have no servants to tend to your horses. Not anymore."

The men shook off their wet hoods, swiping at their rain-streaked faces. They approached Aurelie in the dim stable, the only light being the murky trace of day coming through the open stable door.

Outside, rain continued to beat down upon the flagstones.

Both men were tall and broad of shoulder, both with long, black hair that tangled around their shoulders. She realized as they neared that they resembled one another in what features she could see. They both wore beards that concealed part of their faces, but she could see enough to grasp they were related.

"We will only stay this night," one of them said. "My name is"—he stopped and cleared his throat—"Philip." Nodding to the other man, he said, "And this is my brother, Santon."

Aurelie glanced at Santon, watching as he cast an unreadable look at his brother. Philip's slightly rounder face tensed, and his gaze flicked between his brother and Aurelie.

Santon turned his full attention on Aurelie. His

silvery blue eyes, pale in contrast to his raven dark hair, were hard as his gaze scraped her.

A tingle of alarm crept up her spine, and Aurelie forced herself not to recoil. She suddenly felt very alone with the rain battering down and Sister Berenice so far away on the other side of the nunnery.

She tugged at the corners of her mantle, pulling the material together as closely as she could over the drenched kirtle that plastered to her body, outlining every curve of her breasts and waist and hips.

"What became of your servants?" Santon asked.

"They died." Aurelie took a small step backward.

"The plague?" Santon pressed.

Aurelie nodded.

"Are there any here with the sickness now?" He frowned, and Philip's gaze tightened behind him. They both awaited her answer tensely.

"No, no," Aurelie assured him quickly. "Not for several months."

She swallowed tightly, still uncomfortable beneath the knights' watchful eyes. She wanted to run outside, into the storm, back to Sister Berenice. She didn't want to be alone with these knights. They weren't like the merchant, who had been kindly, fatherly, reminding her of their priest.

These men didn't remind her of the priest. Not at all.

Already, she wished it were morning so that they would be gone.

"We passed through the village," Philip said. "It was deserted."

"Those who didn't die, fled," Aurelie explained, knowing only too well what the men would have seen in the nearby village of Briermeade. The cottages languished vacant, their doors swinging wide. Hens and pigs had scattered to the woods. In the fields, the harvest had rotted for want of workmen, and the cows had starved in the cold pastures.

Aurelie and Sister Berenice had known for some time that no help would come from the village, and they had little recourse to help themselves. The poor convent's own horses had sickened and died in early summer, but even if they hadn't, Aurelie knew Sister Berenice would have refused to leave their small but precious trove of relics and manuscripts unattended to seek out help.

"And the convent?" Santon took another step toward Aurelie as he spoke.

Thunder crashed outside, and she jumped, her heart slamming against the wall of her chest. She lifted a slightly shaking hand to push back the damp, curling tendrils that fell forward onto her cheeks. Santon's pale eyes seemed to follow her every movement.

"We're desperate," she said plainly. "Our food stores have grown low. If you stay here tonight, we ask in return only that you carry our message of need to the abbey at Worcester."

"Worcester." Philip nodded to his brother. "We are traveling south."

Aurelie's gaze shifted to Santon. He merely shrugged, leaving Aurelie unsatisfied. Their lives depended on this message.

"Please," she began, but stopped at Philip's interjection.

"We'll take your message," the knight agreed.

Santon didn't comment, his cold, narrowed eyes

never leaving Aurelie's face. "How many are left in the convent?"

Outside, the rain lessened, but the sky grew darker as night approached. Shadows filled the stable.

What use was there to lie? Aurelie wondered. Before the night was over, they would clearly see the truth.

"Two," she admitted reluctantly. "There are two of us."

The knights exchanged glances.

" 'Twill be dark soon," Aurelie rushed on, eager to return to the security of Sister Berenice's presence. "And our guesthouse is not prepared."

She backed toward the open stable door, thankful that the storm's fierce bluster had abated to steady rain. She continued quickly, "I'll tell Sister Berenice of your arrival. If you'll join us in the refectory after you've tended your horses—"

She explained the location of the convent's dining hall with a few directions, pointing to the dim pathway leading into the cloister.

Aurelie hurried back out into the rain, pulling belatedly at her sodden hood as she tried to cover her already wet hair. She rushed, head bowed to the rain, down the flagged pathway into the cloister. From there, she ran first into the dark, unlit nun's dormitory, through the maze of vaulted corridors. She found her way by knowing touch to the tiny, windowless cell that was her own. Thrusting her soaked mantle from her, she spread it haphazardly in the darkness over a stool to dry and shed her saturated kirtle and stockings.

From a small chest, she plucked another kirtle and new hose. The small cell contained few items. Only a chest for her meager clothing, a stool, a pallet for her bed, and a scratchy woolen blanket for cover.

Another pallet lay across the narrow room, abandoned.

The cell was Aurelie's alone now, without Lorabelle. Lady Lorabelle of Sperling, brought to the convent by her father to be educated by the nuns until she reached marriageable age, was dead.

And dead, too, was the hope that one day when Lorabelle's bold knight came for her and swept her off to his castle to be his bride, she would take Aurelie with her. And that maybe, just maybe, Aurelie would find a bold knight of her own. The love she had dreamed of all of her life.

In her mind's eye, crouched there in the darkness with her hand on the latch of the chest, she could see him again as she had so many times in her dreams. He would be tall and handsome, his powerful body fashioned by years of fighting, his face chiseled with honor. Strong and invincible, yet kind and courtly and in all ways wonderful.

A hot tear splatted onto her hand, and she realized she was crying. *Idiot.*

She dropped the chest lid and scrambled to her feet, swiping impatiently at the tears she would never have let anyone else see. Who was she to dream of love? She would be lucky—*lucky!*—if she were allowed to live out her life in the convent of Briermeade. The alternative could be worse, much worse.

Abandoned at the convent gate, the good sisters had taken in the babe she had been out of charity, and she had endured the strict convent life with just enough obedience amidst her small rebellions to keep her position secure. She knew she was merely tolerated out of pious mercy—and that the goodwill under which she sheltered could be withdrawn at any time, especially as she grew older.

She dreaded living out her life trapped inside the walls of the convent. And she dreaded even more the very real possibility that the abbess would turn her out. Aurelie, unlike most prospective nuns, had no wealthy family to dower her way into the sisterhood with money, land, and goods.

Her future would be decided by the abbess—soon.

And she tried, very hard, not to be scared. She clenched her hands into fists and steadied the quiver that radiated down her arms. She would survive, she reminded herself fiercely.

Aurelie dressed, slipping back on her soft leather shoes, uncomfortably wet now. Clutching her gown in her fists, she ran again through the dark dormitory, through the connecting buildings to the refectory. A small fire burned in the large fireplace, lending warmth and light to the huge, unadorned hall.

Glowing tallow candles added illumination to one of the long, roughly hewn planked tables. The other table sat empty and dark, a stark reminder of the days when both boards had been filled all round by the nuns of Briermeade. Now, the stools were pushed under the tables, and cobwebs crisscrossed the legs.

Sister Berenice and Aurelie had taken to eating in the kitchen, it being until recently the only room with a fire. The convent's rule disallowed fires until the first of November, and Sister Berenice had held strictly to it. But even if that were not so, neither of them could have borne to eat in the refectory, for it was there that memories of those who had died blazed hottest.

At that moment, Sister Berenice appeared in the doorway between the refectory and the kitchen. Aurelie rushed across the hall to the older woman.

"They are knights—two of them. They're not from the abbess!" Aurelie watched Sister Berenice's face fall, and rushed ahead to offer solace. "But I've asked them to take our message to Worcester."

She could see Sister Berenice assimilating the new information, disappointment warring with hope in her old eyes.

"They've agreed?" the nun asked.

Aurelie recalled Sir Santon's shrug. She would write out their message tonight and give it to Sir Philip. And then she would pray.

"Yes," she said firmly, reassuring herself as much as Sister Berenice. "They'll take our message."

She had to believe it. They had no other hope left.

# Two

" 'Tis good to be home, is it not?"

The new lord of Wulfere turned his brooding gaze from the moon-washed scene beyond the castle battlements and faced his friend. Rorke of Valmond stood in the chill air of the wall-walk, watching him. The night was heavy with moisture from the evening's storm.

"Aye," Damon allowed, moving away from the crenelated wall of Castle Wulfere.

He felt the cold through his thick tunic and wool mantle. He pulled his hood up about his face.

"If only it were the home I had remembered," he added quietly.

The familiar scene he had found on his late-night walk along the parapet—the deep, glittering river to one side, the small village of Fulbury to the other, the fields beyond and the thick forests in the distance all around—was comforting and unsettling all at once. For five long years, Damon, with his band of knights and men-at-arms, had joined their king in France, fighting at Crecy and Calais, then assisting in the occupation that followed.

He had spent one of those years shackled in iron on a wet stone floor, shivering in the filth and dark-

ness of a French dungeon. It had been the dream of
one day returning to his beloved Castle Wulfere that
had kept him alive.

Yet now that he was here, Castle Wulfere seemed
different. Perhaps it was only that the eyes with which
he viewed his home were different—older, wiser, no
longer colored by youthful gullibility.

"Five years is a long time to be away," Rorke commented.

Damon's jaw tightened. "A lifetime," he murmured. His elation in his homecoming was mixed
with sadness. His ailing father had died before
Damon could reach home. The castle had been left
in the temporary custodianship of Damon's cousin
Julian, who was also Castle Wulfere's chief man-at-
arms.

"This pestilence has effected every village, every
demesne," Rorke said. "Much has changed everywhere."

And much would never be the same, Damon knew.
Rorke's profile, a shadow against shadows, reminded
him of how much more Rorke had lost than Damon.
Damon still had his four young sisters—intractable
as they were. He still had villagers and castlefolk and
farmers. Rorke had lost everything, and had chosen
to stay on at Castle Wulfere, to help his friend rebuild, rather than return to the abandoned shell of
Valmond Castle—where man and beast alike had
either died or deserted in the past year.

Rorke didn't speak of his pain. He just went on, as
he had gone on in France when he'd lost the nobleman's daughter he'd intended to wed—miring him
and Damon in a web of murder, deceit, and treachery
that nearly destroyed them both. Those terrible times

had bound them as close as brothers. Their mutual loyalty was one of the few things Damon could count on now that he'd returned to a home much changed from that which he'd left.

"It's not only the pestilence that has changed Castle Wulfere." Damon moved along the wall-walk toward the gatehouse.

Something almost a smile, but not quite, quirked Rorke's somber mouth. "Your sisters?" he probed.

Damon didn't need clarification of his friend's meaning. Elayna had run away twice—and that just in the few days since his return, sullen and defiant over a betrothal their father had arranged and which Damon had no honorable recourse but to preserve. Damon's other three sisters were no less trouble. If Gwyneth wasn't clashing stick swords with the pages, she was playing bat-and-ball in the mud or tumbling about with the hunting dogs—all in a boy's tunic with her shorn hair. Then there was Lizbet, who vowed she wanted to be a falconer, not a lady, and had to be dragged from the mews daily lest she sleep there. It was only little Marigold who didn't need to be hauled, kicking and screaming, from some inappropriate activity. But that was only because Marigold was ever hiding under a bed or behind a tapestry. His youngest sister hadn't spoken a word to him since his homecoming.

All four of the girls had been too long unsupervised during their father's prolonged illness, and too long without a woman's touch since their mother had died shortly after Marigold's birth.

But his sisters weren't the only puzzle he faced at Castle Wulfere.

They passed a guard pacing out his watch along

the tower walk, and Damon said nothing until they entered the upper tower room, with its spiral staircase leading down into the bailey. He stopped just inside the building, where they were alone.

" 'Tis Julian." Damon searched his friend's eyes intently in the flickering light of a wall torch.

Any hint of humor completely left Rorke's face.

"He isn't glad to see you home." He voiced the reluctant thought hesitating on Damon's tongue.

Damon's meeting with his cousin had been oddly strained. Julian was distant, their reunion, awkward. Julian had changed. But so, Damon knew, had he.

Did he jump at shadows of treachery past, or was the treachery here, now, real?

Damon studied Rorke. "The Julian I knew was always a man of honor."

"But is he still the Julian you knew?" Rorke asked quietly.

The two men's gazes locked for long seconds before Damon turned to descend the steep tower steps. Together, they walked through the dark outer bailey, past the workshops and stables, the mews and the storehouse. They met only dogs and a few guards, the majority of the castle household bedding down soon after dark.

"I leave for Briermeade at dawn," Damon said as they passed through to the inner bailey. "You and Kenric will come with me."

"Lady Lorabelle doesn't know you're coming?"

Damon shook his head. They reached the stone steps leading up into the huge tower building. "Neither does she know of her father's death."

The two men entered the great hall, quiet now with the evening meal cleared and the trestles put away.

Huge hounds lay before the great fireplace, and the last of the servants flittered away into the pantry and buttery along the back wall.

"She's of marriageable age," Damon went on, approaching the fire's warmth. "It's time."

The instability he had come home to only reinforced his decision that the best way to launch his rule of Castle Wulfere was with a wedding, albeit a subdued one in light of the recent grief and misery. His people needed tradition. And his sisters needed a woman's gentling touch. And he—

Damon scowled at the fire. He had little time for the keeping of a wife, and little sentiment for it, either. Whatever sentiment had once dwelt within his soul had been destroyed in that dark dungeon beneath Chateau Blanchefleur. He had a demesne to rebuild—that was all that mattered to him now.

He didn't need a wife, or want one. But his people and his sisters did, so he would take one—the docile, convent-bred bride who awaited him in Briermeade.


Aurelie and Sister Berenice hovered in the doorway between the refectory and the kitchen. Beyond, in the great dining hall, another candlemark passed as the knights sat over their wine, drinking and talking loudly, occasionally banging their cups on the table to demand replenishment.

They had eaten every last drop of the cabbage soup and the entire loaf of bread, and complained when there was no more. As it was, they had left nothing for Sister Berenice and Aurelie.

Sister Berenice had grown more agitated as the evening wore on. "Let us pray this storm passes and nothing hinders them from leaving at first light," the elderly nun whispered.

"All that matters is that they take our message to the abbess," Aurelie reminded her. The knights made her nervous, as well, but her words were intended to calm Sister Berenice—and maybe herself a little, too.

Sir Santon had grabbed at her kirtle the last time she had refilled their cups. He'd tried to pull her into his lap, but she'd darted away and he'd laughed at her as she'd all but run back to the kitchen. She was glad Sister Berenice hadn't been in the refectory then to see it.

"I fear they won't take the message." Sister Berenice voiced aloud the anxiety that nagged at them both. "Did you see how that one"—she nodded to Santon—"tossed our letter to the side? If the other one hadn't picked it back up, I believe he would have thrown it into the fire."

"Sir Philip will take the message to the abbess," Aurelie whispered back. "He seems more . . . kind . . . than the other one."

The nun, her face pinched, continued to watch the two men. They lounged sloppily at the table near the smoldering fire.

The excitement with which Aurelie had greeted sounds of visitors at the gate had withered to trepidation, and she dreaded the long hours till dawn.

Santon banged upon the table again, and Aurelie placed her arm on Sister Berenice's. "I'll take care of it." While she wasn't eager to serve the men herself, she worried about the nun.

Sister Berenice was old and fragile of health, and

the knights were unpredictable. Aurelie took up the jug and crossed the hall.

She poured only a small measure of wine into Santon's cup.

"We have readied the guesthouse for you," Aurelie said, hoping to gently prod the men into leaving the refectory. "There's a fire burning, and we have pallets prepared." She gave them simple directions to reach the guesthouse across the cloister and down another path, near the gate.

"Thank you, Sister." Philip smiled at her with a lopsided, drunken grin.

Aurelie hesitated to correct him. She knew holy sisters were accorded a certain respect, even amongst low curs such as she was beginning to consider these knights.

"What's your name?" Santon pressed, leering at her. His gaze combed over her, slowly and brashly, putting a damper on Aurelie's reliance on these knights' esteem for the sisterhood.

From the corner of her eye, Aurelie saw Sister Berenice hurrying toward them.

Santon stood, lurching slightly on unsteady limbs. Then he moved with surprising swiftness to reach out to caress a lock of Aurelie's hair. Her thick hair was still tangled and wet from the rain.

"Your name?" Santon demanded softly, twisting the lock in his fingers.

She stepped back, and her scalp stung a little as she pulled her hair through his fingers to escape his grip.

"Aurelie," she said, tipping her chin, forcing a bravado she did not feel. But she would not show him weakness. Something about the man made her feel as if he were looking for that, searching for weakness. And that he would pounce on it if he found it.

He licked his thin lips slowly, and his gaze scraped her body, lifting slowly to her face again. She *felt* as if he'd touched her again, even though his meaty hands remained at his sides.

"Aurelie from whence?"

"I've always lived here," she answered briefly. "Since I was a babe."

"Such beautiful hair." He reached again for the still-damp locks.

"Santon."

The man in front of her turned and dropped his arm at the warning tone in his brother's slurred voice.

"Let her be," Philip ordered. He stood, blinking several times as if the concentration of addressing the situation were almost too much for him in his current inebriated state.

Sister Berenice reached Aurelie's side, her aged face a portrait of distress. She reached out and took Aurelie's hand. Aurelie noticed the nun's hand trembled as much as her own.

"Good eve," Sister Berenice dismissed the men, her voice shaking. She wrapped her frail arm about Aurelie's waist and drew her toward the kitchen.

From the doorway, they watched the men stumble out into the cloister, heading toward the guesthouse. The last thing Aurelie saw of Santon was the dark glower he aimed at Sister Berenice, and then the door clanged shut ominously behind them.

"They're gone," Sister Berenice breathed in relief. She moved to clear the refectory table.

"Not yet," Aurelie whispered to herself, remembering Sir Santon's final glower. "They're not gone yet."

* * *

Aurelie fell onto her hard pallet in the dormitory, her body exhausted, her mind worried and awake. She thought of the knights in the guesthouse. There were no locks on the dormitory, and she was glad in that moment that the knights had had so much to drink. Surely they had fallen immediately into unconsciousness, she reassured herself. They would leave come morning. There was no reason for them to linger. It was obvious the convent had little food, and even less comfort, to offer.

Still, simply knowing they were there, inside the convent walls, left her unnerved. She turned her head in the darkness to the other end of the small cell, to the place where Lorabelle had kept her pallet, wishing fiercely her friend were here now.

She missed Lorabelle, their long talks, their easy understanding, their closeness. They'd been inseparable from the start.

Aurelie had been seven when Lorabelle arrived. The two girls were the same age, both with fair skin and golden hair, but that was where the similarities ceased. While Aurelie survived upon the sisters' charity, Lorabelle was the indulged only child of Gilbert of Sperling, one of the wealthiest lords of the realm. He'd placed his motherless daughter in the care and training of the nuns who, in like fashion, had fostered his late wife as a young girl.

This trust had been accompanied, of course, by the settling of a large sum of money that the small convent had greatly needed. And while the abbess in general looked down upon the education of young ladies in the nunneries due to the disruption to order she believed they caused, she had appropriated the lion's share of the endowment for the abbey and quieted her objections.

And Aurelie's world had come alive. She was brought to Lorabelle's classes with the nuns and the priest, as a companion of sorts for the young lady. Together they learned to read and write, embroider and spin.

At night in their cell, Lorabelle regaled Aurelie with memories of castle life. She told stories of feasts and balls, Christmas celebrations and weddings, stylish clothing and hairdressing, jewelry, and scents. Lorabelle knew songs—some silly, some bawdy, and some that neither she nor Aurelie could even begin to understand in their sheltered convent world.

Lord Sperling had sent gifts—and letters. His interests had veered to the wars on the Continent, and his later missives were filled with exciting tidbits of his successes in France. But most thrilling of all, Lorabelle was betrothed to wed Damon of Wulfere and someday would make her home in his castle.

Often they'd fantasized of that day when he would come and sweep Lorabelle away on his white destrier and take her to his shining castle—and Aurelie along with her, for Lorabelle had vowed she would not leave Briermeade without her dearest companion.

Lorabelle had not seen her betrothed since her childhood at Sperling Castle, but she remembered him in great detail, from the strength of his comely features to his dark brown hair and even darker eyes. Kind eyes, she'd vowed. Together, she and Aurelie had embellished those memories, fashioning Lorabelle's knight into the most perfect of men.

Handsome and tall, strong and commanding. Romantic and chivalric. That had been Lorabelle's knight.

And secretly, he had been Aurelie's knight, too, for she had conjured his very twin in her heart. Her own private fantasy. He was everything Lorabelle's knight had been, only he would love Aurelie instead.

Her cheek resting on the cold sheet, Aurelie stared into the blackness of the windowless cell, pressing the pad of her thumb against the gold ring encircling one finger, twisting the band around till she felt the hard rise of the ruby in its center. Her throat tightened with emotion. Lorabelle had given her the ring the day she died, tugging it from her thin finger and pressing it weakly into Aurelie's palm.

Lorabelle's betrothal ring.

She was gone forever, and so should have been Aurelie's dreams. But for a little while, alone in the darkness, she let herself dream again.

A scream woke her.

Aurelie's internal hourglass told her it was time for sunrise prayers, even without the ringing of the bells that had been silent these last months. She listened, but heard nothing more. Nothing but her own harsh breathing, and the drumming in her ears.

*Had she truly heard a cry?*

She'd had nightmares, many of them, in these last months. But this didn't feel like a nightmare. This felt real.

Sitting upright on the pallet, she pushed back the woolen coverlet and reached for her thick, warm kirtle. She pulled it on over the chemise in which she had slept. Grabbing her worn cloak, still damp from the night before, she rushed out into the dormitory, her pulse racing with apprehension.

Sister Berenice was already gone. To the chapel for prayers, she assumed. Had that scream been hers?

Had she fallen?

Or—something worse? Aurelie swallowed thickly, panic swelling up as she thought of the knights.

She had to find Sister Berenice.

Hugging her cloak tight to her body, she raced down the stone steps and out into the cold of the cloister. She pulled the hood up about her face, taking in the deserted courtyard bathed in new morning light. Usually, it was a serene scene.

Today the cloister looked frightening, haunted, far too empty.

She ran, her soft-shoed feet silent over the still-damp stones. Her breaths came sharply, and by the time she reached the whitewashed stone chapel her throat hurt from the chilled air.

The building lay in shadows, the sanctuary lit only by pale rays of dawn streaking through the side windows and over the altar. Aurelie pushed back her hood, struck by the emptiness of the chapel. Not of worshippers—she was accustomed to that by now—but of ornament.

Gone were the rich brass candlesticks, the silver chalices, the old illustrated book of the saints' lives, the treasured sliver of wood from the true cross and the chip of bone from John the Baptist that they always kept in a place of honor—

Aurelie's gaze darted about, confused. She ran forward, then stopped halfway down the narrow aisle. She gasped in shock as she spied a small foot protruding from behind the altar.

Racing ahead again, she found Sister Berenice, her neck crooked at an odd angle, lying still and pale on the stone floor. Dead. She was dead. Aurelie had seen enough death of late to know it instantly.

Her heart hammered sharply in her chest, and her throat closed up so tightly she could scarcely breathe. She staggered back and bumped into something immovable. Something hard.

She jumped and spun around in terror. Sir Santon towered over her.

Aurelie screamed.

# *Three*

"Greetings, sweet Sister," Santon said softly. He reached out and caressed a lock of Aurelie's hair.

Aurelie ducked instinctively from his touch. She took a step away from the knight, then another, willing herself not to run. Not when she was yet so close to him.

Her mind worked wildly for a way out. He was blocking the entry. Behind her lay the altar, the priest's rooms—and a door to the back path.

"You killed Sister Berenice!" she whispered hoarsely, her heart banging so loudly she could scarcely hear anything over the clamor of it.

The knight's face puckered into an apologetic moue that was eerily detached at the same time.

"A necessity, I'm afraid," he murmured, stalking her lazily, as if he had all the time in the world. He reached into his braided belt now and unsheathed a small dagger. The blade shimmered in the cool morning light. "But you—you're different. 'Tis naught to fear for you."

Aurelie bumped up against the altar. Her legs quivered and she felt cold and strange, almost as if her body were not her own. She took a deep breath, prayed, and spun around toward the priest's rooms.

The knight bore down on her from behind, and Aurelie screamed as he snatched at her long hair, tearing her to a tortured stop, his fingers tangling into her curls.

He twisted her around to face him, and she felt the deadly stroke of the dagger against her throat. Terror burst inside her, sick and clammy.

"Where are you going, sweet Sister Aurelie?" he asked, his voice still deceptively soft though his breath came more quickly from the brief exertion.

"Let me go!" she demanded, pushing at his chest, kicking him. She might as well have been trying to kick down a castle wall.

The knight laughed at her for an awful moment, then in a sudden move, he extricated his hand from her hair. Aurelie nearly fell from the abruptness of the release.

She took one stumbling step back, anxious to put any distance she could between herself and Santon. She was afraid to run, afraid he would grab at her again. Inching away slowly, she hoped, prayed, for help. But she knew in her heart there would be none. She had only herself to depend on.

They'd reversed positions, she realized. The way to the chapel entrance lay free.

"Let me go," she urged him again.

She was getting closer, closer, to the door. What she would do once she'd gained the cloister, she had no idea. She only knew she couldn't give up.

She knew the honeycomb of passages beyond, Santon didn't. She could hide.

"You have what you want," she said, forcing a calm she didn't feel into her voice.

"No," he said, his insinuating glance dropping to her breasts. "Not all that I want. Not yet."

Aurelie had no time to run now. No chance to hide. He pounced forward, spinning her in his grasp so that he pressed her back hard against his chest, and with the knife at her throat again, he pushed open her cloak to cup one of her breasts. He fondled it roughly through the thick material of her kirtle.

"Do you like that, sweet Sister?"

He squeezed the soft mound, chuckling when a desperate, hoarse "No!" tore from Aurelie.

"Ah, but you will, sweet Sister," he promised, pinching the tender bud of one breast through the coarse material. "You will."

She bucked and kicked, twisting in his grip. The blade slipped in his hand as he struggled to hold on to her, and she heard him grunt when one of her wild blows connected fiercely with his codpiece. He stumbled back, cursing. She heard the dagger clatter onto the stone floor and she surged forward, but only for a pitiful instant. He roared forward, snatched her back by her hair, and slammed his fist into the side of her face.

Aurelie crumpled to the cold floor, hot tears stinging her eyes, her head ringing. She wanted to stand again, to run, but she couldn't move at all. Through blurry vision, she saw Santon peering down upon her. His angular face was set in a hard scowl.

The pounding of booted feet filled the church, and Philip appeared in the arched chapel entrance. He stopped short, his gaze snapping from Aurelie to his brother.

"What are you doing?" Philip demanded at once, moving toward Aurelie. "Leave her be!"

"Back off!" Santon pushed the other knight away. He nodded toward the rear of the church. "There are more chalices in there, and a silver mazer. Go, get them." His gaze returned to Aurelie. "I'll take care of the sweet sister." One corner of his mouth curled upward. He knelt beside Aurelie, reaching out a finger to skim along her jawline.

He lowered his hot mouth close to her own, adding, "She's beautiful, is she not?"

"Leave the girl alone," Philip warned. "You already murdered one holy sister in this church. Is that not enough?"

"I'm not going to kill her," Santon mused, drawing his finger from her jaw to her cheekbone. "Yet," he added softly.

Aurelie watched the brothers argue, forcing herself to lie perfectly still, her eyes darting everywhere for some way of escape.

She saw none. From the corner of her eye, she spied Sister Berenice. A huge sob welled up in her throat, and she gulped it back painfully.

At that moment, Santon reached down to the hem of her kirtle and thrust the garment up, revealing her slim stockinged calves and pale bare thighs to the cold air of the chapel, and to the view of both men.

"No!" Aurelie shouted, struggling to scramble up and push down on her kirtle at the same time.

"Don't fight me!" Santon grated, and shoved her down, slamming the back of her head onto the unyielding stone.

Pain radiated through Aurelie's entire body. The chapel ceiling spun overhead. She battled for the consciousness to fight as Santon straddled her hips, his knees trapping her arms, his heavy body confining her legs. He reached down between his thighs for her kirtle, grasping it viciously.

Aurelie drew a breath to scream, but stopped in a choked gasp of shock when a sword flashed between them to bear directly down on Santon's throat.

"Damn you, Philip!" Santon snarled, snapping a glare at the man who stood over him.

"Leave her be, I said," Philip warned, his face a mask of tension. "It is enough that one nun is dead, and that we are stealing the church's treasures. You will not rape a holy sister! And you will not kill her. Leave her be, or I swear I will cut open your throat."

Santon glowered at his brother. The sword pressed deeper into the flesh of his neck. He didn't move for several moments, then he looked again at Aurelie.

He released her kirtle and hefted his huge body off of her.

Philip withdrew his sword and lowered it. He looked scared, Aurelie realized with a jolt. As scared as she. And he looked relieved.

Aurelie felt no such relief. The frustrated rage in Santon's eyes made her cold, and terrified.

"Let's get the rest of it," Santon ground out, nodding over his shoulder toward the priest's rooms where the remaining treasure lay. He looked back at her again, still very near.

She recognized the intent in his eyes before he lifted his fist, but knew Philip—behind him and now moving toward the priest's rooms—wasn't even aware of it.

"Fare thee well, sweet Sister," he said in a low voice meant for her alone.

There was no time to cry out, or even to flinch. She barely felt the blow when it came.

Hooves clattered in the still air, ringing out hollowly over the stones and through the empty passages as Damon and his men swept into the convent. The gate stood wide, seconding the desolation he had found as they had ridden through the village.

They rode straight into the cloister before Damon brought his mount to a halt. Rorke arrived beside him, with Kenric.

"I fear we are too late." Damon slid from his horse. He'd seen entire villages wiped out by plague, and feared Briermeade and its small nunnery had met that same fate.

He walked across the cloister, the two knights following. The remainder of his men-at-arms waited, horses stamping in the cold air. He entered the refectory first, and found it empty.

"Search everywhere!" he ordered as he emerged, sending the men scattering.

They began, the empty buildings telling the story. From the dormitory to the chapter-house to the parlor, they combed every room. In the enclosed field behind the church, they found plots in large numbers, many of them new, the grass having not yet grown over the earth.

Damon stamped into the chapel, angry and frustrated as he prepared to search the final building. He had lost Lorabelle! He knew she was not at Sperling Castle, having sent word there first to make certain of her location. Her uncle, the new lord of Sperling, believed Lorabelle to remain at Briermeade. If she was not to be found here, she was indeed dead.

He stopped just inside the door, Rorke and Kenric nearly crashing into him from the suddenness of his halt. Then, just as abruptly, Damon rushed forward.

She lay before the altar, her heavy sun-bright hair splayed around her pale face. Kneeling beside her, he saw the shallow rise and fall of her breasts beneath her gown. Her cloak lay twisted beneath her. He immediately slid his own heavy cloak from his shoulders and draped it over her body to protect her from the chill air, then turned his attention back to her face. He noticed the dark purplish splotches on both cheeks, her forehead, and beneath one eye.

She was slender, soft-looking, and sweet-featured. And some savage, inhuman wretch had beaten her. Damon stared at her, stunned by the depth of his anger. He was so accustomed to feeling nothing that emotion was almost unrecognizable when it came.

"There is another one over here," he heard Rorke speak from behind the altar.

"She's dead," Kenric pronounced, joining Rorke. "Her neck is broken." After another moment, he added, "The church is bare. They've been robbed."

Damon shook himself and left the young woman's side to study the older nun. "Murdered," he murmured. "This morning?" He glanced around the church, noticing the starkness of the altar. "It can't have been long." He exchanged glances with Kenric and Rorke, knowing they were as cognizant as he of the danger of marauding bands of thieves. The pestilence that had ravaged England had left behind it a rampant lawlessness not known in generations.

Returning to the young woman's side, a shaft of

light from the window above the altar sparked red fire on one of her fingers as he knelt beside her. Damon's hand moved to touch the ruby ring encircling her finger, recognition jolting him.

"Lady Lorabelle?" His gaze narrowed, his brow furrowing, as he took in her appearance. Dressed in plain homespun, he had at first assumed her to be one of the nuns. A young novice, perhaps.

But he knew that ring. His father had sent that very ring to Lady Lorabelle of Sperling upon their betrothal. He didn't recall Lorabelle well from their meeting long ago, but he knew the ring. It had been his mother's.

He touched her cheek, her skin like cool silk. The bruises were beginning to mottle and swell along her cheekbones and below her eye. As he touched her face, he felt again that rush of anger, but this time with it came something else, an emotion that confounded him even more—because it wasn't anger. It was something that felt almost like . . . *need.*

But that was illogical. How could he need this helpless woman? She needed *him,* and his people needed her. He, Damon of Wulfere, needed no one.

Rising, he spoke quickly to Kenric and Rorke, directing the arrangements for the elderly nun. She would have to be buried without the aid of a priest. It was clear from the evidence of the cemetery behind the church that of late many had died without benefit of holy sacraments in the convent at Briermeade.

Kenric and Rorke dispatched, Damon returned to the young woman, lifted her head onto his lap, and called out her name.

\* \* \*

*"Lady Lorabelle?"*

She heard a man's voice echoing off the stone walls surrounding them, filtering through an odd ringing in her ears.

Opening her eyes, she lifted her lashes slowly, blinking against the light streaming through the side windows of the stone building. Her head pounded, and fuzzy vision met her attempt at sight.

A dark form peered down upon her. A hand touched her face.

"Lady Lorabelle?" she heard again.

Closing her eyes, she sought retreat and solace from the relentless pain. She felt lost, alone, somehow disconnected from her own body. A strange, awful dizziness spun through her. She recalled knights, cruel knights. She remembered terror and pain—

She bolted upright, her eyes flashing open again. New agony shot into her temples and she collapsed backward, onto something firm and warm.

"Easy, Lady Lorabelle. You're going to be all right now."

She blinked several more times. The ceiling of the chapel came slowly into focus, and closer, she saw that the form peering down at her was a man.

He was calling her Lorabelle. Her thoughts spun about wildly, her senses scrambling for some foothold in reason.

The man was thoroughly fearsome. His features were harsh, all planes and forbidding angles—but for the slightly crooked nose and the thin, ghastly scar that sliced across one sun-bronzed cheek all the way down from his temple to his cheekbone, then twisting back behind his ear, where it disappeared into thick brown hair. His huge body was clothed in a white sherte and black tunic covered by a thin hauberk of interlaced rings, but it was his eyes that compelled her, pulled her back. His eyes were dark yet somehow alive with light—and at the same time shadowed with something she couldn't read.

A memory slipped through her mind, an enchanted tale Lorabelle used to repeat of a bespelled prince trapped within the body of a beast, and for an instant it seemed as if that prince were he, and then she blinked, and the memory slipped away and she saw that he was just a man, a most terrible, fearsome man.

Still dazed, she stared up at him, battling to place what was happening, who he was, why he was calling her Lorabelle.

He was a knight! They were back! Or had they indeed left? She attempted to scramble up then, her will to survive outpacing the agony ripping through her head at the too-quick movement.

They were back, and they had brought more knights!

"No!" She fought to her feet, faltering, reaching to the pews for support. The cloak she hadn't even realized was draped over her fell to the floor.

The knight rose up before her, and his height was enormous. He was even more terrifying than the ones who had come before him.

"No!" she cried again, stumbling into a run, her heart pummeling madly.

"Lady Lorabelle!" the man called out from behind her, his voice registering surprise. He caught her to him as if she were no more than a butterfly. "Lady Lorabelle! Stop!"

"No!" Her breath came in short gasps, terror and

confusion roiling within her. Despite herself, she fell against him, her legs no longer able to support herself, the flight's end inevitable even before it had begun.

He smelled of leather and horses. His chest felt hard beneath her cheek.

Pain sliced through her head, returning with greater force, following her exertion. "Don't hurt me," she whispered.

He drew her away from him and stared down at her. "There's naught to fear. I won't hurt you."

There was a ring of truth to his iron voice, and she wanted to believe his words, cling to them. But his promise evoked an appalling echo in her mind.

*'Tis naught to fear.*

The explosive recall of another dark knight making that same vow shot through the haze of her consciousness, crashing to the surface.

She couldn't escape this knight—she could no longer run, no longer fight. She closed her eyes, awaiting a blow, or worse, his hands upon her breasts or pushing up her kirtle.

But he only lifted her into his arms and carried her to a pew. He set her down, and she opened her eyes, stunned.

"I don't know what has happened here this day, but I'm not here to hurt you," the knight insisted.

She stared at him, responding at last from somewhere deep within her to the knight's clear, steady voice, accepting in that moment that his arrival was somehow separate from the terror that had come before. In his eyes suddenly she saw something stunning, a flicker of gentleness that belied his harsh features.

He reached out and took one of her hands, and touched the ring on her middle finger.

A thread of fire trickled up her arm, a sensation of something unfamiliar and mysterious, something just beyond her ken. She'd never been held by a man, and the mere act of this fearsome man's hand upon hers seemed intimate. She knew that it was unseemly, that she should draw away.

But she couldn't move, and not because she was afraid or because he was preventing her. She realized, vaguely, she didn't want to move. Her thoughts grew only more garbled as the unaccustomed awareness of this strange man rushed over her.

"You're safe now," he said. "You understand?"

She blinked, nodded mutely, and the knight released her hand and raised his eyes to study hers.

"The convent was attacked, robbed?" he probed quietly.

Her mind clicked with disjointed images, echoes of terrible screams. Her own screams, she realized—as Sir Santon towered over her, brutally shoving up her gown. Sir Philip holding his sword to his brother's throat. And Sister Berenice—

"Sister Berenice!" Full recall came upon her, sharp and shocking. "They killed her!"

The knight nodded. "Yes, she's dead." He went on grimly, "The men who killed her—how many were there?"

"Two," she whispered. "Two knights." Her mind swam, and she couldn't think straight. Her head felt as if it were on fire, and the harder she tried to think, the more it hurt.

"It's possible they could be part of a larger band of criminals," the knight was saying. "Knowing the convent to be unprotected, they may decide to return, to search it more completely for valuables. I have good, strong men with me, but we are few. You're in danger here, Lady Lorabelle. I must take you to safety. Without delay."

*Lorabelle?* Dazedly, she remembered then that he'd called her Lorabelle several times already.

"Who—" she began.

He spoke over her. "You don't know who I am."

"No, but—"

"My name is Damon of Wulfere."

He waited. Aurelie's mind raced, stumbling, searching. Something snapped, and her gaze slipped to her hand, to the ring there. Lorabelle's betrothed!

He thought *she* was Lorabelle!

She heard, as if from a great distance, "The pestilence took your father, Lady Lorabelle. He's gone from this world. I'm here to take you to Castle Wulfere, to be my bride."

She felt hot in the cold chapel. The pounding in her head increased tenfold. She opened her mouth to speak, but no words emerged.

Only another second passed before the world went black.

# Four

Her eyes blinked slowly open. Damp, heavy clouds streaked the sky above, hiding the sun. Chill air bit her cheeks, tasting metallic in her mouth.

The ground on which she rested swayed rhythmically beneath her, rocking her against something warm and strong that held her tight and made her feel somehow safe and comforted in a world that wasn't safe, wasn't comforting—although she couldn't remember why.

She was cold, so very cold, and there was a deafening ringing in her ears that seemed to come from inside her head rather than outside. Her eyes began to drift shut as she sought again the succor of oblivion.

"Lady Lorabelle."

A voice parted the vapors in her mind, compelling her. She slid her head toward the sound, toward the warm strength, and stared.

Intensely dark eyes, lit from within as if by some secret fire, gazed down at her from a warrior's visage. The fragile light swirled around him. He looked to her like a magical hero called out from the mist. Called out from years of girlish dreams that sang somewhere deep inside her heart.

She kept staring, comprehending in small, baffling increments that the swaying motion beneath her was a horse, not the ground. And that the warm hardness on which her head rested was the powerful shoulder of this big, strange, magical knight.

Without moving her gaze, she realized that she sat sideways before him, held against his body intimately as they crossed the murky slopes. She should not sit so close to a man, was all she could think. She shouldn't let him hold her. She shouldn't let him take her away with him. It wasn't allowed. The next time the sisters met in the chapter-house, they would chasten her severely for her dishonor.

Yet she didn't move. The sturdy cradle of the man's arms sparked a peculiar longing deep within her, and she turned toward it. She burrowed closer, seeking his warmth, his comfort, the peculiarness of this longing. His heat enfolded her shivering body. She knew she wore her own too-thin cloak—she could feel its familiar scratchiness around her. But she could feel another cloak wrapping her body, too. A huge, thick, rich one—and that still wasn't enough to quell her shuddering.

She wondered if it was sunrise or midday or dusk. The thick lacing of gray clouds bewildered her sense of time and place. Her whole existence seemed focused on the knight who held her in his arms.

Suddenly, she remembered other knights, cruel knights, and she gave a choked half sob of fear and twisted in his arms.

"No, no, easy, my lady. You're safe now," the knight promised, and he held her tighter until she believed him. "I'm taking you home. And I swear you will be safe," he repeated under his harsh breath.

*Home?* She had no home, naught but the convent of Briermeade, and even that was not a true home to call her own.

She knew then that she had to be dreaming, so she closed her eyes and slept. Again and again, the cruel knights tore through her dreams, clawing at her, dragging her into some black nightmare—but every time, the dreamlike knight pulled her back into the light.


Their horses thundered over the bridge, breaking the peaceful twilight. Damon and his men dashed through the village, onward to the castle. It rose in the loamy darkness, towering above them. He heard shouts, and the clang of the portcullis rising to greet him as the watch recognized their lord.

He didn't slow, storming through the gatehouse and outer bailey toward the inner courtyard and keep. He'd woken Lorabelle periodically, pulling her out of the tormented sleep that claimed her and promising her that she would be all right, that she would be safe. And each time she had been more difficult to rouse.

A stablehand ran toward him, alerted by the commotion of his arrival.

"You! Hurry!" he shouted in a hoarse voice that didn't sound like his own. He called for his squire and roared orders at everyone in shouting distance. It seemed to take them a lifetime to respond. His battle-honed destrier knelt at his bidding, and he dismounted with her in his arms.

He took the hall steps in bounds.

\* \* \*

*Heavy hands were everywhere, holding him, tying him. The clang of chains came with them, then the crack of whips, then always, always, the eyes came again. Eyes filled with glittering hatred, eyes that promised Damon pain and took sick pleasure in the giving of it.*

*"Confess!"*

*The dark voice underscored its demand with the agonizing flick of the whip.*

*"Confess, I say to you!"*

*The voice carried through the blood, sweat, and semiconscious nightmares. With practiced skill, Damon gritted his teeth to keep from confessing a lie to spare himself this torture, transported himself to Castle Wulfere in his mind, to the foothold in sanity that had taken him through innumerable nights of torment.*

*"Confess!"*

*Icy-hot pain flew through the air at him again. He heard a disembodied scream. "No!" Endless moments passed before he realized that dead voice was his own. The whip came again and again. He would die if they tore into his flesh one more time. Then he was alone in the deep black Hell— but she was there, Angelette. Always Angelette. "Help me," she whispered into his agony. "Help me, help me, help me—"*

Damon opened his eyes with a choked gasp. His body ached and his chest pounded. Tormented pulsebeats passed as he came aware of where he was. Castle Wulfere. It all came back to him, the nightmare, the horror, and despite the draft of the wintercold room, the fire dying now in the middle of the night, he was covered in sweat, trembling still.

All these months had gone by since he'd walked away from Blanchefleur, and he trembled still. He blinked, battling to rid his waking mind of his nightmare. He concentrated on Lorabelle, who lay sleeping in his bed.

She moaned, and he sat up in his chair. It was the second night since he'd brought her home to Castle Wulfere. She turned toward the sputtering candlelight, revealing the discolored bruises that covered her face. She moaned again, and this time her eyes fluttered. *Would she wake?* There was no physician at Castle Wulfere, and he had none to depend upon other than the maid Eglyntine, whose skill with herbal medicines was well-known among the castle's inhabitants. She'd been his mother's maid and his father's nurse, and he'd called upon her immediately to tend the lady Lorabelle through this time, and to be her maid when she recovered.

When, not if. Her wounds, severe though they were, did not appear mortal. But still she slept, peacefully most of the time, but occasionally—as now—broken by fitful moans and cries that stirred compassion and rage within him. He knew much of nightmares, of pain, and would not wish the same upon anyone. It was those nightmares that compelled him to her side these two nights, to be the one to sit by her bed, to calm her in the night.

There was no logic to it, only need, only something inside him that had to make her feel safe.

She sat up in the bed suddenly, her eyes wide and wild, flailing at air.

"No! No—" she gasped.

He rose quickly to take her shoulders in his arms, hold her until she stopped flailing, her wide, wild eyes staring straight up at him, so clear, so hurt, so vulnerable.

"Don't," she whispered hoarsely.

He swallowed thickly. "I'm not going to hurt you." Yet still she twisted in his arms, and he held her tightly, afraid she would hurt herself. "Lorabelle. It's Damon." He repeated the words over and over, until she calmed, slumping against him. "It's all right," he whispered, stroking her hair. She fell back onto the bed, her eyes closed, her chest still heaving.

She mumbled something he couldn't make out. He took the cloth from the bowl of herbed water and bathed her forehead, gently ministering to her wounded flesh and by the time he stopped, she was asleep again.

Finally, he left her to feed the dying fire, to warm the huge chamber for her. When he finished, he returned to his chair by the bed, but not to sleep.

Pale wands of sunlight slid across the room from the narrow window slits. Aurelie's head ached dully, seeming too heavy to lift from the bolster. She lay still, and her surroundings drew slowly into focus.

She lay in a great bed in the middle of a large, airy chamber. Someone had tied back the bedcurtains with thick, braided gold cords. Beside the bed was a chair, a table, and a stool. A small bowl with some kind of mixture of herbs and water, with a cloth draped to the side, sat on the tabletop. At the end of the bed stood a bench, and in the corner, a chest and a sturdy pole with dark tunics hanging from its arms. Tunics that clearly belonged to a man.

She reared straight up in the bed. Her head swam from the sharp motion, but she compelled her senses to function.

Hazy, semiconscious memories of arriving at a castle pierced her mind. Shadowy images of a great gatehouse perched beside a cliff, dark towers rising above them, horses clattering beneath enormous portcullises, then the sensation of sweeping out into one expansive bailey after another toward a huge, towering keep. Gentle arms had carried her. Then there was nothing else, until now.

She looked down and saw that she wore a chemise, simple but of sheer material. It wasn't her own—yet how it came to be on her body was an unfathomable mystery to her.

Chillbumps rose on the bare skin of her arms despite the crackling warmth emanating from the fire in the massive hearth across the room.

*Where was she? And how long had she been here?*

A knock sounded on the arched wooden door of the chamber. She pulled instinctively, ridiculously, at the soft muslin sheets and warm wool coverlet for the scant protection they offered—protection from what or whom, she didn't know.

The door cracked open. A small-statured, plump, bright-eyed woman appeared in the portal. There was a cup in her hand, a pewter goblet.

"Oh, milady! Ye're awake!"

She spun around and stuck her head back out into the corridor long enough to call for a tray of food. Someone must have been immediately in the vicinity for she didn't have to step all the way out. She turned and shut the door then.

"Aye, ye are much improved this morn, that ye are." The older woman clucked cheerfully as she bustled toward the bed.

Her short, rotund body was clothed in a dress of

coarse linen. Wiry gray hair curled out around her comfortably lined face, escaping the confines of her veil.

" 'Tis God's own grace smiling on ye, milady, that ye have survived so much. The Lord in heaven must have great plans for ye."

When her words of encouragement achieved no response, the woman nodded down at the goblet she held in her pudgy hands. "I have something for ye to drink, Lady Lorabelle. 'Tis a draught to soothe yer pain."

*Lady Lorabelle.*

Aurelie blinked. "What did you call me?"

The maid's brow furrowed. "Lady Lorabelle."

The echo of another voice, deeper, harder, richer in timbre, seared upward in her memory. She remembered a dreamlike knight. He had brought her to this castle, carried her in his arms.

He had called her Lorabelle, too.

She stared down at the ring on her hand. Its ruby-red fire gleamed in the fresh morning light. It felt heavy on her pale, slender finger.

Something inside her brain stretched, searched, and clicked.

A wave of impressions, fragmented memories, washed over her—the convent, the terror of the brutal knights, the murder of Sister Berenice. It was tumultuous and disconnected, real and fantastical all at once.

"Where am I?"

"Why, ye're at Castle Wulfere, milady." The servant watched her with eyes squinty with concern. She set the goblet down on the table by the bed. " 'Tis the home of Damon of Wulfere—and ye're to be his bride."

Aurelie's heart pounded.

Damon of Wulfere. He was the dreamlike knight who had carried her. More hazy spots of memory surfaced. She remembered him here, too—in this chamber, bathing her face with cool, healing cloths, holding her, whispering reassurances in her ear. She remembered tenderness. Or did she remember a dream?

One thing speared through, indisputable. He had possessed a fearsome visage that had made her shiver.

She couldn't bring the two bewildering impressions together. He was hero, and he was beast—how could he be both?

She was overwhelmed by the realization that he believed she was Lorabelle.

"How long have I been here?"

"Ye've been here these two nights past, milady."

*Two nights.* She struggled to breathe. The stone walls of the room closed in on her, and a burning ache shot through her skull.

"My clothes," she whispered hoarsely. She had to dress. She had to leave. She didn't belong here. But she didn't belong in Briermeade anymore—not without Sister Berenice!

She couldn't go back there alone.

A gulp of sorrow at the memory of what had happened to the elderly nun choked her throat, but she pushed it back. *Don't cry,* she warned herself fiercely. She couldn't let herself fall apart. She had to think.

The abbess had ever begrudged her presence at Briermeade, but had shown her mercy all these years nonetheless. Surely she would not forswear her now.

If she would not let Aurelie join the order, she might still let her stay at the abbey for a time, find employ in Worcester. Her mind spun at the prospect. She was woefully inexperienced in the world.

But she would survive. She would do whatever she had to do, but first she had to get to the abbess—before it was too late.

Before the one person left on God's Earth who had any reason to care whether she lived or died thought she had perpetrated this fraud deliberately.

"Where are my clothes?" she repeated, desperate.

The servant watched her with eyes that were squinty with concern in her plump face. "Yer clothes have been taken away to the laundresses, milady. The seamstresses will come to measure and fit ye for new ones. In the meantime, there are gowns in the chest. They belonged to Lord Wulfere's mother. Ye're to wear them till new things can be prepared.

"My name is Eglyntine," she went on. "I am to be yer maid."

There was a soft knock at the door, and she went to it. She returned with a tray of food. She held it out toward Aurelie. "Come now, milady. Ye must be famished."

Aurelie stared at the maid, then at the platter. There was a hunk of bread and a generous wedge of cheese. Her stomach rumbled in reaction.

Eglyntine laughed.

"It seems yer belly speaks for ye, Lady Lorabelle." The maid placed the platter on her lap.

"I have to see Lord Wulfere." Aurelie pushed the platter aside, and climbed off the bed. Her knees buckled and she would have fallen if Eglyntine had not rushed to her side.

"Milady! Ye must stay abed!"

"I must see Lord Wulfere!" Aurelie insisted through gritted teeth, pushing away from Eglyntine to stand on her own feet. Her legs felt unfamiliar, not her own.

"Lady Lorabelle." Eglyntine wrung her fleshy hands. "Drink. Eat. 'Twill nourish yer strength."

Aurelie sucked in a gasp of new pain as she moved past the maid. She sank down at the chest, pulling the lid up. She touched a soft rose-colored samite garment with embroidery and studded gems that rested atop the piles of clothes inside the chest. Never in her life had she seen anything so exquisite, much less donned such a thing. She rummaged beneath it, pushing aside piles of beautiful barrettes, ribbons, and other ornaments to find an ungarnished gold gown that resembled a nicer version of her own plain kirtle.

She had no right, not even to this simplest of gowns. But they had taken her own, she reminded herself. And she had no choice.

"Help me put this on," she ordered, turning to look up at the gaping maid. "Please," she added softly, ashamed at having spoken harshly.

She stood too fast, and pinpricks of black dotted her eyes. She felt herself sway on her feet, and she reached blindly for support, clinging to a tapestry hung from the wall beside her until she steadied.

"Lady Lorabelle, ye aren't fit! Ye must eat. Please, milady."

Aurelie blinked away the dark pinpricks by sheer force of will, and hated to admit the maid was right. Hated to admit any weakness. Nothing scared her like vulnerability. Her entire life had been one exer-

cise after another in vulnerability, and she knew how
to fight it.

"I'm fine," she said, still gripping the gown, "but
perhaps you're right. I should break my fast first."
Moving hurt more than she'd expected, and her legs
felt as if they belonged to someone else. Fragile, as
if they'd break beneath her. She needed strength.
Food wasn't a bad idea. She must not have eaten in
two days. No wonder she felt weak.

She would eat, then she would put on that gown
and, with or without the protesting maid's assistance,
she would find the lord of Wulfere and then—God
help her, she had no idea what then.

# Five

Damon repeated his prayers by rote as he kneeled in the dank coolness of the chapel, his men-at-arms and castle staff crowding in around him to murmur their own. More corporeal matters than the welfare of his soul consumed his mind, but responsibility for his household, especially his intractable sisters, brought him here each morn.

If anyone needed prayers, 'twas his sisters.

Castle Wulfere had been without a priest for months, since Father Lambert had been taken by the pestilence, and the routine of daily prayers had lapsed, only adding to the general lack of discipline.

Glancing sideways, he took note of each of his sisters' dark bowed heads. Their meekness was a sweet falsity.

He could see now that Marigold was sliding down, down, down, and in a minute would likely crawl away to hide if he didn't grab the hem of her gown and hold on to her.

Lizbet's soft boots were dusty with sandy gravel and there was a feather caught in the back of her hair—revealing an illicit early morning visit to the mews.

Gwyneth had a wooden stick hung from a belt at her waist—the better to practice her swordplay.

And under her breath, Elayna was humming a tune performed by the minstrels who had passed through Castle Wulfere a few days before and with whom she'd made her latest getaway attempt.

He would see to it that one of the maids escorted his sisters upstairs to do something ladylike, practice their embroidery or some such. And he said an extra prayer that there was even one maid strong-minded enough to keep them there. But it was his conference with the steward that held his thoughts for the moment.

After breaking his fast and seeing to it that his sisters were forcibly installed in the solar, he proceeded to his first occasion to examine the book of accounts. When he completed his inspection, he turned his gaze to the man sitting across the table.

The thin face of Eudo, the balding steward, held prideful expectation as he awaited his new lord's judgment.

"All goes very well, I believe, milord," Eudo prompted. "As the ledgers attest, we have benefitted from substantial profits and are well prepared for winter. With the many extra fines accrued—"

"Extra fines which will be returned," Damon interrupted.

For a moment, he thought his shocked steward would fall off his chair.

"Mi—milord?" he sputtered. "Surely you don't mean that."

"I mean precisely that, Eudo."

"But milord, it's your duty, your right—"

"It's my duty and my *right*," Damon found himself emphasizing the word *right* as he spoke to the slackjawed servant, "to guard the interests of this demesne as I see fit. And I don't see fit to exact death fines at a time when more than half of the families in the village have suffered loss in the space of a few months."

"But—but 'tis custom, milord." The steward's voice cracked. He cast an imploring look at the man seated beside Damon.

"Cousin," Julian spoke in the measured, overly reasonable tone one employed with a stubborn child, " 'twas I, in my custodial duty, who approved the collection of the death fines. Eudo merely carried out the responsibilities of his office. Now, more than ever, the people's respect must be commanded."

Damon looked at his cousin, gazing into eyes as light as his were dark, yet set in a face he knew to be a striking reflection of his own.

"I will command my people's respect through just and merciful governance," he said, measuring his own words in return, resenting the deference his steward paid to his cousin.

Julian's expression tightened. "As custodian of this castle and its prosperity in your absence, I sought only to pursue its advantage."

Damon knew he walked a fine line between exercising his lordship and placating his cousin's ego. Experience had taught him how easily Julian's pride could be pierced.

He had realized only upon his return that his cousin's custodial care of Castle Wulfere went back more than just these last few months. Damon hadn't realized the extent of his father's infirmity in his final years, and the extent to which he had relied on Julian.

Orphaned as a boy, Julian had been raised with

Damon as if they were brothers. But their status as adults was not, and never would be, equal.

Damon disliked their new roles as superior and subordinate, but he couldn't allow his authority to be undermined.

"I'm grateful, Julian, for your faithful custodianship," he stated. "And I remain grateful for your continuing, steadfast service as Castle Wulfere's chief man-at-arms."

"You know that there are already rumors of freemen making ludicrous demands in the face of the great shortage of workers," Julian dared to press his argument. "There are even reports of serfs abandoning their lords. The surplus in fines collected this autumn will ensure Castle Wulfere's ability to attract labor come spring. It would be ill-considered—"

"I have *well* considered the entire situation, and I will put my trust in a reputation for fairness and justice to hold Castle Wulfere in good stead." Damon prayed he was right in his decision at the same time that he resisted the frustrated urge to rebuke his cousin for continuing to challenge him before the steward. But his relationship with his cousin was uneasy enough without open confrontation, and he would avoid it if he could.

He rose, pointedly closing the discussion before his irritation could boil over.

"Inform me when the fines have been returned," he instructed Eudo.

The steward stood, bobbing and bowing.

Damon nodded to Julian, and strode out of the steward's chamber, through the great hall where maids swept the floors. They scattered at his passage, but he was well accustomed to such reaction, knew full well he terrorized the castle populace with naught but a glance.

He couldn't help it, and didn't try.

He'd seen children cry and bury their faces in their mothers' breasts at his approach. Even grown men had been known to tremble upon facing him. The shocking gash that scarred his face had altered forever how he was greeted—but only Damon knew it was what people didn't see, couldn't see, that had truly changed him.

But it was the scar that kept people at a distance. And that was more than all right with Damon. He liked it this way.

The scar had become more than a badge of torment, it had become a shield.

He stepped outside the hall and drank in several deep, full breaths of the cold, crisp air of the bailey. After days of rain, this morn was proving to be of unusually dry, moderate weather. On what might be the last tolerable day before winter struck in force, the daily life of the castle bustled around him. Stableboys led horses to the smith for shoeing, laundresses dipped tablecloths in the trough for cleaning, maids carried fresh rushes up the stairs to the hall.

He surveyed it all, the tension of the encounter in the steward's chamber easing from his frame as he observed the domestic scene. It was this normalcy, this peace, he had craved during those dark days in France.

His gaze alighted on the narrow window slits in the third floor of the keep. There, in his chamber, his bride had awoken this morn, finally, from that deep, fitful sleep that had claimed her for so long.

He could not take one more night at her side, one

more night when he held her, touched her, soothed her. He should not have done it, for it had broken open a part of him that was better left closed, forever, and he would close it again, now.

It had made no sense—there was naught he could do for her that he hadn't already done. He had perfectly good servants to tend her here. Servants who could have sat by her bedside, reassured her in the night, bathed her face and opened their own hearts to her, not his. His heart was ruined and holding her, bathing her face, tenderly whispering those reassurances to her, had only crushed it that much more.

But he was the one who'd left her so long at Briermeade, and whether it was logical or not, he felt responsible for what had happened. He clenched his fists tightly at his sides.

*It could have been worse.* She'd been attacked, beaten brutally, but there had been no sign that she'd been raped. That relief had been keen. Already, he had men hunting for any trace of the knights who'd defiled the convent at Briermeade and assaulted his bride.

If found, he knew he would have killed them with his bare hands if he'd discovered they'd raped her.

But they hadn't, and so far, they hadn't been found, either. And now his bride had awoken—not just rearing in fitful sleep, but true consciousness. Something to break her fast had been brought to her room. Eglyntine had rushed down to report his bride's condition, as he had ordered.

The crisis was past, and now he had to place his bride in proper perspective. She was safe now, and her recovery was assured. He had spent days preoccupied, attending the training of his men and the holding of court in his great hall with only half his attention.

His men were already looking at him as if he'd lost his mind. And perhaps he had. He was known for his single-minded focus, a focus that a thousand men could not break in battle.

These past few days, it had only taken one woman to break it.

He didn't want to feel anything for this lovely girl he would take to wife. It was easier to feel nothing. He had learned that lesson well at Blanchefleur. Slowly, lash by lash, he had learned to feel nothing— for the beloved father figure who had betrayed him, for the tormentor who had whipped him, for the fellow prisoners whose distant cries could have driven him mad deep in the thick, black nights of that hole beneath Blanchefleur.

But he had not gone mad. Instead, he had gone dead.

To feel again, now, was to risk every bit of strength that had sustained him. It was all he had left, this coiled knot of inner control.

He could not give it up.

His blunt nails were cutting into his palms, and he unclenched his fists when he realized it. Resolutely, he turned his thoughts in a more productive direction. This temperate day would be a perfect opportunity to evaluate his men-at-arms in the practice yard—those who had returned with him from France, and those who were new to him since his arrival home. This time, with the full measure of his attention.

He had barely turned to stride toward the outer bailey when a page burst into the inner courtyard and ran, puffing, across the beaten grass to the hall steps.

"Milord! A message just arrived from Worcester!" The boy timidly held out a parchment.

Damon took the note and unrolled it. He had left several men at Briermeade to secure the convent while others had been ordered first to comb the surrounding countryside for the thieves while the trail was fresh—and then go on to Worcester to inform the abbess of the fate of Briermeade.

His men would have arrived in Worcester yestereve, and they had clearly wasted no time in assessing the situation and sending word back. The thieves had not been found, and his message had arrived too late—for the abbess, and for Briermeade.

"The messenger waits at the gate for word to take back to Worcester," the boy said.

Damon snapped the parchment back into a tight roll and looked at the boy. "Tell them to keep searching."

The young page ran back toward the outer bailey.

"Lord Wulfere."

He pivoted at the unexpected sound of a voice that sparked instant recollection. His heart beat low and hollow in his ears, a mocking reminder that it existed despite the fact that Damon chose to deem it dead.

Gold hair fell around her shoulders in wild abandon, framing sweet features that struck him anew with their enchanting, clear beauty. Her body was small-boned, yet there was something strong, resilient, about her. She was tall for a woman, and she stood with her spine straight and her pale face tilted up at him, her blue eyes uncommonly bright.

Yet for all her spirit, she looked as if her legs might well collapse beneath her. She wore no cloak, and she shuddered in the chilly air, hugging her arms to the soft, gold gown that made her look like an angel.

The maid Eglyntine clattered down the hall steps after her, huffing and holding her heavy skirts up, her face pinched with distress.

Damon pulled off his mantle and quickly tucked it around Lady Lorabelle's delicate shoulders. The weather wasn't nearly so temperate without proper gear, and now he found himself shivering and irritated because of it.

Though he knew what he truly resented was not that he had to give her his cloak but that he had to see her at all. He planned to be an honorable husband to his bride, to provide for her and protect her, and to create an heir with her. He would do his duty—to her, to his forefathers, to the people of his demesne. The duty that he had lived for all those dark months.

But he wanted his focus back. He wanted his dead heart back. He wanted to protect her and forget her all at once, and he knew full well that what he wanted was impossible—but that didn't stop him from wanting it just the same.

"Lady Lorabelle, you should not be about," he said curtly, annoyed because what he felt when he met her gaze was not duty, not protection, and it was far from forgetting her. It was some kind of . . . neediness again. Not her need, but his. And that was naught but foolishness. It was a deep-of-the-night sort of need that he would not allow to face the light of day.

He shook it off with every bit of that inner will of his.

"You've been through much, and you need your rest," he added, feeling awkward and more irritated because of it.

He could sit by her bed, bathe her face, tenderly whisper to her when she was unaware. But she was not unaware now.

Now she was too aware—watching him with such vivid eyes that he could scarcely meet them. There had been something unreal about the nights. He could forgive himself that lapse in will. But not now.

It was too dangerous in the light of day.

He noted the bruises on her skin, concentrating his thoughts. The wounds were still ugly even as they faded, and he couldn't stop himself from reaching out, instinctively skimming his fingertips over the wounds to examine them. She didn't flinch at being touched by a man with a face straight from Hell, as he'd overheard himself described.

He was the one who flinched, not her, dropping his hand back to his side. He turned his scowl on Eglyntine.

"What were you thinking, letting her out of the hall? Can't you see she isn't fully recovered, woman?"

The maid wrung her pudgy hands.

"Milord, she—"

"It wasn't her fault, my lord," Lady Lorabelle interrupted the maid. She clutched at the clasp of his mantle, tugging it closer, still shivering even beneath its protection. "I must see you. There's been a mistake—"

"What you *must* do is return to bed," he spoke over her.

"Nay, I cannot."

"Yes, you can," he retorted, his irritation only growing with her resistance. "You look pale. You're trembling. Hie thee to bed, Lady."

He shot her a frown known to send knights quaking in their mail. He didn't know how to explain to her that as grateful as he was that she was recovering, he'd be even more grateful if she'd do it out of his sight henceforth.

Since he was the one who'd paced around her room the past two nights, he knew that would make little sense even if he could figure out how to express it. But there were several things that weren't making sense since he'd found her at Briermeade, and he couldn't express any of them adequately, so he glowered at her instead.

She didn't move one step back to the hall. She should have been scared of him—but she wasn't.

"I must speak to you," she announced, her voice every bit as sure as her legs were not. She had her chin jutted out at him stubbornly. "I must go to Worcester."

"Worcester," he echoed, puzzled.

"To the abbess," she continued determinedly. "Maybe she'll still let me join the order," she explained. "You see, there's been a mistake. I'm not who you think I am. I'm not your bride."

Damon stared at her. What nonsense was this? Not only was she not as meek as he'd expected, she was daft to boot. She had no business in Worcester—

A thought flashed into his mind. What if she *was* daft? What if that beating had caused some wound to her wits? She certainly didn't look sound, and she wasn't acting like it, either.

But he'd known many men to take powerful blows in battle, and though he'd heard of men losing their senses as a result, he hadn't known any firsthand. Mayhap she'd been daft to start with. Or—

His next thought took him aback.

Was this some scheme to break the betrothal? Mayhap she truly wanted to join the sisterhood. She didn't seem the submissive sort to wed the Church, but what did he know of women's desires? His sister Elayna's litany of ruses to escape her own intended match rose fresh in his mind. Elayna didn't want to join a nunnery, though he wouldn't be surprised if she pulled that one next.

Especially if it worked for Lady Lorabelle.

He narrowed his gaze on her, and was stunned by the bleakness in the shiny depths with which she met him. An unwelcome sense of kinship surged in his chest. He recognized pain and he saw it in his bride.

Nay, more than saw it, he *felt* it. He didn't want to feel her pain.

Damnation, he didn't want to feel his own. And he had a demesne to rebuild. He had no time for figuring out a woman! He'd already spent too much time on her—though he couldn't blame her for that.

She hadn't asked to be attacked, and he still blamed himself for that—so much that he had risked everything by holding on to her for two desperate nights.

Those nights had been a mistake; he knew that now more than ever. Something inside him knew too much of her now. He knew her pain, connected to it too easily. He knew her nightmares.

Those nights were over now, and so should be this connection. But he had a terrible intuition that it was not gone, and if he could have, he would have gladly greeted her desire to return to Worcester, to the abbess, and taken her there this day, himself, to be free of her and of this painful link he felt when he looked at her.

But he couldn't. His people needed a wedding, and his sisters needed . . . He had no idea, but he prayed that this pure bride of his would. She was his only hope. Without her, he would have to do what perhaps his father should have done long ago—send his sisters away, to be fostered. They didn't want to go, he knew that. And despite his better judgment, he didn't want them to go, either.

"What are you talking about?" he demanded.

"I must go to the abbess," she repeated.

"The abbess is dead!"

She went even paler and her face fell. "Dead?" she whispered.

"Dead," he repeated ruthlessly.

Every bit of light went out of Lady Lorabelle's eyes.

# Six

He carried her in, ignoring her protests. She could have walked, but he wouldn't let her.

"I'm fine," she told him, though she knew she was not. The words came instinctively. She was afraid she would never be fine again.

He placed her in a chair by the fire in her room. She shivered uncontrollably despite its warmth. She felt as if she'd never stop shivering. He cursed and tore a blanket off the bed and tucked it around her shoulders, over his cloak, which she still wore.

"Your hands are like ice," he said to her grimly, rubbing them between his. He turned to give curt orders to Eglyntine. "Bring her something warm to drink. Now."

The maid rushed out of the room to do his bidding.

"Damon."

The voice came from the hall and she turned to see a knight she recognized in the open doorway. He was tall, with burnished gold hair and strong features. It clicked in her mind that he had been at the convent. She only remembered snatches of the attack, and the aftermath—of Damon and his men. This man was one of the knights who had accompanied him.

"Rorke." Lord Wulfere straightened.

"There's a peddler at the gate," the knight, Rorke, said. He flicked a glance at her, seeming to measure his words as he continued. "He's heard of your search, and has information he says is urgent to that cause."

Eglyntine puffed back in. Damon took the cup from her and Aurelie let him press it into her hands.

"Drink that," he said grimly, "and I'll be back."

The abbess was dead.

Aurelie willed her hands to steady as she held the cup. Eglyntine, thank God, had gone away.

She needed to think.

Lifting the cup, she took a drink. Whatever was in it, she needed it.

The bouquet of herbs struck her. She knew a little of healing plants from the convent. Tending the gardens and assisting the apothecary had been among her varied assignments. She guessed it might include a syrup of woundwort and poppies. The apothecary at Briermeade had often prescribed a like potion for all manner of pains.

Aurelie had never had need of such, but she prayed it worked. She needed her strength.

Damon's fearsome visage rose in her mind. He was the most shockingly handsome man she'd ever seen, and she'd seen enough of them from hidden perches as they entered the convent guesthouse to know that the lord of Wulfere was something out of the ordinary, that he affected her differently.

But she'd never been touched by any of those men, held by them, carried in their arms. She *had* been touched by Damon of Wulfere, carried in his arms.

She didn't belong in his arms. She didn't belong in his bed, his chamber, or even his castle keep.

She could still go to Worcester—if she could convince Lord Wulfere to take her there. But with the one person at the abbey who cared anything about her dead, she would be simply another beggar.

They would just as likely cast her an end of bread and shut the gates on her as take her in. Winter was nigh upon her, and she could end up alone. At the mercy of men like Sir Santon.

Aurelie gripped the cup in her hands tighter.

*She could beg shelter at Castle Wulfere.* She latched on to the idea. She wasn't without worth—she could sew, cook, launder. Well, she wasn't very good at any of it, but she would manage.

That was it. She just had to explain to Lord Wulfere, again. She'd throw herself on his mercy. Then everything would be all right.

She refused to think about the fact that she wasn't sure there was a speck of mercy in Lord Wulfere's harsh soul. It had taken every ounce of courage she'd earned in the stifling atmosphere of Briermeade to face him on the hall steps.

*And yet had he carried her so gently in his arms? And had he bathed her face while she lay sleeping?* Clouded memories tangled in her mind. She had woken, and he had been there. He'd held her with tenderness, caring. Or had that been part of some misty dream, not real at all?

She heard the sound of a voice, and steeled herself for his return.

Then she realized the voices were outside her chamber, that they had been there all along. Two voices, rising and falling, as if they were pacing outside her door.

She sat very still, listening, thinking she might learn where Lord Wulfere might be, and when she might expect him.

Or just what these men were doing outside her door.

"—daft—" she heard one muffled voice through the thick door.

Aurelie's brow furrowed and she rose, leaving the cloak and blanket behind on the chair, and tiptoed to the door to press her ear against it.

"—damaged her wits, they say," the other said. "Pity, her being the lord's bride and all."

Aurelie's frown deepened. *What?*

"—blows—"

"—addled her brain—"

"That, or she's trying to break the betrothal—"

"He'll likely lock her in the tower if that—"

She couldn't hear the rest of the man's comment, but she heard the other say, "Aye," in agreement and she heard the word "tower" again.

Aurelie blinked. Lord Wulfere thought she was daft—or defiant. And she had the very distinct feeling that those two knights were guarding her—from what? Surely not from someone coming in. . . .

So it had to be from someone going out. From *her* going out. Lord Wulfere was afraid his bride would run away from him!

A bubble of hysteria rose in her throat and she pressed her fingers to her mouth to hold it back. She didn't know if she wanted to laugh or cry, but she was pretty sure if she laughed, she *would* cry, so she held her arms tightly around herself to still the awful trembling that seized her.

If he thought she was daft now, what would he think when she offered to be his laundress? She could end up in Lord Wulfere's tower for who knew how long!

She had no proof that she was *not* Lady Lorabelle of Sperling.

Her gaze swerved to the betrothal ring on her hand. And he had certain proof that she was.

She could explain. She would tell him everything, every detail of her life at Briermeade. There was surely someone, somewhere, at the abbey who would remember there had been an orphan raised at Briermeade.

Or a passerby to the convent, someone who'd stayed at the guesthouse. The merchant who had promised to take word to the abbess—

Where had the merchant been from? She didn't know. He could be on the other side of England by now for all she knew. But no matter, Lord Wulfere might be harsh, but he was not dim-witted. She would explain, and somehow she would make him believe her.

*Or she could not explain.*

She felt as dazed as if a load of stones had dropped atop her head. *She could, quite simply, marry the lord of Wulfere.*

No one would know. They were all dead—all those who would have known the difference between herself and Lorabelle of Sperling. The traveling merchant was long gone, and Sir Santon and Sir Phillip—they were gone, too, were they not?

They were thieves, roving criminals. They would have moved on.

*No one would know.*

Then she snapped out of the moment and horror squeezed her chest. She would have to be truly daft to embark on such a course! She would survive. She would do whatever she had to do—

*You will be safe,* Damon of Wulfere had promised. Could she ever be safe with a man such as he? Half beast, half hero. The knight of dreams and destiny, magic and miracles. She'd waited for him all of her life. *But this man was no dream, and what she was considering was wrong, very wrong.*

She squeezed her eyes tight and prayed in desperate whispers, but she couldn't hear her own words over the memory of his terrible, dark voice.

Then she realized his voice was outside her door—not in her mind. Her breath clogged in her throat. She had just enough time to scramble out of the way before he burst through the portal. Clutching her arms about herself as if they were some protection—from what?—she faced him from the middle of the sunlit room.

Whatever breath she'd been holding, she lost immediately. She fought the desire to leap back. Where would she go?

She tipped her chin and held her ground for dear life.

He paced toward her relentlessly, his face cast in harsh lines. How could he be even larger than she remembered, even taller, broader, more fearsomely beautiful?

There was no sound, not a breath, only the hiss of the lowering fire. And then blunt words, close and low. Her heartbeat thudded over them, but she read them on his lips.

"Lady Lorabelle."

She swallowed very hard, and there was no more time to think. "Yes?"

# Seven

"You should be abed," he said hoarsely, because he knew not what else to say. She faced him from the middle of the room, lovely and proud and hurt. Every time he saw those bruises, he had to close his eyes to control the overpowering and inconceivable emotion that swelled his chest. Anger, but also illogical regret that he hadn't somehow protected her.

And something even beyond that, but he forced himself to open his eyes again and not feel it. He'd lost whatever naive innocence had once allowed him to feel, and the undeniable truth that looking at this woman made his chest ache meant nothing more than the shuddering exhale of a dying body on the battlefield. 'Twas the last gasp of life escaping its earthly shell.

"I'm fine," she said. "Much better. I'm not accustomed to lying abed and I—"

"You don't look fine." She looked beautiful, despite her bruises, but he was doing his best not to notice that, or to remember how light and soft her body had been in his arms when he'd swept her up those hall steps.

He could see how she clutched her arms protectively around her body, protecting herself from—*him*.

There was a part of him that wanted to rail at her that he was her betrothed, that in the eyes of the Church he had every right, even now, to see what that angel-gold gown shrouded, and in fact to bed her if he so desired.

And God help him, he did desire. 'Twas as if she'd bewitched him, like some sweet faery from his dreams. From those hopeless, searing dreams he'd known deep in the blackest nights at Blanchefleur.

Before he'd stopped dreaming or hoping or feeling.

He closed the distance between them and reached out, cupping her chin in his hand. He felt rather than heard the soft intake of her breath, but she didn't shift her eyes from his.

He turned her face just slightly to the light, to catch the glow of the glazed windows. To prove she was no faery, but flesh-and-blood woman. Her skin was fine as silk, warm and delicate beneath his touch.

The want pounded back, fiercer than ever, and he had to fight the urge to crush her to him, sweep her straight to that great bed. It was inevitable; they would share it soon, anyway.

But not this day. She was still hurting, and he was not so despicable yet as to ignore that to satisfy his carnal desires. Because it *was* carnal. It was lust, pure and simple.

It couldn't be more. *He wouldn't let it be more.*

"You look pale," he said curtly. "And you're still trembling."

He dropped his hand back to his side.

Had he felt her tremble? Or himself? He barely recognized his own body all of a sudden. How did this slip of a trivial woman cause his seasoned warrior's body to quiver?

Perhaps she was a faery, after all.

"I'm still cold, that's all," she said, and her clear, light voice sounded hesitant suddenly, as if loath to request a thing from him, as if she had no right. "The fire—"

The fire was dying, he realized. He was at once exasperated and boggled by her seeming hesitance, and it occurred to Damon that she seemed more than one woman—proud and unpretentious, confident and shy.

He wondered again, quite seriously, if her mind had been touched.

"I'll see to it that more wood is sent up," he said abruptly, irritated by the entire plethora of confusing impressions she unfurled inside him. "You should have informed someone of your need. My servants are here to do your bidding."

He would fetch the servants, and then he would hear for himself whether she had suffered some wound to her wits. He had every intention of settling this matter of their marriage, and then he could put it—and her—out of his mind. His duty would be discharged.

For surely 'twas naught more than this unsettled business, this duty—not his bride herself—that distracted him.

And yet even now, he was distracted, bedazzled, by those vulnerable yet unflinching eyes of hers, and the way she both tip-tilted her chin in pride and clutched her arms over her breasts in modesty.

He was living in a dangerous situation, he knew grimly. The desire he felt for this woman defied logic.

Whipping around, he pivoted for the door. He would find a guard and order them to fetch servants and wood.

The sooner he could be done with this matter, the better.


Aurelie let out the breath she hadn't even realized she'd been holding. She'd felt stunned, pinned by his dark gaze—naked, not her body, which was modestly covered in this gold gown that didn't belong to her, but her very soul. She had never seen such eyes, so cold and yet so alive with fire they all but blistered her. They seemed hardened to shut her out, but piercing straight to her deepest heart at the same time.

Relief soaked her now that he was gone, but just as quickly panic stormed back.

The enormity of what she had done overwhelmed her. She was chilled, but she knew that wasn't why she trembled. She heard the low sound of his curt voice in the corridor, and she prayed that it would be Eglyntine who returned, not the man who would be her husband.

*Her husband.*

With little more than a single perilous word, she had set upon a dark, daring course from which she couldn't turn back. She had saved her life, and had put it at more risk than it had ever been before—all at the same time.

She had placed her future, her very life and limbs, in the hands of this fearsome lord, cold and harsh and surely more beast than man.

And now he would be her husband.

She perched on the mattress's thick, padded edge, pulling an extra cover from the foot of it and wrapped herself in it.

A boy scurried in with wood, and if she'd had any doubt that his servants leaped to his bidding, it would have been gone now.

"Leave us," he commanded the boy, and knelt to feed the fire himself.

The boy ran out, and with the loud thunk of the door behind him, Aurelie was alone again with the lord of Wulfere.

She set her feet on the floor. Leaving the blanket behind, she approached the warmth of the now-blazing fire. He rose but didn't turn, yet he must have known she was there.

"There will be no more talk of Worcester." He pivoted to face her.

*She couldn't lose her nerve now.* "No."

"You will not be retiring to a convent," he went on, almost as if she hadn't spoken. Or as if he didn't believe her. " 'Tis not your fate, not what your father wished for you. We are betrothed. You belong to me, and to my people. We will be wed."

"I don't desire to join a convent." At least in that, she could be honest.

"You bid me take you to the abbess," he said, and he took a step toward her. As he closed the gap between them, his expression became clearer—and it was remote and curious at the same time. "It seemed very important to you. If you were not trying to escape this marriage, then why?"

She didn't—couldn't—reply to him.

"Those blows to your head," he began again, then stopped for a long moment filled with nothing but

the crackle of the now-roaring fire and some stormi-
ness in his eyes she couldn't read.

He looked uncertain and unhappy, almost desperately so, and she fought an unexpected urge to reach
out to him, stroke away the harsh lines on his brow.
She longed to offer him comfort, to ease this pain
she saw—nay, *felt*—within him.

It was laughable, of course. There was naught of
tenderness in this severe lord, and she doubted her
comfort would be welcomed. He demanded obedience of his bride, but she had no reason to believe
there was a chance he would demand love or accept
it.

Or that he was even capable of such soft emotion.
And yet there was this longing within her, and it
was so deep and real, it stole her breath.

"Do you recall what happened in the chapel at
Briermeade?" he asked.

She swallowed hard at the memory. "Most of it."
It seemed like a bad dream, as if it had happened to
someone else. There were parts of the attack she
genuinely didn't remember at all. And there were
parts of it she knew she would never forget. *Sir Santon's cruel eyes, his hard hands, his hot breath as he leaned
over her, pushing up her gown—*

"The knights, do you remember their names?"

Aurelie forced her gaze to be steady on him as she
controlled the choking fear her memories wrought.
Sir Santon was gone. It was the lord of Wulfere she
had to fear now.

"No." Her veins hummed with dread as she spoke
the lie, half expecting him to call her on it, to know,
somehow, with that piercing gaze of his.

It was foolishness. He didn't know she wasn't Lorabelle. He didn't know she knew the knights' names, either. And she could never tell him that she knew their names. What if he had men searching for them? What if he found them?

Still, she almost collapsed with relief when he accepted her answer and moved on.

"Do you recall aught else of your life at Briermeade, or before that at Sperling Castle? Do you remember that you were betrothed to me?" He gave her no time to answer between the questions, as if the entire conversation was somehow painful to him and best completed quickly. "Do you know who you are?"

He finally stopped.

"I don't remember everything," she forced herself to say, hating the web of deceit that spun her deeper and deeper into something so dire, and now so deliberate.

*The less he thought she remembered of her past life, the less she would be expected to know—of Sperling, of Lorabelle's family and home.*

"The past is . . . fragmented," she went on. "There are things I don't remember about . . . myself. But I know who I am." She swallowed thickly. "I'm Lorabelle." Guilt slammed into her, but there was no turning back. It was already too late.

She saw something in his gaze. Some flicker of emotion—pity, or something deeper. It was fleeting and mysterious.

"Perhaps your memories will return to you in time," he said now. "However, we will be wed as soon as a priest can be fetched. We have a duty to our people, who have been long without cause to celebrate. Our marriage represents a new beginning for Castle Wulfere, and cannot be long delayed."

He stepped closer, and she found it hard to breathe, hard to think.

"Do you understand?" he asked, as if not quite sure her touched mind followed his words.

But she did understand, so much more than he knew. And she was ashamed and shameless at the same time.

It had been easy, and it had been unplanned. But oh how she wanted this new beginning, too.

"Speak now, if you would protest this marriage."

Her heart clanged a last, frantic warning. "I'll marry you," she whispered in spite of it.

He stared down at her for a long moment, and she saw a struggle within him that she didn't understand, but could no longer resist.

Instinctively, she reached out and touched his arm.

Pain flared bold and bright in his gaze, like a fire leaping to life, and she would have flinched from it herself if he had not turned away from her on his own.

She covered her mouth with her fingers, only realizing then how much they shook, and she knew there was a small, perilous part of herself that wanted so much more a new beginning.

That small, perilous part of herself wanted a dream.

He was gone before the servants had put up the tables from the midday meal. Damon and his men clattered through the shadowed tunnel beneath the portcullis and out again into the new dawn. The home he had longed to never leave again a few days before was the home he couldn't wait to get away from now.

He rode hard, his men forming a close half circle of chainmail and horseflesh at his flanks. His audience with the peddler had given him a lead that couldn't wait. He could have sent his men without him, but he wouldn't—and not because he didn't trust them.

But because he didn't trust himself.

His lovely faery-bride, without so much as the full measure of her own wits, was nigh to robbing him of his—and perhaps much, much more. More than he could bear to lose.

Damon of Wulfere had never run from anything. Till now.

# *Eight*

The rest of the day passed in a fog. She wanted to believe she was fearless, but she wasn't. What she was doing was desperately dangerous, and her mind worked over it again and again, taking her in fatiguing circles.

Eglyntine had pressed herbed draughts upon her relentlessly. They must have contained more than woundwort and poppies, for they brought heavy sleep, stilling the torturous thoughts. The sun pouring in the long narrow windows now hurt her eyes, and she blinked against it as she sat up in the bed, adjusting to the bright day. Morning, she assumed. Time had taken on a strange insignificance.

A sound alerted her that she wasn't alone.

Two pairs of eyes peered up from between the folds of the heavy curtains at the foot of the bed's great frame.

The eyes blinked, and the curtains snapped together.

Aurelie's breath trapped in her lungs and she grabbed protectively at her covers. Then the obvious hit her. They were children. She felt foolish for the instant of panic. Whoever her secret visitors were, they couldn't harm her.

The fabric rustled, as if one pushed another. Loud whispers followed.

"Lackwit!"

"Dolt!"

"You're a dolt!"

Aurelie climbed out of bed noiselessly, slipped around the corner of the bed, and whisked the curtains apart. Three—not two—children dropped their jaws and jumped backward almost onto the bed. Two girls, and a boy.

The littlest girl quickly darted behind the other two, snatching back a bit of curtain to boot. Also clutched in her arms was a well-loved doll, with a painted wooden face and cloth body dressed in a miniature kirtle.

"Hello," Aurelie said, at a complete loss for what else to say. She knew naught of children. She and Lorabelle were the only girls who had lived at Brier-meade during her years there.

The children stared back at her with a curiosity that seemed to equal her own.

"Are you Lady Lorabelle?" the boy asked. He appeared to be the oldest of the three, ten years of age at most. His oldest sister was a year or two younger, she figured. And the little one couldn't have been more than five.

Aurelie swallowed hard. She would have to get used to being called Lorabelle, and a myriad of complicated emotions tangled inside her heart, not the least of which was grief.

She pushed it back into that dark place where she had shoved all the pain of the past months at Brier-meade, those awful months of misery and death that bore no rational explanation. The priest at Briermeade had at first declared the calamity a result of a particularly sinister alignment of the planets, then later proclaimed the world was surely coming to an end. But it had not.

Morn still broke each day, and people went on, no matter how difficult it was to do so in the emptiness of those they'd lost.

Aurelie could do no less. It struck her that with every bit of honor in her soul she owed it to Lorabelle to be the best lady of Wulfere she could be.

Lorabelle deserved no less. And neither did the man behind those depthless eyes who would be her husband.

"Yes," she said, and it all felt so real suddenly. "I'm Lorabelle."

"Are you truly going to marry our brother?" asked the boy.

Of course, Aurelie thought, struck now by how much the children looked like Damon. They were his brother and sisters. And she wondered how she hadn't realized it instantly. They were mere miniatures of him in their features.

Their clear, fair countenances were what his scarred, grim one must once have been. The middle child had long, thick brown hair that fell loose around her shoulders. Her apple cheeks held the kiss of the cold morning air, proving, along with the straw poking out of the back of her hair and her belt and even her gown, that she'd been outside already. So had her brother.

The boy had the same lustrous dark hair, only his was poorly cropped, shorn in clumps—some of which stood straight up from his head. A wooden stick stuck out of his belt, and his boots were wet with fresh mud. More splats of muck speckled his tunic.

He looked more like a stableboy than a son of the castle. They both looked spirited, and she'd wager they were a handful for whoever was in charge of them.

Obviously, they'd escaped their minder this morn already.

"Yes," Aurelie answered the boy. "I am going to wed Lord Wulfere. I didn't even know he had a brother and sisters. What are your names?"

The girl with the straw poking from her hair snorted. "She's not a boy!" she crowed, smacking her sister—not brother!—on the arm. "She's Gwyneth. I'm Lizbet. And that's Marigold." She thumbed over her shoulder. "We have another sister, Elayna. But she had another fight with Damon before he rode away yesterday so she's locked herself in her room. She doesn't want to be betrothed to Lord Harrimore, but Damon won't revoke it."

Gwyneth leaned forward just a bit. "He's mean," she whispered loudly. "Damon, I mean," she clarified. "Lord Harrimore is just old."

Aurelie didn't know how to respond to Gwyneth's comments. She wasn't reassured by the girl's assessment of her brother. She sifted through the information Lizbet had provided instead, coming around in the end to the news that Damon was still gone. He would be back soon, she supposed, since he'd stated their marriage would not be long delayed. But he hadn't told her any more than that, or even that he would be leaving. She'd found out about that from Eglyntine. She knew no more what to make of his absence than she did of the girls before her. Gwyneth with her cropped locks and mud, Lizbet with straw poking from every fold of her clothes, and Marigold—

The little girl had pulled the curtains completely back over herself now.

"Don't hit me," Gwyneth snapped at Lizbet.

"You weren't supposed to bother her," Lizbet said. "She's sick and she's supposed to rest. It's all your fault. She wouldn't have known we were here if you hadn't had to stick your fool-born head out—"

"You're not bothering me," Aurelie broke in before the two could come to blows again.

"Sir Kenric and Sir Beldon will be in trouble with Damon if he finds out we sneaked past them," Lizbet said.

Aurelie had found out that Sir Kenric and Sir Beldon were the two knights posting the watch outside her door. She wasn't sure if her husband-to-be feared it unsafe to leave her unguarded with her confused memories, or if he still suspected she might run away from him.

*Or did he suspect something else altogether?* She couldn't dismiss the possibility that he didn't trust her, that somehow she'd given herself away already.

She was completely unnerved by what she'd done.

"Off with their heads!" Gwyneth made a sweeping arc with her stick sword. "That's what Damon would say if he was here." She looked at Aurelie. "I told you, he's mean."

"You'd be in big trouble if he was here," Lizbet said, crossing her slender arms and glaring at her sister.

"So would you," Gwyneth countered. "Lucky for you, he's gone."

"Lucky for *you*," Lizbet replied heatedly.

"Lucky for *him*," Gwyneth said now, and pulled the stick out of her belt. She jumped to the side, flourishing her makeshift weapon again. "I don't have to do what he says."

Aurelie stepped in again. "Well, it doesn't matter what anyone says. I'm glad to meet you. I'm feeling much better today." And she *did* feel better physically. Her strength was back, and the pounding in her head had settled to a dull yet tolerable ache.

Gwyneth and Lizbet stared back at her, solemn. Aurelie felt the weight of some judgment she didn't understand. Although they fought each other with energy, they appeared unified in some silent test.

Gwyneth stuck her stick sword back in her belt then. "Is it true?" she asked, still staring at her in a measuring way. "Are you mad?"

"Gwyneth!" Lizbet cried. "She's not mad. There's a difference between being mad and being daft." She placed her slender arms akimbo and turned to Aurelie. "Isn't that right?"

Aurelie considered the absurdity of finding herself cast as either mad *or* daft and yet at the same time being called upon to clarify the difference.

"I hope I'm neither mad nor daft," she told the girls, struggling for a way to explain, and feeling ashamed and dirty. She didn't want to lie to these children. "There are some things I can't quite remember, that's all." That much was true. There actually were moments during the attack that were completely clouded to her now—but she knew full well that her words carried a broader implication. *She was surviving*, she reminded herself. But it didn't make her feel better about it. "I hurt my head—"

"Some bad men hit you," Lizbet spoke up.

"Some very bad men," Aurelie agreed. The thought of Sir Santon shot a cold shudder through her body. She forced her mind to shake off his image. "But I'm feeling better now, and you don't have to worry about bad men. You're safe here at Castle Wulfere, aren't you?"

Gwyneth and Lizbet didn't answer, but the littlest girl peeped out from between the bedcurtains again. She hung back, the edge of the bedcurtain kept clutched in her little fingers.

"She doesn't talk," Gwyneth explained.

Before Aurelie could question this revelation, a knock sounded on the door.

"Milady." Eglyntine poked her head in. "Are ye ready to break yer—Oh my goodness!"

The maid glimpsed the children and her round face pinched into a scold, but Aurelie had to bite back a grin as she realized Eglyntine's chiding was not directed at the children.

"Sir Kenric! Sir Beldon! Ye have let these mischievous elves into yer lady's room!"

She went on for several more full minutes in the corridor but Aurelie missed it, distracted by Gwyneth and Lizbet as they dove behind the curtains again with much pushing and conferring of "pea-brain" and "beetle-head" between themselves.

When Eglyntine returned, there was naught but the peeping of three sets of boots beneath the curtains to reveal their continued presence. The maid whipped the curtains back briskly with one hand, balancing a tray of food in the other. "Out with ye," she ordered.

The girls made a run for it. At the last instant,

Marigold looked back, an infathomable expression in those enormous eyes of hers.

Something stirred in Aurelie, and she wanted to do something, she wasn't sure what. Tell the child to stay. Hug her. Comb her wild mop of hair.

See if she could make her smile.

There was something about the girl that reminded her of a skittish cat that had once found a home in the convent kitchen garden. One of the nuns had rescued it from boys in the village of Briermeade who'd been kicking it between them like a ball.

"I hope those imps didn't wake ye, milady," Eglyntine said as the door closed behind the girls.

"No, no, they were fine here, really," Aurelie said, thinking she was probably being overimaginative. But then why didn't Marigold talk? "I enjoyed meeting them," she added. "I suppose their nurse must be looking high and low for them."

"Oh my, no," Eglyntine replied with an exasperated expression. "There's no nurse. No tutor, either. Not since their lady mother passed away." She tsked as she set the tray of food on the table by the fire and took a moment to feed its low flames another piece of wood before approaching Aurelie. "Methinks his lordship has got his hands full with the lot of them now, that he does!"

"Why doesn't Marigold speak?" Aurelie asked, still gazing after the closed door. No nurse. No tutor. No mother. Who took care of those girls?

She heard Eglyntine sigh and glanced back at her. The maid's cheerful face sobered and she shook her head.

"If anyone knows, they haven't told me, milady.

The mite stopped speaking about three months ago, 'tis all I know. She's turned skittish, runs away before anyone can take hold of her. She lets her sisters touch her, that's it."

Aurelie's throat tightened, and she yearned to do something, anything, to help the little girl. It was, she realized, similar to the pang she felt when she looked into the lord of Wulfere's dark, depthless eyes.

What had she gotten herself into? This castle, this family—there were secrets, painful secrets, and she found herself longing to uncover them, heal them.

But that was ridiculous. She had her own painful secrets, didn't she? Her throat tightened more, and she felt confused and lonely, and she missed Lorabelle more than ever.

Eglyntine was regarding her worriedly. "Are ye feeling pain, milady? I can bring ye another draught, if ye wish," she offered.

"No, thank you. I'm fine. Really." Aurelie didn't want more draughts. She didn't want to sleep. She needed her wits about her.

She had to learn all she could about Castle Wulfere.

"I feel quite rested and strong," she assured the maid. "Actually, after I break my fast, I'd like to see the castle—if that's all right."

Eglyntine stared at her as if she'd sprouted a third eye. "Of course it's all right, milady."

Aurelie stared back, realizing her mistake. The lady of this castle didn't need her maid's permission to tour it. Luckily, if Eglyntine thought anything of it, it would simply reinforce the impression that the lord of Wulfere's bride wasn't quite right in the head.

But she needed to be more careful in the future.

"Good," she said, and made an effort to sound more authoritative. "I'd like a bath brought up. After I break my fast, I'll bathe and dress to go downstairs."

# *Nine*

"And here we are at the kitchen, milady," Mistress Betha, the steward's wife, recited as she led the way down a stone-walled passageway that linked the domestic buildings to the castle keep.

The kitchen was timber and thus a fire hazard, which explained the separation of the buildings, Aurelie noted as she continued struggling to build a map in her head of the mazelike plan of Castle Wulfere.

It was Sir Beldon who had fetched Mistress Betha, and he'd accompanied her as they toured. The steward's wife was polite, though she seemed impatient at being distracted from her work. Aurelie had been sore-pressed to keep her mental map straight as they'd taken a circuitous tour of corridors, sweeping into a tower, past room after room, up twisting stairs, along winding corridors to another tower, then back down through the service area and now to the domestic range. It was evident there had been a series of building periods wherein each new addition to the castle had added layer after layer of complexities. She was frankly bewildered at this point, with one corridor after another breaking off in every direction.

She'd made careful note of several things, one of

which was a schoolroom, dusty and unused, and the location of the stables. One, in case she stayed; the other, in case she fled.

Over an hour had been spent being painstakingly dressed and coiffured by Eglyntine. She now wore a green camlet gown with an exquisite pearled belt with buckled leather shoes. Her hair had been pulled back in twists over her ears with silver pins, and covered overall with a fine veil that trailed down her back, held in place with a circlet of more delicate hammered silver.

When Eglyntine had held up a small, circular mirror of glass over metal, Aurelie had looked into the face of a woman she didn't recognize. A woman capable of things she'd never suspected.

The servants had been just starting to break down the tables as she'd arrived belowstairs to begin her tour. She already felt strange within herself, and even stranger still at the way they reacted to her. They'd all immediately curtsied and backed away, disappearing like mice through doors behind the screens in the great hall.

She didn't know whether the servants were daunted by the reports of her lost memory, or if 'twas her soon-to-be status as lady of the castle that created the awkwardness. There hadn't been a lady of Wulfere since Marigold's mother had died soon following her birth.

And perhaps a lady of the castle was not welcome.

There seemed naught for her to do in spite of the fact that the castle was clearly understaffed as a result of the pestilence. She inquired of the steward's wife, but it seemed everything at Castle Wulfere had been taken care of for many years without a lady, and Mistress Betha seemed uneager for intrusion now—perhaps thus the speedy, bewildering tour.

As Aurelie passed down the steps to the kitchen after Mistress Betha, she glimpsed steps going down in another direction. A cold, damp-feeling draft swept her as she came even with the passage and she shivered. Here, the torches that were set everywhere at regular intervals to light the way sputtered and burned low.

"That's the storage basement," Mistress Betha explained. "It goes straight down to the river, where we have a dock to unload supplies. That's why the chill here, milady."

She pushed open the door into the kitchen, and waited for Aurelie to pass through. Inside, heat hit her immediately. A fireplace big enough for a tree trunk covered one wall. A boy used a crank to turn spitted meat over the flames while a young woman stirred something in a huge cauldron with a ladle nearly as long as her arm. Two enormous tables took up the center of the room where a parade of servants worked under the direction of a burly man with an exasperated look about him. He stopped short in the middle of barking orders and stared at her. Glared, more like it. She was interrupting preparations, and it occurred to her that there were more servants in the kitchen than anywhere else.

Were these preparations for the wedding feast? She didn't have the nerve to ask. She didn't want to know. Whenever she thought of the wedding, she felt sick, and so she avoided the entire line of contemplation.

The servants dropped their tasks and sprang to their feet to curtsy at Mistress Betha's introduction. Aurelie felt the weight of her new status. A few days ago, she'd been boiling pottage herself in the con vent kitchen and now she didn't belong in the kitchen at all. In fact, she sensed she was making everyone there extremely uncomfortable.

The warmth of the kitchen felt suddenly stifling and she wondered how she would ever fit in at Castle Wulfere. Its inhabitants were oddly serious and aloof.

"Ye've seen everything, milady," Mistress Betha said, ample arms jabbed on her hips with her fists.

It occurred to Aurelie that perhaps the woman was afraid she would be ousted from her place of signifi cance in the household. The big burly cook stared at her and the servants waited as if unsure whether or not to return to their tasks.

"Thank you," Aurelie answered. "I see that I have You have everything . . . well in hand." She forced a smile.

Mistress Betha turned away and said something to the cook, seemingly content to leave Aurelie to find her own way back to the great hall as she was accom panied by Sir Beldon.

"You there!" Aurelie heard the cook bellow to the boy as she made her way back into the drafty corridor. "Get that spit turning. I want those fowls—"

The kitchen door clanged shut and the cook's voice faded behind them. Aurelie made her way back up the passage they'd just come down, and stopped at the point where it broke off to another passage leading down to the storage basement and river dock.

"We didn't go down there," she said, rubbing her hands over her arms against the chill.

" 'Tisn't a place for you, my lady," Beldon said quickly. "Damp and slippery." He shook his head, frowning fiercely though there was naught else fierce

about him. He was young, not much older than she.
"His lordship wouldn't like it if I let you down there,
scarce recovered as you are," he went on.

"I'd like to see the river," Aurelie said just the
same, and peeked into the corridor. The idea of
goods arriving by boat intrigued her.

The entire castle intrigued her.

Away from the uncomfortable eyes of the steward's
wife and the servants, and alone with the rather
timid, for all his fierce frowning, Sir Beldon, her natural curiosity took over. She felt like a child.

How often had she dreamed of seeing the inside
of a castle? She'd always had an enormous curiosity
about them, and had so many times fantasized about
living in one.

Now she had the chance to explore one firsthand,
not just listen to tales spun late at night from across
the small convent cell she'd shared with Lorabelle.
For a few moments, she forgot her unfamiliar status
in this castle, and merely enjoyed the sense of adventure. If she could, she would have cheerfully lost Beldon and not cared how long it took her to find her
way back to her chamber.

The passage took a sharp turn as she stepped into
it, then immediately began its twisting descent.

"My lady—" Beldon sounded very vexed now. "By
the rood, my lady, have a care on those steps, at
least!" He hurried to catch up with her.

Aurelie placed her hand on the cold stone for support when she almost slipped. Beldon was right; the
steps were slick, and even the wall itself felt moist.

"I'm fine," she called back to him, feeling quite
safe. There were smooth grooves in the wall and her
fingers slid along them, using them for balance. The

wall torches fluttered in the wind that swept up the twisted passage and provided little in the way of illumination.

She only half listened to Beldon's continued grumbling as she felt her way around two more descending turns. Light met her round the next curve, and she smelled the dank tang of river water and heard a thunk—a boat rocking against the stone wall, perhaps.

She almost ran into a tall man at the base of the spiraled steps and stopped short without leaving the passage.

He was dressed in black and was extraordinarily handsome, powerfully built. Beyond him, she saw a ledge and men moving bulging sacks.

She couldn't see the river, and guessed there had to be some sort of drop.

"How now, my lady," the knight said in surprise, and looked past her at Beldon. "What do you here?"

"Sir Julian. This is Lady Lorabelle," Beldon explained hastily. "She wished to see the castle and its environs. I couldn't convince her this wasn't a place fit for ladies."

"I see," the other knight said. "Then I will reassure you, Lady Lorabelle, that Beldon speaks you true. 'Tis naught but a storage dock, and a freezing one at that."

As he spoke, the dark knight—by taking a step up—caused Aurelie to step back in order to avoid finding her nose in his broad chest.

"Let me introduce myself," he went on. "I'm Julian, Damon's cousin."

He had extraordinarily light eyes, she noticed. He looked remarkably like Damon, yet different as well.

It was more than that his cleanly planed face was smooth and unscarred. The difference was in his eyes, his silvery blue eyes that seemed to reflect light but not absorb it—in a weird reverse of Damon's deep, nearly black eyes that seemed to smolder from somewhere deep within.

"Welcome," he said, "to the family."

He put his hand beneath her elbow and ascended the first step, coming alongside her, then taking the next, guided her relentlessly along with him. It was evident Julian was bent upon escorting her in the opposite direction to which she wanted to go.

"Thank you," she said. "But I was curious to see the river—"

"There are better views of the river," Julian interrupted, smoothly tucking his fingers more firmly under her elbow. "Let me direct you." He continued up the steps and she had little recourse but to go along with him unless she wanted to dig in her heels like a mule. "I hope you are much recovered from your ordeal."

"Yes, but—"

"These steps are perilous," he continued. "Too steep, and ever damp from the river air. I would not wish you to be exposed to such a hazard."

They'd reached the top of the stairs, where it joined the main passage.

"I would advise you to try the north tower." Julian nodded over her head to Beldon. " 'Tis the most glorious point in the entire castle to behold the river. You can see the bridge from there as well. Go thee now, my lady. 'Tis quite a sight."

He was looking at her as if she were a bothersome

child for all his chivalrous tone. His smile didn't extend to his silvery eyes.

" 'Twould be a pity were anything to happen to you on these slick steps," he added. "I would be sorepressed to explain it to my cousin, would I not?"

She felt cold suddenly. And quite foolish.

"Of course." She glanced back at Beldon, who appeared relieved. "I appreciate your concern."

The turret chamber of the north tower was evidently an unused room, with odds and ends—spinning wheels, and broken tables and chairs. But Julian was right—the view when she opened the narrow window was breathtaking. From this vantage, she could see where the liquid ribbon of river curved to come alongside the castle. There was a bridge in the distance, beyond the village, and then the land rose sharply on one side as it approached the castle.

She wondered how far the drop was to the river.

Based on the descending corridor toward the domestic buildings, and the spiraling steps down to the storage basement and dock that she hadn't quite reached, she suspected the drop was enormous at its apex. Clearly, Castle Wulfere took complete advantage of its imposing geography.

Snow fell, swirling inside the open window, and flakes dotted the green camlet of her gown. Beldon stepped around her and pulled the window shut.

"You'll catch your death, my lady."

He turned back to her, and the look in his steady eyes suddenly reminded her somehow of Julian's, and her heart beat out a warning. It was more than annoyance. It was animosity.

But just as suddenly, the look changed, and Beldon seemed as friendly as before. She was chilled, that

was all. Her temples throbbed. She was tired from all
the walking and the climbing of stairs so soon after
her ordeal. Her imagination was getting away from
her.

She returned to her room. Eglyntine was there,
tidying up. Aurelie slipped into bed, not even bothering to remove the camlet gown, and closed her
eyes. Eglyntine hummed something light beneath
her breath as she worked, and soothed by her comforting presence, Aurelie slept.

The next two days were overtaken by a procession
of seamstresses who measured and poked and fitted
her for fashions she had never realized existed. The
colors and fabrics of the gowns they created amazed
her. The seamstresses were talkative and she listened
with seeming disinterest while she took in every word,
determined to learn all she could about her new surroundings and its people. Of Damon, they spoke little. He hadn't been home for years—and even before
he left for the Continent, he'd been fostered at a
neighboring lord's castle. It was clear the seamstresses were intimidated by him, so much so that
they didn't even speak of him without whispering.

They spoke of Sir Rorke often, with sighs and
smiles, and Aurelie discovered that there were no ladies about the castle because the many knights in the
garrison were landless, unable to offer anything to a
bride—except for Sir Rorke, who in fact was a lord
in his own right. But whatever the mysterious circumstances of his tenure at Castle Wulfere, it was of little
interest to the seamstresses who spoke instead of the

blue of his eyes, the breadth of his shoulders, the comeliness of his jaw.

He was clearly the object of infatuation at Castle Wulfere.

They were excited about the wedding, too—and about having intricate gowns to create again. The old lord had been ill for a long time before his death, and in grief over the loss of his wife.

Aurelie came away with the impression that Castle Wulfere had been a merry place at one time. It was hard to imagine now. There was nothing merry about the servants or certainly Damon. Eglyntine alone was a cheerful presence, though even she retained a certain distance.

Of Damon's sisters, she saw little. Elayna remained locked in her room, and the other three seemed to vanish each time she spied them, like little ghosts that only she could see. No one else seemed to pay them any mind, and this bothered her. She'd seen something vulnerable and secret in their eyes, and it haunted her in spite of everything.

The idea of getting close to anyone here scared her—especially getting too close to Damon—but she couldn't ignore the pain in his sisters' eyes. They had no parents, and she knew too well how it felt to be an orphan.

They needed supervision, at the very least. They should be studying—reading, writing. The value of education had been instilled deeply in Aurelie at Briermeade, where the nuns took such activities earnestly. She would speak to Damon. Perhaps a new tutor could be brought to the castle for the girls.

Until that time, she had been well-educated at the

convent and she could teach them. The thought shook her—she was making plans, thinking of the future—a future she had no promise would be hers.

# Ten

During the days that followed, Aurelie found she didn't have to worry about getting too close to anyone. No one seemed eager to get close to her.

In the great hall, she felt as if a hundred eyes were on her back each time she entered. All conversation would cease at her approach. She returned to taking meals in her chamber. Everyone was polite, but she felt awkward and very alone.

There was a whispering voice in her heart that told her they knew she didn't belong, would never belong. Somehow, they all knew.

Twas as if the entire castle held its breath, waiting. . . . For what? She was being silly, she told herself. And yet she couldn't shake the uncomfortable feeling, and wasn't sure she should try.

The sun broke through the misty snowfall on the third afternoon after Damon had ridden away. Light shone against the glazed windows, and Aurelie couldn't resist pushing one open. Vast curtain walls, crenelated towers, and mighty ramparts soared against a backdrop of forest and pearl gray sky. Between the castle and the woods, the foreground was dotted with the snow-laden thatched roofs of a village. Open white fields spread out beyond it. She could just glimpse the river from this angle.

She leaned over the sill, inhaling the crisp yet sweet air. From nowhere came a sensation of natural buoyance she barely recognized. It had been so long since she'd felt happiness. Since before the pestilence had come to Briermeade. The feeling surprised her, and saddened her. She hadn't realized till now how she missed being happy.

She'd spent too much time trapped in this chamber, watching servants tiptoe around her—and tiptoeing around them in return. She had to get out of here. She had to find a way to live in this strange, enchanted castle without hiding—or she would surely go mad.

In the courtyard below, she heard a shout. She saw Gwyneth and Lizbet, chasing each other on booted feet. Beyond, soldiers paced the wallwalks far across the outer bailey, but no one paid any heed to the girls.

"Can't catch me!" she heard Gwyneth cry as she darted out of the path of a snowball hurled by Lizbet, whose hood flew back as she ran, scooping up another handful of snow as she dove behind a frozen trough to escape her sister's vengeance.

Without taking the time to second-guess herself, Aurelie pulled the window shut and grabbed her cloak. She pulled her hood over her head, tied it neatly beneath her chin, grabbed her new gloves, and hurried out into the corridor. She headed for the stairs, saw Sir Kenric there, engaged in conversation with another knight, and turned in the opposite direction. Lord Wulfere's knights made her nervous, the way they seemed to—what? Protect her? Watch her? Wait for her to reveal herself? She had no idea.

Not having taken the most direct route out of the hall, she found herself in a circuitous passage that boggled her. Somehow, eventually, she came out behind the screens at the back of the great hall.

A servant charged out of the pantry, carrying a tray of stacked bowls, and almost fell over her. She grabbed the tray, barely saving it from tipping its load.

The hall bustled with the castle populace seeking relief from the cold. She saw groups of knights throwing dice by the fire while others crowded round to watch and make wagers.

Outside, the courtyard was empty. It had taken her too long, she realized, and knew she shouldn't be surprised. Damon's sisters, she had noticed, had a way of evaporating into thin air.

She reached the bottom of the hall steps and stood there for a moment, enjoying the feel of the light, fresh air on her face. She closed her eyes and just breathed in.

The inner courtyard was unusually quiet, though she could hear voices and sounds from the outer bailey, men shouting at each other, and the distant clang of a smith hammering at his forge.

Then she heard another sound, ethereal, almost like the wind, and she opened her eyes. Marigold gasped and stopped short in the middle of the courtyard. Her cheeks flushed bright and her eyes widened. She was unkempt, dirty even, Aurelie realized. Beneath the flapping folds of her cloak, she could see that her kirtle was on backward. How long had it been since the little girl had had a bath, been dressed in clean clothes—and not dressed herself? Her hair poked stringily outside the hood of her cloak, and she looked like a tiny ice statue, she stood so still.

She must have gotten separated from her sisters, Aurelie thought, and she was afraid to run past her. The little girl shifted her gaze, the only thing moving in her tiny face, searching beyond her, no doubt for Gwyneth and Lizbet who seemed to be long gone.

"Hello," Aurelie said softly, afraid to step toward the child. Afraid she'd run. This was the closest she'd come to Marigold in days.

The child stared back at her.

"I'm Lorabelle, Marigold. Remember?"

The girl bit her lip and said nothing.

"It's a beautiful day, isn't it?" Aurelie asked casually. "I saw your sisters playing, and I was hoping to join them."

Marigold continued to watch her with her sad, shining eyes. She was a pretty girl, Aurelie thought. And would be prettier if she smiled.

There was something about the little girl that made her think she hadn't smiled in a long time.

"I love the snow," Aurelie continued conversationally, as if she weren't the only one participating in this particular conversation. "At Briermeade, the sisters made skates from bone, and they would glide around the pond every Christmas, as a special treat. It was the one day a year no one worked."

She smiled, the pleasure of the memory mixing with a certain sadness because she couldn't think of those days at Briermeade without thinking of how they were all gone now.

"Perhaps when the village pond has frozen, I can show you how. Would you like that?"

Marigold didn't respond.

"Want to make snow angels with me?" Aurelie asked, thinking fast. Something inside her drove her to break through the shell of this little girl. There was so much brittle pain on the surface, and she felt it more deeply than she would have expected—or wanted to.

All her resolve not to become too attached to anyone or anything at Castle Wulfere fell apart as she met Marigold's clouded eyes. Something in them pulled her.

Maybe she could do some small bit of good here. It was guilt and shame and madness, but it compelled her.

She plopped down on the snow, and promptly flung herself on her back. Sweeping her arms and legs in arcs, she couldn't help smiling. When had she last engaged in such nonsense?

She knew the answer. A year ago, Christmas.

The final Christmas at Briermeade.

Tears stung her eyes, lingering heavily on her lower lashes. She swiped at them and carefully picked herself up and stepped out of the pattern she'd created.

The little girl watched her with those big solemn eyes of hers.

"Now you make one," Aurelie suggested. For a moment, she was certain the child would run rather than respond, but she surprised her. She bit her lip, avoiding Aurelie's eyes, but she did plop down in the snow, stretch her arms out, and wave her tiny limbs in arcs. When she was done, she jumped up to inspect her work.

Suddenly, she grinned. Aurelie's breath caught.

"What are you doing?" came a voice from behind her, and Aurelie swung around to discover Lizbet and Gwyneth.

"Making snow angels," Aurelie said, and smiled at them. "Want to join us?"

The two older girls seemed to hesitate. They looked at each other, then Aurelie, then flung themselves down in the snow, giggling, waving their arms, racing each other to make the fastest snow angel.

Pretty soon, they were all racing, making circles of snow angels around the courtyard. Maids hustled to and fro on occasion, huddled in their cloaks and hoods, and stablehands and soldiers passed by, but no one paid any attention; they were all too busy hurrying wherever they were going. Aurelie wasn't sure they even realized it was their soon-to-be lady who was sprawling about so madly in the snow.

She felt anonymous for a time, and she took pleasure in the freedom of it.

Marigold never said a word, but her eyes shone with something like delight, and Aurelie sensed she'd made some crack in that dark shell of hers. She was reluctant to push further. There was a part of her that knew the little girl wasn't ready to be pushed further, and a part of her that wasn't sure she *wanted* to push. Marigold touched her, and that was an unsettling thing.

"I'm glad Damon isn't here," Lizbet said when they were all tired, flung back into the snow, too worn out to rise for a minute. "He doesn't want us to play."

"He wants us to work," Gwyneth put in, and she lifted her stick sword in the air above her. "Off with his head!" She flicked her sword in imaginary thrusts and parries.

"He wants us to study Latin and embroider tapestries and learn to be ladies," Lizbet said. She sat up in her snow angel and tugged her hood tighter. "I want to be a falconer. I don't want to learn to sew."

"I'm going to fight battles for the king when I grow up," Gwyneth added. "Like Damon. I don't need to learn to read. I need to learn to fight."

Aurelie sat up, brushing snow from her cloak. She rose, holding a hand out to Marigold. The little girl hesitated, then accepted it. She held it for just a moment, appreciating the tentative familiarity the girl allowed, then let go of it to brush the snow from Marigold's cloak. She could feel the slender fragility of the little girl's shoulders beneath the thick layers of clothing.

"Even a falconer must sew," Aurelie commented casually to Lizbet. "What if your falcon is wounded? Who will tend him?" One of the wealthiest noblewomen who had come to Briermeade had brought a sparrow hawk with her, receiving special dispensation from the abbess to keep it. The noble lady had allowed Aurelie a chance to observe its care on occasion.

She turned to Gwyneth. "Men such as your brother must be able to read, and so must you if you truly wish to be like him. What happens if the king sends important siege plans to you, his trusted commander. What will you do if you can't read them?"

Aurelie avoided pointing out that the chances of two young noblegirls being allowed to become a falconer and a warrior were nonexistent.

Gwyneth and Lizbet stared at her.

"Damon says you're to teach us," Lizbet said after a minute.

Aurelie blinked, the fact that the girls were, if not acquiescing, at least no longer arguing the notion of lessons, superceded by the full impact of Lizbet's words. So the charge of his sisters was yet another reason for the lord of Wulfere's haste to wed.

It seemed there were many reasons the lord of Wulfere needed a wife—and none of them had anything to do with his heart. And of course she'd known that. Marriage among people of Damon's station was a matter of business and convenience, and often of the king's will as well.

There was a hollow ache in her chest.

She knelt, packed a ball of snow in her hand, and shoved away the ridiculous emptiness. Purposefully, she tossed it so that it passed a breath from Gwyneth's ear.

"Oops, I missed," she teased. "But not next time."

Gwyneth's eyes lit up, and she started running, scooping snow at the same time. Lizbet shrieked, and was off, as was Marigold. In seconds, snowballs were flying like missiles from trebuchets. Laughter echoed across the courtyard, and Aurelie realized with a sense of startlement that she was laughing, too. It was at this moment that she became aware of the sound of pounding hooves, muted by thick snow and screams and laughter. Marigold was running, her little cheeks red, her eyes shining, toward the gate that stood open between the inner and outer courtyards. Snowballs crisscrossed the air, and Marigold ran, looking back over her shoulder. A huge destrier appeared in the gateway. Aurelie's heart thundered in her ears.

She lunged straight into the path of the horse, pushing into Marigold, hooves flying mere breaths from their heads.

# *Eleven*

Damon fought to control the powerful destrier, pulling back just in time. The horse tossed, snorted, rearing on its hind legs. Stablehands came running, and men on horseback reined in short behind him.

He felt his heart stop. For a split second before he realized his horse hadn't touched his bride or his sister, he thought he'd killed one or both of them.

Later, he didn't remember dismounting. He only remembered air, bitter in his lungs, and the sharp taste of something else. Panic.

He reached Lorabelle as she struggled to rise and, without thinking, he put his arms around her. She was holding on to Marigold—or Marigold was hanging on to her, and she staggered, half falling again from the burden of the child's weight and her own shock. He grabbed both of them, fierce protectiveness surging inside him. Marigold clung tighter to his bride. Lorabelle looked up at him, her eyes wide and stunned, full of pride and spirit and something that might have been fear.

Her hair grazed his cheek and he felt shaken to the depths of his ruined heart. What was it about her eyes that made him feel as if he looked into his own?

"Are you all right?" he demanded hoarsely, fighting the completely unwelcome rush of recognition. How could he recognize anything in her eyes? It was illogical.

He became acutely aware of his hands on her, of her warmth through the material, her softness, her pliant body. And of how he wanted to pull her closer still.

"I'm fine," she gasped, and she got to her feet, turning to the child. "Marigold," she said softly, and he swallowed, stunned as the sister he'd seen run from everyone buried her face in his bride's breast.

"You saved her life," he said. He could hear men talking, shouting, gathering behind them. "Thank you."

"Thank God she's all right," Lorabelle said, making nothing of the risk she'd taken or his gratitude, still holding Marigold tightly, stroking the girl's wild hair.

Gwyneth and Lizbet stood frozen in their tracks beyond her. They didn't approach him, and he knew better than to try to take Marigold into his arms or to try to comfort any of them.

"We were—" She stopped, took another breath. "We were laughing, playing. We didn't hear you coming. I should have warned her to stay out of the path of the gate. I should have—"

"We should have taken greater care. I'm not accustomed to having children about." He threw a look back at the men who'd ridden in with him, desperate to defend himself against the turmoil he knew must show in his eyes, turmoil he couldn't let anyone see, much less his bride. She wouldn't understand it, and he couldn't explain it other than to put it down to exhaustion. In three nights, he'd barely slept.

"Take these three inside," he ordered. His squire stepped forward reluctantly, taking Gwyneth's hand. Another squire took Lizbet's, and Lorabelle bent to set Marigold down between them. She whispered something to the little girl, and Marigold went acquiescently enough. Gwyneth whacked his squire with her stick sword, though, and the momentary commotion was such a relief that Damon didn't even reprimand her.

When again he was certain his face showed nothing of the turmoil inside him, he returned his attention to his bride.

"What do you here, my lady?" he asked gruffly, ushering her from the gateway, away from the prying eyes and ears of the company of men behind him. "It's bitter cold and you should be in the keep." He sounded like a mother hen, he thought, and felt foolish and frustrated. He took the courtyard in great strides, then stopped short, realizing he was forcing her to almost run to keep up with him. "You're still recovering."

He could see the faint outlines of those bruises, and yet still she was beautiful—full lips, dark gold brows, perfect nose, thick lashes. Dark magic, sweet desire. Hell and heaven, waiting for him here at home.

"I'm perfectly warm in my cloak," she responded argumentatively. "And besides, I'm fine."

"What of your memories?" he asked, changing the track of his thoughts deliberately. He began walking, at a more reasonable pace, toward the keep again. "Have you remembered more of the attack? A name, or even a description?" The search grew bleaker by the day. His men had little to go on, and the peddler's seeming fine lead had turned to dust. His best hope was that his bride would recall something crucial.

There was something frightened and fragile in her eyes then, but it was swiftly gone, covered up somehow. Her gaze was indecipherable again, and he wondered if he had imagined that fear, that fragility.

"I'm sorry," she said, with a slight shake of her head. "Perhaps I'll never remember their names. You were searching for them, for the knights who robbed Briermeade?"

"My men are still searching," he told her. "But I can't spare them much longer, not with winter coming on hard. The trail is cold." He hated to accept defeat in this quest that seemed more hopeless all the time.

He'd learned that the attack at Briermeade hadn't been the first such incident—but rather that there had been a series of robberies and murders in a growing circle encompassing Briermeade, Castle Wulfere, and Worcester.

Lorabelle was lucky to be alive.

There was that something in her eyes again, and he fought his reaction, his desire to pull her into his arms again.

That would be a mistake.

He stopped short at the hall steps and regarded her grimly.

"You're safe here," he said. "This is your home now."

She lifted her face and gazed up at the towering keep. His eyes were drawn unwillingly to her mouth, to those full lips. She took a long breath, just the sound of it an enticement that made no sense. She couldn't be aware she was doing it, driving him mad.

"It's beautiful," she said softly, and her gaze swung back to him. "Proud, and secretive, and so strong."

Her description shocked him with its familiarity. He thought of Castle Wulfere the same way, almost like a woman. *A woman like Lorabelle.*

"You must have missed it all the years that you were gone," she ended.

She could have no idea how deeply true her words were, but he had no desire to discuss it with her.

" 'Tis just a castle," he said, more bluntly than he intended. *And she's just a woman,* he added mentally, his thoughts swerving back to her against his will.

He was lying to himself, of course. She wasn't just a woman. She was like as not his own corner of purgatory.

She said nothing for a long moment, averting her gaze.

"I would speak to you of your sisters," she said. "I understand they have no nurse, no tutor. I would like to take charge of them." She turned her head, slowly, her gaze connecting with his again. "As is what I understand you expected of your wife."

The look in her brilliant eyes of sky was unreadable. Did she expect a declaration of romantic love? There was challenge in her eyes as she faced him. She confounded him in some deep way that bordered on insanity.

"I'm not a sentimental man, my lady," he said harshly. "And this marriage was not set upon for sentimental reasons. I have a duty, and so do you. That doesn't come as a surprise to you."

It was a question, though he didn't pose it as such.

She answered, "No." A smile almost quirked her mouth, but not quite. "That doesn't surprise me." She lifted her chin. "I understand perfectly."

"Do you?" He lifted a brow.

"Of course," she said, still leveling her clear, proud gaze at him. "What more would I want, my lord?"

He stared at her for a long moment, trying to decipher her soft voice—was that bitterness, mockery, meekness? She staggered him, putting the lie to his own words while leaving him baffled as to the truth of hers.

It was unsettling and bothersome. He had no use in his life for such a conundrum, no matter how fair or enthralling the package it came in.

No matter how painfully something inside his chest twisted.

"What more indeed," he said tiredly, exhausted more from the effort of dealing with this enigmatic beauty than from the long hours of riding and nights without sleep. "Very well. I've brought a priest back with me. Prepare yourself. Tonight, we wed."

Their conversation in the courtyard unnerved Aurelie in more ways than one. She had known the lord of Wulfere would not expect love from this marriage, but what had surprised her was the bewildering sense of hurt she'd felt when he had made that very plain.

Oh, she'd hidden it, she knew. But the emotional reaction frightened her just the same.

*What was wrong with her?* She was in no position to allow emotions to run away with her.

The continuing peril of her position had been made plain to her, too.

*He had been searching for the knights from Briermeade.*

She woke every night, seeing that last blow coming toward her, feeling terror sucking the air from her chest. She could see Santon's face, those glittering, cruel eyes.

What if Santon and Philip were found?

Thank God the search would soon be called to a halt, that bitter winter was nigh upon them. The knights would have more time to elude the chase, more time to disappear forever.

Except from her dreams.

From where she stood inside her chamber, she could hear Eglyntine in the corridor ordering a tub and hot water. She opened her eyes to look at the huge curtained bed that had been hers alone this past sennight—but which was not hers at all.

It was his, this fearsome lord's, and tonight they would share it.

There was a knock on the door.

She jumped, her heart in her throat.

It was only Eglyntine, bustling back in with a line of servants. She directed the boys who carried the bath and the buckets, then they quickly left again, except for Eglyntine. Aurelie stood motionless as the maid began untying the laces that bound her newly fashioned blue woolen kirtle.

It was simple, much like her convent dress, and yet of much finer work. But she knew the seamstresses had devoted the bulk of their energies to a purple silk gown, closely fitted at the bustline, with long, wide sleeves and fashionable slits to reveal the ivory underdress they were working on at the same time.

She wondered if they were even finished, fixing her mind on something, anything, that would take her thoughts from the man who awaited her below, from the overwhelming culpability of what she was about to do. She closed her eyes, concentrating on the comforting cleansing, the warm water and gentle hands that scrubbed and soothed.

*Was this really happening, or would she yet awake, find herself alone in her tiny cell, Sister Berenice in the kitchen, stirring their evening pottage?*

"Milady," came a soft voice intruding upon her imaginings.

She opened her eyes to find Eglyntine gazing at her with a look of worry.

"Ye must not fall asleep, milady," she said, her pudgy eyes crinkled. "Yer lord awaits ye in the chapel, and there is much to be done. Ye cannot be late."

Aurelie pulled her knees up to her chest, and nodded, not explaining to the maid that the tension throbbing through her body could not possibly allow sleep. She put her hands over her eyes as Eglyntine lifted the bucket and she felt the water pour down, rinsing her soaped, fragranced hair.

When the maid was done, Aurelie wrapped herself in the large drying sheet she was offered. A fire blazed, but she was colder now than she'd been in the courtyard.

Another maid came in, followed by the seamstresses, and her body was powdered and creamed, her hair combed and woven with purple ribbons. She was primped and poked and pulled as last-minute touches were made to the hastily prepared wedding garments.

At last Eglyntine held up the silver-framed mirror and Aurelie looked down into her own eyes, huge with fear.

"Milady, are you ready?"

# Twelve

Every man, woman and child of Castle Wulfere and its tiny village of Fulbury who could squeeze into the courtyard of the keep were there to stand witness to their vows, with even more crowded onto the wall-walks.

Aurelie shivered, not so much from the cold wind that blew up to the chapel door where they stood but from the unnerving enormity of what was too late to stop.

"I charge thee by the Father, and the Son, and the Holy Ghost, that if any of you know any cause why these persons may not be lawfully joined together in matrimony, he do now confess it," the priest intoned.

His flat, somber voice thinned, carried off by the bitter breeze.

"Damon of Wulfere, wilt thou have this woman to be thy wedded wife, wilt thou love her, and honor her, keep her and guard her, in health and in sickness, as a husband should a wife, and forsaking all others on account of her, keep thee only unto her, so long as ye both shall live?"

"I will."

She stole a glance at the lord of Wulfere's harsh profile. From this side, she couldn't see the scar that

ravaged his face, and he was breathtakingly handsome. The lines around his eyes told of years spent
squinting into the sun. Brackets framed his mouth,
but they held no memory of smiles—instead, they
hinted of pain. His unnerving eyes remained fixed
forward. He looked tired.

He had changed into a heavy, formal tunic, which
only added to his remote, coiled aura. The garment,
fitting snug to his muscular shoulders, tapered to
lean hips which were set off by an ornate jeweled
girdle. His warrior's body was intense, intimidating,
molded by battle as was his face. She could easily
imagine him atop a mighty warhorse, brandishing a
gleaming sword, violent and ruthless. He was built to
shed enemy blood.

She prayed that she would never face his wrath.

"Lorabelle of Sperling, wilt thou take this man to
be thy wedded husband, wilt thou obey him and serve
him, love, honor, and keep him, in health and in
sickness, as a wife should a husband, and forsaking
all others on account of him, keep thee only unto
him, so long as ye both shall live?"

Her mouth was dry. She did not allow herself to
look at Damon again. She could not allow fear to
overtake her, and if she looked at him at this fateful
moment, it would.

"I will," she whispered.

The priest nodded to Lord Wulfere, and she felt
the knight take her hand, enclose it in his own. His
touch was hard warmth, rough skin, constrained
power. For an instinctive second, she relaxed, felt
safe.

Then her chest tightened again. Damon of Wulfere
was anything but safe.

He repeated after the priest.

"I, Damon of Wulfere, take thee Lorabelle of Sperling to be my wedded wife, to have and to hold from this day forward, for better, for worse, for richer, for poorer, in sickness, in health, till death us do part, if Holy Church will ordain it. And thereto I plight thee my troth."

The priest turned to Aurelie, and she stumbled through the recitation of her vows in a muted voice, shaking. It seemed strange, unreal.

The priest intoned a lengthy series of blessings and then they went into the chapel for the nuptial Mass. Her knees were locked and sore by the time it ended.

*She was the lady of Wulfere.*

He took her hand again and helped her to rise. She had to look at him now.

"You may honor your bride with the kiss of peace," the priest finished.

Time lost consistency, seeming to completely stop yet hurtle forward at the same instant as Damon's depthless eyes fastened on hers and his mouth descended toward her. The very air seemed to burn, singeing her skin, her eyes, her mouth.

Then the heat was real. It was him. His hands slid up her arms, to her shoulders, as he placed his lips on hers.

*Don't feel anything,* she warned herself in that last desperate instant.

*Don't feel. Don't feel. Don't—*

The chapel swam around her, taking reason away with it, leaving only the marvel of this newness. Her eyes closed tight in wonder and in that moment fear had no place in her mind. She felt unbalanced, dizzy, and she reached for him, his unyielding form beneath his tunic, pressing her hands against his chest for support.

His lips were warm and firm, his kiss little more than a brush of flesh to flesh, a caress, but it was astonishingly intimate. She felt him draw back, and she opened her eyes.

He was very near, and for the space of a heartbeat she thought she saw something lost and dazed there, as if he were a man coming alive again from the dead.

Then the look was gone and she was simply cold and alone in a crowd with this stranger, her husband.


The great hall was alive with noise.

There had been no time to arrange for entertainment—jugglers, dancers, musicians—but their lack was not felt at Castle Wulfere this night. The hall filled instead with laughter and shouts and joy. For the first time since Damon had been home, he saw joy.

He took in the scene from his position at the high table. Wine flowed freely, and the numerous courses were consumed with gusto as man-at-arm and villein alike sat down together. No seat was left untaken. The soaring walls were radiant with swords, pollaxes, maces, halberds, hammers, and falchions, glittering down upon the tableau like stars. Three enormous fireplaces blazed and the keep fairly glowed.

Servants scurried between tables, arms laden with an endless procession of delights—lentils and lamb, spiced tripe, fish cakes, and turkey-neck pudding. He had ordered preparations to begin a week ago when he'd set out for Briermeade, and Castle Wulfere's cooks had done an admirable job under the time constrictions.

For this night, his people could forget the darkness and death of the months past and look forward to the promise of the future. *The future.* He glanced at his bride beside him.

He watched as she bit into a succulent morsel of lamb, her tongue reaching out to lick her sweet lips of its juice. She cast a self-conscious look in his direction and caught his gaze.

She had been quiet throughout the feast, thinking her own mysterious thoughts. The purple of her gown lit up her eyes with violet glimmers amidst the blue, and he felt himself caught in them and in the way her chest rose and fell as she breathed and in that mouth.

That perfect, luscious mouth of hers.

He couldn't let himself think of kissing her again, of how soft, untried, that mouth had been, how she had made him desire her, want her, with nothing but innocence as her tool.

*Don't think of it,* he warned himself.

He had eaten almost nothing. It wasn't food he craved tonight. It was a damnable thing, this desire. Somehow more than physical, more than the lust he had expected, and it was that which made him understand fully the danger of this innocent bride of his. He couldn't lose control. He couldn't give her that power.

Not now, not ever.

He had worked too long, too hard, to gain it in the first place to lose it now. And yet, there was no turning back. They were wed. And she was so perilously sweet.

*His wife.*

"Does the feast please you, my lady?" he asked, covering his disorientation with the meaningless question.

"Your people are pleased." She had stopped eating.

He toyed with the cutting knife perched on the edge of the trencher they shared, trying not to gape at the radiance of her even as he was ensnared. Torchlight and shadow defined the swell and dip of her breasts, dark and light, rise and fall, magic and madness.

*Stop.*

"It has been a desperate year," he commented with deliberate care. "They are easily pleased."

She picked up a slice of apple and held it between her fingers delicately. She lowered her lashes, avoiding his stare, as if she knew better than to hold it for too long, as if she, too, felt this intensity, this power, this *something* that was too strong.

He felt his willpower slipping away.

"And you?" he asked quietly, his blood humming despite his inner warnings. "Are you easily pleased, my lady?"

Did they still speak of the feast? Or something else? He wasn't sure. When she looked up at him, there was caution and trepidation on her face, as if she weren't certain, either.

But when she spoke, there was nothing to reveal her thoughts.

"It has been a desperate year," she said simply, repeating his own words back to him. She set the slice of apple down without tasting it.

He was relieved and dissatisfied at once. She

turned away, letting her gaze sweep over the crowd
below the raised dais, and he allowed the clamor of
the feast to fall between them.

From far across the hall came unintelligible shouts,
laughter, conversation.

Closer in, down the table, rose the voices of his
men as they argued the relative virtues of the pollaxe
and the mace.

The attention of the table was seized by Sir Beldon,
who commenced a gory retelling of a recent tourney
at a nearby castle. Damon didn't know whether to be
amused or worried by Gwyneth's avid attention to the
tale.

He was, he decided, simply grateful that she was
wearing a proper girl's gown and had left her stick
sword in her chamber, though she remained a sight
with her poorly cropped hair sticking up in all directions, completely unamenable to the simple fillet cir-
cling her small brow, which made a valiant effort to
tame it.

It had taken every maid that could be spared from
the castle staff to bring his sisters to this semblance
of decorum. Even Elayna, who had not spoken a word
and had barricaded herself in her chamber for days,
ever since he had reiterated his intention to hold
firm the betrothal their father had set in place for
her, had deigned to make an appearance, albeit with
her pretty nose in the air, her mouth set in recalcitrant lines.

He had no idea what to do with her. She was four-
teen, by God. Too young to know her mind, what was
best for her.

He only wished he were more certain *he* knew what
was best for her, for any of them. The role of guardian

had been thrust upon him suddenly, and he was ill-prepared for it. His sisters were strangers to him—and he to them. They should have been sent away to foster years ago—and indeed, it would be the easiest thing to do now. Only guilt held him from it. His father had been remiss in their education, their training.

And Damon had been busy, too busy to know or care that his sisters grew up neglected and abandoned in their own home. He'd fought for his king for four years, and been buried beneath a French chateau for another.

He hadn't given a thought to his sisters, not until he'd arrived home. The weight of that failure fell heavily on him, and he gazed in an unfocused way across the hall, anywhere but at his sisters.

"Enough," barreled his old friend Ranulf from the end of the table, interrupting Beldon's involved discourse of the gory joust.

Kenric's brother, Ranulf of Penlogan-by-the-sea, was the one guest in attendance at this hastily laid wedding feast. Time had been too short and weather too dire to send the invitations far and wide that would normally be delivered for such a celebration. And Damon was glad.

This feast was for his own people, and he had no wish to socialize.

Lorabelle's parents were dead, though her uncle had sent gifts of cloth and jewels to mark the occasion. She had no family close enough to brave the winter's harshness for this one night.

Even Ranulf would not be here if not that Damon had stopped at nearby Penlogan Castle before returning home to inquire as to whether they could spare their priest. Ranulf had accompanied his cleric for the opportunity to spend an evening with his comrades again. Ranulf, newly vested with the lordship of Penlogan-by-the-sea after his exploits in service to the king in France, was one of the few men Damon trusted. One of the few men he was glad to have as guest in his home these days.

As with Rorke, Ranulf and his brother Kenric were friends without whom Damon might still be in that dungeon beneath Blanchefleur. Or dead.

"Enough of this talk of violence," Ranulf announced again as Beldon tried to continue his tale. "There are not such bloodthirsty pursuits on our friend's mind tonight." He raised his goblet. "To the lord of Wulfere and his beauteous bride!"

The other men raised their goblets and repeated the toast, cheering and drinking. Damon noticed Rorke, at the end of the table, toy with his goblet, his face set in strained lines. His bride's cheeks flamed, though she nodded her head graciously.

Julian drained his wine and set his goblet down with a thunk and called for more.

Dessert was arriving—servants emerged from behind the screens loaded with trays of sugar comfits, candied pine nuts, cream custards.

The priest from Penlogan Castle leaned across the table toward her. "Lady Wulfere, my dear child, do you remember me?"

His bride gave the priest a quick, nervous look. "Father, I'm sorry, I—"

"Father Almund," he supplied. "I served a time at Sperling Castle. In fact, I presided over your parents' wedding. It honors me to have presided over yours as well."

"Father Almund," Lorabelle repeated his name in her soft, careful voice. "Of course. I see."

But she didn't see. Damon sensed it at once. She was uncertain, lost. He realized the priest had no knowledge of his bride's fragmented memories.

"You were a beautiful child," the priest continued, and much of the table listened as the drinking in the wake of Ranulf's toast had left a brief break in conversation. "A tribute to Lady Sperling. 'Tis a pity she did not live to see this day. My lord Wulfere will be a fortunate man if you have inherited her talent with gardens."

The priest looked around at his audience at the high table, apparently seizing upon a favorite topic as the enthusiasm in his voice rose. "I spent my boyhood in a monastery, and spent many hours toiling in the plots of master gardeners, but Lady Sperling possessed an extraordinary gift. She designed a most exquisite park at Sperling with groves of trees and ponds. Songbirds of all sorts flocked there, and there was a small timber summer house in which the lord and lady would reside at times. It was a most peaceful place."

He looked at Lorabelle again, his round face settling into somber lines.

"Yes," she murmured finally, gazing into her goblet. "It was very beautiful."

"But you never saw your lady mother's gardens, did you?" Julian interjected. " 'Tis to my recall that Lady Sperling passed from this world when you were but a babe, and that Lord Sperling had the park razed in a fit of grief."

A tint of rose swept Lorabelle's cheekbones again. She raised her gaze, but looked beyond the priest. It was a hunted look, secretive and painful. Yet she had nothing to hide, to feel shame about. Her broken memories were not her fault.

A burn in Damon's chest grew as he locked his gaze with Julian's now. The priest might not be aware of Lorabelle's recent injuries, but his cousin was.

And yet deliberately, it seemed, Julian had made his bride uncomfortable.

Damon turned to the priest. "My bride suffered an attack at the convent of Briermeade before I brought her back to Castle Wulfere. There has been a certain effect upon some of her memories. It will pass in time, we hope, but her memories of her home and family are not complete. You understand."

He sensed Lorabelle's tension, but she didn't look at him, didn't meet his eyes. Elusive, guarded, so controlled and yet so vulnerable just the same. It was absurd to feel pain for her. Had he not pain enough of his own? And yet he couldn't resist hers.

Over the noise in the hall, he could hear the beating of his own heart, alive and defiant, damn her. He clenched his jaw and turned away, exhaling slowly.

He lifted his goblet and drank, barely tasting the wine. Across the table, the priest's expression was pained as he made his regrets.

But it was not the look of the priest that stopped the harsh beat of his heart. It was the look of his cousin.

Julian's eyes met his through the flickering torchlight and shadows, and he saw for the first time plainly what he had only suspected before. Loathing.

# *Thirteen*

"Bless, O Lord, this chamber and all that dwell therein, that they may be established in thy peace and abide in thy will, and live and grow in thy love, and that the length of their days may be multiplied."

Father Almund moved from the doorway of the bedchamber, blessing the bed itself, before turning back to dash sprinkles of holy water on the bride and groom.

Aurelie flinched at the cold, wet flecks, but the man who was now her husband remained fixed as a statue, no emotion, no movement to betray life.

Here in this candelit room, the light around Damon shaded his face into but an outline of a man she didn't know and scarcely comprehended. What a mystery he was to her. His kiss had been the most amazing thing she'd ever experienced and she hated it for the sweet helplessness it wrought.

And yet she wanted more.

Nerves bubbled through her—fear, or anticipation, she wasn't sure which—and she breathed deeper, slower, trying to control them.

She had chosen this path of her own free will. She might convince herself at times that it was the other way around, that this path—some hand of fate—had chosen her, but it wasn't so.

*At least be honest with yourself,* whispered a knowing voice inside her. She longed for this fearsome knight from the depths of her soul. And she didn't know what would happen next as a result, couldn't trust what her reactions would be anymore. When he had kissed her, her body had responded without her consent, ripping all her careful plans away, shredding them. She'd wanted to taste him again, inhale him, consume him. Want. Desire. It was shameful, base. Weak.

It was she who was consumed, lost to these new, overpowering sensations. Throughout the feast, she'd been unnerved by what she'd done, and even more unnerved by that kiss. So unnerved, she'd come close to disaster in that conversation with Father Almund. *Damon had rescued her, protected her.*

She wasn't accustomed to being protected. All her life, she had felt alone. At the whim of the abbess, she could have been set aside at any time. She was more alone than ever here, at Castle Wulfere, where she had no right to be. And yet she felt protected, too, and it was that feeling that rushed to her heart now, breaking down barriers she so desperately needed, complicating everything.

How could Damon be both her savior and her peril at the same time? How could she know which was truth, which was lie, when her entire world was a lie?

She watched as the priest bid them good eve and withdrew, leaving her alone with her husband and the snapping fire and chilled night air of the immense chamber that was now theirs to share. She stared at the paneled arch of wood as it shut.

The intimacy between a husband and wife wasn't completely beyond her understanding. She had been shielded from much at the convent, but there had been forbidden snatches of talk between nuns who had been wed previous to giving over their lives to the Church.

How could she make love to him, do those things the nuns had spoken of with him? And how could she not? She was his bride.

She turned and found his extraordinary, depthless eyes fixed on her. Something hot and thick, like warmed honey, unfurled inside her stomach, spreading outward to every end of her body. They faced each other for a timeless beat. She smelled beeswax and smoke and lavender, and the faintly leathery scent that made her think of horses and heat and him.

He continued to look at her with an intensity she felt down to her toes. It was a terrible risk, even the smallest bit of pleasure she took in this moment.

"Thank you," she said, blurting out the first thing that came to mind, heedless, wanting only to break this charged awareness. "Thank you for what you did, what you said to Father Almund, to explain—"

"He didn't know." He dismissed her gratitude with a shrug. "It was nothing."

Nothing. Of course. Had she imagined more? Had she imagined the protectiveness? Only yearned for it, dreamed of it, concocted it out of her fantasies?

She couldn't know. Too much of what she was living now was fantasy twined with nightmare for her to untangle it anymore.

"Your sisters surprised me," she said, trying again. Looking for some way, any way, to delay what was to come, what was inevitable, what she exploded with longing for. "They looked like different girls tonight. Sweet and gentle and compliant."

Something nearly a smile but not quite twisted those hard lips of his.

"You see the good in them," he murmured, holding her gaze as he moved, walking around the table to the fire.

"How did you manage to get Gwyneth to leave her room without her sword stick?"

He shrugged again. "The same way I managed to get Marigold bathed and Elayna to unlock her door and Lizbet to come out of the mews. I gave them a choice: obedience, or departing tomorrow to be fostered."

"Would you truly send them away?" she asked, surprised.

He looked over at her for an extended moment.

"It's not what I wish," he said eventually, and he faced the fire, gazing into the flames, his profile set in sober lines.

"They need their home," she said instinctively, fighting for these girls she barely knew. Or perhaps fighting for the girl she herself had been—a girl who'd had no home at all. "They're hurting. You must have seen that—or you wouldn't have—"

"Perhaps I made a mistake," he interrupted.

It was difficult for her to imagine him as a man who made mistakes. He was deliberate and deadly, quiet steel.

Did he ever feel uncertainty? Vulnerability? Weakness?

She didn't know what she was searching for as she examined his face through the shadows. Some sign of that uncertainty, vulnerability, weakness that would tell her he was human, that he was like her? Some sign of that need she almost believed she'd seen after they'd kissed?

"Why doesn't Marigold speak?"

If he was surprised by her question, he didn't show it.

The small table before the fire and a few feet separated them. A pitcher and two silver goblets rested on an ornate tray.

His eyes blazed across the darkened space.

"Stubbornness." He shrugged, making the movement casual, but its stiffness belied the gesture.

"You don't believe that."

His mouth almost tilted, and she realized he'd almost smiled again. Did her contentiousness amuse him? It couldn't be the topic of conversation he found laughable.

Of course, his hard mouth didn't make it all the way into a smile. She wasn't sure he *could* smile.

"When it comes to my sisters, I don't know what to believe," he said, circumventing her question.

He lifted the pitcher and poured wine into the two goblets.

"It will take time to become a family, to know each other again," she said. "They must have missed you all these years you were gone. Thought of you. And now—"

He set the pitcher down. "Now what?"

His irises glinted in the darkness, and a strange discordant hum of excitement filled her. *Now what?* Were they still talking about his sisters?

"Where is Elayna's betrothed?" she persisted, hanging on to anything that kept her from falling into this pit of longing that threatened to pull her down.

"In the north. Waiting, for her sixteenth birthday." He picked up one of the goblets. "Wine?" he offered.

She shook her head. "Why does she protest?"

"She's intractable."

"She's romantic," she countered, guessing. She knew what it was to be Elayna's age, what it was to dream.

"She's foolish." He set the goblet down and came around the table toward her. "He's older than she, but he's a good man. A good match. 'Tis common practice for girls to be betrothed to strangers, as it is for them to be sent away to be fostered," he added in his unemotional, low voice. "You were sent away to be fostered. Betrothed to a stranger."

He was close now, so close. She could feel his energy, palpable, taut. Her stomach seemed to drop away from her body.

"You are wed to a stranger," he continued softly.

Her breath clogged her throat.

"Is it so terrible?" he asked in a husky whisper.

She felt herself reduced to a single, throbbing heartbeat, violent and perilous.

"What is or isn't terrible for me has nothing to do with Elayna." She battled against falling into those hard-vulnerable eyes, this bone-melting weakness. Her own sickening need.

He must have seen it, recognized her need. He reached out, touched her cheek.

"You have a fierce heart, Lorabelle of Sperling."

"Your sisters are confused, troubled. Anyone would be touched by them. Even—" She took a breath, difficult to do with him touching her at the same time. "Even you."

She didn't know where that had come from. She wasn't sure it was true. For a moment he said nothing. Then very close, very low, he spoke.

"You think I have a heart, my lady?"

"Everyone has a heart."

His eyes, dark with something—desire?—pinned her, and she couldn't breathe much less move.

"You're bold," he said in a voice that deepened her peril.

He brushed his thumb over her lips with a rough feathery lightness that made her want to do something stupid, like sigh or swoon.

"But you're innocent, Lorabelle," he continued. "You could almost make me believe you speak the truth."

She could feel the warmth of him, the heat of his body, the softness of his breath. She wished she'd taken the wine. She wished she could think of something else to say. She wished for anything but what was about to happen, what she feared would strip the last bit of her will from her forever.

The power of her desire for him terrified her. She needed him. She wanted him, God help her.

But she was beyond God's help.

"Almost," he repeated in a whisper, and he leaned forward—

*He was going to kiss her.* She was everything he could never be again in this life, and his body throbbed for the touch of her, the feel of her. His need for her was illogically complex, and it consumed him in that moment.

His hand moved behind her neck to clutch a handful of fragrant, thick hair together with the fragile material of her veil, still draped in dainty folds from the gleaming circlet on her head.

She tipped her face up, her eyelids fluttering, and he kissed her, a confusion of things that could be and couldn't be flooding his senses. She tasted like hope and hell rolled into one, all sweetness and need, innocence and sensuality at once. He deepened the kiss, claiming full possession of her mouth.

Hot and cold need coursed through him, and he ached to bury himself inside her, to seek that perfect satisfaction, that sweet peak that was both simple and so very complicated.

His hands stroked her, down the curve of her back and lower, pulling her closer. He had never wanted any woman this badly before. She made a sound against his mouth, a moan, and he broke the kiss.

"My lord," she whispered.

He closed his mouth over hers again, invading, hungry, but he could hear that sound in her throat once more. Anxiety. He tore his lips from hers with effort.

"Lorabelle?" He blew her name across the skin of her cheek, breathing deeply of her, woman and innocence. He pulled away from her completely now, leaving her staring up at him. In the firelight, he could yet see the faint outlines of her bruises. And she was shaking, he realized. *She was shaking.*

Was she afraid? The thought slammed into him, almost knocking him off his feet. He'd expected her to fear him in the beginning, had been shocked when she hadn't. But now— Now, the reality of it shattered him. This was his life now. This was his truth. He was feared, distanced from the rest of the world forever. Even from his bride.

When he was certain he had control of himself, he let go of her. She wobbled slightly, as if she, too, had trouble keeping her balance.

He turned away from her and looked at the fire again, anywhere but at her. "You never answered my question."

"I— Your question?" Her voice was thin but strong, and he knew if he turned, he would see nothing of her thoughts, nothing of that vulnerability he'd heard in her gasp against his mouth. She would have it all under control now. And he understood that all too well, knew too much what that kind of control could hide.

"Is it so terrible?" he repeated grimly, and forced himself to pivot and face her through the shadows. "Is it so terrible to be wed to a stranger, to me?"

"You aren't a stranger," she said in that careful voice of hers. "You're my husband."

"And yet a stranger," he argued in a low voice.

A long beat passed.

"Yes," she said softly. "And yet a stranger."

He swung away from her, clenching and unclenching his hands at his sides to keep from turning back to her. "You aren't completely recovered. And it will take time, as you said, to know each other. We will wait."

He had been so close to quenching his secret torment for her, his hunger, his need.

*Need.* Was that truly what it was?

"Go to bed, wife," he said, knowing if she didn't,

if he looked at her again, it would be too late. His head pounded, his blood stung in his veins.

She hadn't moved. He could hear the faint sound of her breathing.

"Go to bed," he said again, harshly, and this time, she went.

# *Fourteen*

The days fell into a routine. Aurelie had the school-room cleaned the day following the wedding, and set out a regime for the girls. They were sulky at first, but she tried to make the lessons pleasant and the moodiness wore off in time.

She woke early every day, before morning prayers, to oversee the girls as they dressed, taking care with their hair and seeing that they bathed. The maid Damon had arranged to come to attend them from the village was young, barely older than Elayna, and had no control over them at all. The first thing Aurelie did was bring in the seamstresses, who made new gowns for all four of them.

Gwyneth would have nothing to do with the pretty new kirtles, however, despite having acquiesced briefly for the sake of the wedding, so Aurelie ordered new boys' tunics made to replace the worn, patched ones Gwyneth had filched from the pages' quarters.

Aurelie had taken the beautiful barrettes and ribbons and fillets from the chest in her room, the one that had been packed with gowns that had once belonged to Damon's mother, and given them all to the girls. She didn't ask anyone's permission, but simply did it. She was beyond asking permission anymore for taking things that didn't belong to her—and she figured after all that they did belong to the girls since they had been their mother's.

The only thing she kept was a chatelaine's chain, which she hung on the belt she wore at her hips. The chain of keys had belonged to Damon's mother and was a talisman of sorts to her, making her feel closer in some way to the previous lady of Wulfere as she worked to fit into this new life.

Along with cleaning out the schoolroom, she'd also turned her attention to the girls' quarters. Their chamber itself had been a dreadful mess.

Gwyneth, it was discovered, had an entire collection of stick swords, makeshift bows and arrows, bats, balls, and other unrecognizable items—most of which Aurelie let her keep as long as Gwyneth agreed to stack them neatly beneath the bed.

She did have to return two gauntlets, a gorget, and even a helmet. She'd been working toward a complete suit of armor which she'd been secreting away, piece by piece, from the guardroom.

Lizbet was required to return a number of items to the mews—jesses, leashes, even a small perch and tiny leather hood—which she had been assembling apparently for some time and which it was discovered the falconer was greatly missing. Aurelie was simply relieved she didn't discover a bird—particularly a dead one—although she suspected that the acquisition of a baby hawk might well have been next on Lizbet's list if she hadn't been stopped.

Aurelie did allow the girl to keep a string of tiny bird bells which Lizbet had fashioned into a necklace of sorts that she liked to wear.

Gwyneth, Lizbet, and Marigold shared one huge bed together, and Elayna slept in a connecting, smaller room that had once been a maid's but which Elayna had turned into a private bower. It was, Aurelie soon came to realize, only one of the ways in which the eldest of Damon's sisters sought to create a differentiation between herself and the other children. Elayna's room was relatively clean already, and contained a stack of small, bound manuscripts of romantic poetry that had belonged to her mother.

Other than her clothes, Marigold's only possession seemed to be her beloved doll. She was rarely separated from it.

After they'd attended prayers and broken their fast, Aurelie began their day with study. Freshened up after its long disuse, the schoolroom was tapestried, and when the small hearth was lit, it turned out to be a warm and cozy place to study.

There were huge, deep windows with cushioned seats built into the thick stone recesses. They could be unshuttered to look out over the river and fields and woods, and she thought the room would be an especially delightful place to be during the spring and summer.

Aurelie wondered if she would still be at Castle Wulfere for the spring and summer, and the thought brought with it a measure of both sadness and apprehension.

At no time since the night they'd been wed had her husband touched her again.

She had lain there in that great bed alone that night, surrounded by the pillows and blankets they were meant to share, with her nipples hard and achy, her mouth dry, her arms empty, and had felt light-headed with unquenched desire.

It was absurd, she had told herself over and over, but that knowledge hadn't stopped the burning in her veins.

Her life was in danger. She had a role to play as Lorabelle, and any vulnerability could be a mistake.

And yet her heart had stormed in her ears that night, drowning out other concerns that should have been more important.

*You aren't completely recovered. And it will take time, as you said, to know each other. We will wait.*

His words reverberated in her mind, and she poured over them again and again, trying to understand them.

It was a reprieve, and she should have welcomed it. She'd been more frightened than she'd ever been in her life in that moment.

His touch had cast a spell on her, stealing her breath, causing her limbs to tremble. She'd felt heat, dampness between her legs. Did he know what he'd done to her so easily? So shamefully easily?

Had *she* affected *him* at all?

He'd taken a blanket and slept in one of the large chairs by the hearth, and had continued in this way every night since. He couldn't be comfortable, she knew that. And he was wakeful, restless, as much as she.

Yet he didn't seek the solace of the bed, or of his wife.

She had the dream every night, still. She'd wake, sweating, shaking. *Sir Santon.* She couldn't rid herself of the nightmarish vision of his eyes coming at her.

They were endless tormenting dreams that left her gasping in the night, frightened and alone.

Her husband dreamed, too. She'd heard him, more than once, come awake with a horrible groan, and sometimes she caught a word. A name. *Angelette.* But whatever haunted him, he didn't share that information with her. He spoke to her very little at all. After prayers, he disappeared—to the training room where the men worked during these bitterly cold days, or to the wall-walks where he inspected the watch, or the hall where he held court for the villagers.

She would see him again at meals—or sometimes not. Sometimes she'd see servants take bundled bread and meat pies down the hall steps and know he was eating where he worked, not stopping.

At night, he would again sleep in the chair by the fire, often arriving long after she'd crawled into that great curtained bed alone.

But why? Yes, she'd still carried the bruises on their wedding night, but they'd faded more every day until they completely vanished. And her physical energy had been fully restored for some time.

Was it truly that he wished to give them more time to know one another? If that were so, he was certainly making no effort to bring about any meaningful progress in that direction.

Three possible conclusions left her unsettled. One was the prospect that her husband simply didn't desire her.

Another was that he suspected her.

A third was that he was in love with another woman. *Who was Angelette?*

"Do you love him?"

Aurelie startled, blinked, and focused on Elayna. There were several desks with benches in the schoolroom, but they had set aside their Latin verses and their slates and chalks to settle into the padded chairs that were drawn up in a circle around the hearth to work on their embroidery. Elayna had quite a repertoire of stitches, having been trained by her mother in happier days.

Gwyneth, Lizbet, and Marigold had no sewing experience at all, though Aurelie hoped eventually to teach them to at least ply a needle through cloth without making a bloody mess of their fingers.

"He's my husband," Aurelie evaded.

Elayna watched her intently. She was a curious mix of woman and child, keenly independent, and yet awkwardly vulnerable, and just beginning to show the promise of the beauty she would be.

She was all long arms and legs and contentiousness now.

"So you don't love him," Elayna pressed.

"I don't know him," Aurelie told her honestly. "Yet," she added.

*Would she ever know him?* she wondered.

"He's mean," Gwyneth put in.

"Has he said anything mean to you?" Aurelie inquired, recalling that Gwyneth had said she wanted to be like Damon. She suspected the girl admired more than abhorred her brother, though Gwyneth wasn't ready to admit it. There were so many things about the boyish girl that baffled her.

"He said he would send us away," Gwyneth answered.

"Only if you didn't obey him," Aurelie countered. "He doesn't want to send you away."

"He doesn't?" Gwyneth's eyes rounded.

Before Aurelie could answer that question, Lizbet piped in, "If you don't love him, do you kiss him?"

"She kissed him at the wedding," Gwyneth reminded her.

Aurelie was relieved when Elayna brought the conversation full circle, cutting off more exposition on whether or not she and Damon kissed.

"I'm not going to marry a man I don't know," Elayna announced firmly. "No matter what Damon says, or even the king."

It was the first time she had directly referred to her betrothal. It was the first time she had engaged in a conversation more meaningful than a discourse on the weather.

"Your brother wants what's best for you," Aurelie said. She wasn't sure the king cared what was best for her, but Elayna was the eldest daughter of one of the most powerful families in the realm, and her marriage came under the dictate of royal will. Damon could not easily alter the course already set down for Elayna's life.

"How do you know what he wants? You just said you don't know him." There was a damp shimmer in Elayna's beautiful, dark eyes, but she held her head high in her rebellious way.

"I know that he's your brother."

Elayna made an indelicate snort. "Since when? He just comes riding back here like he's the ruler of the world, telling everyone what to do—"

"I thought your father was the one who arranged this betrothal," Aurelie corrected gently.

Elayna shrugged, and Aurelie could see her blink back the moisture that was accumulating in her eyes.

"It doesn't matter," she said with a sniff. "I'm going to run away again, so far away he won't find me this time." She bit her lip. "I hate him," she tacked on in a rough whisper.

She swiped at her eyes and attacked her sewing.

Aurelie's heart squeezed at the pain in the girl's voice, and she knew more and more, every day, she was growing entangled in these girls' lives. She wanted to live for herself, for Aurelie, to be aware every minute of her own need, her own danger—but every time she looked into any one of these four girls' eyes, she let herself down.

She couldn't be here, at Castle Wulfere, and not try to do something for them—even though she wasn't quite sure *how* to do anything for them.

"You feel very strongly about this, don't you?" she said.

Elayna looked up, surprise flickering across her expressive face. "Yes," she said quietly, staring at Aurelie. She bit her lip again, crinkled her forehead, and seemed about to say something else when her sisters interrupted.

"If you run away again, I'm going with you," Gwyneth said. She put her sewing down, and was looking at her big sister with something close to panic for all her big words.

"Me, too," Lizbet said. "We have to stick together."

Marigold crawled under her seat with her doll, and Aurelie's heart squeezed tighter.

"Come on," she said resolutely. "Let's be sensible. It's much too cold to go anywhere—except downstairs to eat. I'm hungry. How about you?" It was time for the midday meal, and she didn't think this conversation was doing anything to make Marigold feel more secure in her world.

She hadn't made any progress with Marigold at all. The little girl would let her hold her hand, put her arms around her, but she didn't speak, not one word, even to her sisters.

There was nothing wrong with her hearing, though, and it was obvious this line of talk distressed her. At the moment, Aurelie didn't have the slightest idea how to deal with Elayna's situation. Like Gwyneth's desire to be a knight and Lizbet's to be a falconer, Elayna wanted something that was impossible. She was a noblegirl, growing into a woman soon. She would be wed—not for love, but for convenience and property. Aurelie couldn't change that.

She directed the older girls to put their sewing away neatly in their baskets while she slipped down to the rush-covered floor, heedless of the herbs and straw that stuck to her gown, and held out her hand to Marigold.

The little girl's big eyes watched her, shiny and dark.

"Come on," Aurelie urged softly. "Aren't you hungry?"

The little girl shook her head.

"Well, I am," Aurelie tried. "I won't go down to the hall without you." She sighed loudly and sat back, gazing up at the high stone ceiling above them. "Unbelievable. I'm going to starve to death right here in the heart of Castle Wulfere, surrounded by all this plenty. Perhaps you can see how long it takes. It could be a study project." She swerved her gaze to the child beneath the chair again. "Marigold, you're in charge."

With that, she made a dramatic collapse back onto the rushes in front of the hearth. The rushes weren't as thickly laid as she'd expected.

"Ow." She sat back up, rubbing the back of her head ruefully. "On second thought, I think I'll starve sitting up."

Marigold peeked out from under the chair. Gwyneth and Lizbet gathered close, staring down at her, and then they started giggling. She realized even Marigold was smiling.

"What?" Aurelie demanded.

"Your hair," Elayna put in with a laugh. "You've got straw poking straight up out of your hair."

Aurelie picked at her hair, and Marigold and all of her sisters came around behind her to help. Smiling to herself as she stood, brushing off her gown, Aurelie didn't mind at all that the back of her head felt like it had a knot growing on it.

"All right," she said, finally satisfied that she looked presentable. "How about we save that project for another day then?"

She stretched out her hand to Marigold, and the little girl took it. Together, they headed for the great hall, where the midday meal was already being laid. Sausage pies and peas with bacon water.

"Mmm," Aurelie said, squeezing Marigold's hand. As usual, she carried on conversations with the little girl as if there were two of them in the dialogue. She'd noticed that, aside from her sisters, other people around the castle didn't bother to speak to Marigold at all since she didn't respond, so she'd made a point of holding extensive conversations with her. "Good idea coming down to eat. We wouldn't want to miss this."

No one was seated at the high table, and there was a maid already on her way out of the pantry, carrying a bundle Aurelie knew would be meant for Damon.

She thought about Elayna's reaction to her simple validation of her distress. It hadn't been much, but it had meant something to Elayna to know that Aurelie was listening, that she recognized how much this betrothal troubled her. And she hadn't missed the hurt beneath Elayna's disdainful dismissal of her relationship with her brother, or Gwyneth's eager need to hear that her brother didn't truly want to send them away.

But for her to do anything about this gulf between Damon and his siblings, it would mean she would have to brave the fearsome lord herself. Damon's sisters didn't have the confidence to approach their brother, and it was clear that he— Did it even occur to him to approach his sisters? He'd told her on their wedding night that he didn't know what to make of them. But they needed him.

And if there was a tiny part of her that needed him, too, she was going to disregard it. She was going to survive, and that meant not falling head over heels for a stone-cold knight even if he was her husband. And she was going to help these girls, too—because somehow, just surviving wasn't enough anymore.

She had to do something good here.

Yes, she was good and truly entangled. But it was one thing to be entangled with his sisters. Another thing to be entangled with Damon. If she could just keep her perspective, she would be fine.

And she *would* be fine. She *had* to be. So that meant she *had* to keep her perspective.

She could do it.

"Where are you taking that?" she asked, nabbing the bundled meat pie from the maid as she passed by. Elayna, Gwyneth, Lizbet, and Marigold froze in the process of seating themselves at the high table.

"To his lordship," the maid answered, her expression stunned. "In the training hall."

"I'll take it to him," Aurelie told her. "And have more sent, please, with something to drink." She nodded authoritatively to the maid, who was still looking stunned, and the girl pivoted and headed back toward the kitchen. Aurelie thought she was getting better at playing lady of the castle. At least the servants had gotten to where they didn't shy away from her so much, and she'd learned to give orders rather than asking permission.

She was making some progress. And she hoped she was about to make some more, in another direction.

Either that, or she was about to make a really big mistake. But she forced herself to banish the fretful thought and move on.

After all, she'd made one really big mistake already, so why stop now?

She smiled at Damon's sisters. "Let's get our cloaks," she said.

Lizbet, Gwyneth, and Elayna spoke together.

"What are we doing?"

"Where are we going?"

"Why?"

Aurelie took a resolute breath and squeezed Marigold's hand for luck.

"We're going," she told them, "on a picnic."

# *Fifteen*

"You have company, my lord."

"Send them to the keep. I'm busy." Damon couldn't imagine what sojourners would be braving this wintry weather to stop at Castle Wulfere. Ranulf and his priest and men-at-arms who'd traveled with him had departed the day after the wedding and no one else was expected.

Or wanted.

Damon parried, clashing swords with Rorke, both of them enjoying the mock battle. Most of his men had broken training to fill their bellies at the midday meal, allowing Damon and Rorke a chance to leave off their coaching to take on one another in a friendly bout.

From the corner of his eye, Damon saw the gangly squire shifting from one foot to the other.

"My lord—" The squire started again nervously. "It's not that sort of company."

Now Rorke lowered his sword.

Damnation. "What is it?" Damon demanded, frustrated. Here, in battle with a foe of equal merit to himself, the lines of engagement were clearly drawn. Life made sense. Life felt as whole as it got for him.

He lowered his own sword, his breath coming fast,

his blood pumping, and followed Rorke's gaze up, to the gallery that surrounded the cavernous, boxlike training hall that connected to the armory and guardroom within the outer bailey of the castle.

"It's your wife," Rorke commented, with a mix of amusement and mischief lightening his usually serious voice. "And your sisters."

Shifting his gaze again, Damon noticed Julian, in consultation with the armorer, stop and look up, his gaze narrowing on the group in the gallery. Damon knew Gwyneth had made a particular pest of herself of late by sneaking into the pages' training sessions, but his bride had seemed to keep control of the girls over the past week.

Julian turned back to his discussion with the armorer, but Damon watched him for another long beat. He hadn't been able to forget the look on Julian's face the night of the wedding, but he hadn't made any headway in figuring it out, either. He just knew that something had changed in Julian while he'd been away, and that while Julian was Castle Wulfere's chief man-at-arms, he often inexplicably disappeared during training periods.

Rorke had in large part taken over charge of the training of the men, while Damon had retaken the business demands of the demesne. And yet still Julian seemed busy, constantly out of pocket.

Damon turned his attention back to the flock of female trouble in the gallery. Truth was, he wasn't any happier to see his sisters and his bride braving the male bastion of the training hall than Julian was.

Here, he could forget the sweet temptation of his wife. He could forget how every night he went nearly mad with unsated desire. Vivid thoughts took him in an instant.

Lorabelle's clear sky eyes, the curve of her mouth, the honey of her taste, the seduction of her touch . . .

*Stop.*

He didn't know how he was going to make it through another night, and now she was here, damn her.

He strode across the immense room, took the winding steps up to the gallery. They would have come in through the tower, the only direct entry to the gallery from the bailey, and taken the circular tower steps to the upper floor.

The gallery ran all the way around the long, unadorned hall, about halfway between the floor and ceiling. The only warmth came from the twin crackling firepits against each far wall.

On this narrow second level, the only furniture consisted of long bare benches. He noticed his younger sisters were already removing their cloaks, laying them over the benches. As if they intended to stay.

His bride still wore her cloak, and stood there, spine straight, chin jutted forward in that shyly earnest way of hers, clutching a bundle that looked suspiciously like his meal.

"What are you doing here?" he asked, plainly unwelcoming, his gut clenching immediately at the tentative yet purposeful look of his wife.

*His wife.*

He still hadn't gotten used to thinking of her that way, wasn't sure he ever would.

He hadn't allowed her to become his wife in deed,

and he couldn't stop thinking about that. It was better when he didn't have to look at her, like now.

By the saints, she was a beauty. He seemed to forget that in between times, and it would be as if he saw her afresh every time.

"We've brought your midday meal," Lorabelle said.

His midday meal.

"Why?" he asked. Where was the maid who usually brought his food? "We have servants for that."

Lorabelle seemed unswayed by his cool greeting. "We're having ours brought over, too."

"Why?" he demanded again.

"We came to have a picnic with you," Elayna put in.

Her face held the general wary-sullen look of all his sisters, the one that reminded him that he'd failed them, couldn't make it up to them, and there was no point in trying. The look that he'd planned on his bride blocking him from ever having to take in again. And yet here she was, putting herself and his sisters right in his face, in his domain, his defense. The training hall.

Elayna hadn't removed her cloak yet. She glared at him as if waiting for him to order them out of the hall. Which was exactly what he was about to do.

A maid appeared, emerging from the well of the tower stairs, another servant coming along behind her. They carried more bundled pies and a pitcher and goblets.

"It's going to be an indoor picnic," Lizbet clarified, watching him guardedly even while a light of childish enthusiasm gleamed in her pretty dark eyes.

She fingered a ribbon around her neck that was strung with—were those bird bells?

"Because it's cold outside," Gwyneth said.

Was that a boy's tunic she was still wearing? A *new* boy's tunic?

"Well, no kidding, you beef-wit," Lizbet said and elbowed Gwyneth in the arm. "He knows it's cold."

Gwyneth jabbed back. "You're the beef-wit."

Lorabelle did nothing more than lift a brow, and Gwyneth and Lizbet sighed in unison.

"I meant to say, *dear sister,*" Lizbet said in a monotone.

"You're the *dear sister,*" Gwyneth returned in an equally lifeless voice, then they both broke into a cascade of giggles.

Damon followed the exchange with a sense of bafflement—both at seeing his young sisters actually laugh, and at the amazing control Lorabelle had gained over his sisters in a very short time.

Not much different from the amazing control she'd gained over him. All he had to do was look at her to feel the clumsy thickness in his blood, the ache in his chest, the lightness in his head.

He didn't want to look at her, didn't want to feel all those things that were exactly why he stayed so carefully away from her. But she was standing right in front of him, so he had little choice at the moment.

"Right here is fine," Lorabelle was saying, turning to instruct the servants on placement of the food and drinks on the benches. "Well, are you hungry?" she asked, shifting back to Damon. "Because we are. And we've come all this way to join you. The kitchen made sausage pies, and they smell just wonderful. I can hardly wait to taste them."

She gazed at him, so sweetly, so earnestly, and his sisters stood around her, watching him in much the same fashion.

The words *go away* died on his lips. Damnation.

He took her cloak, and Elayna slipped out of hers in the meantime, and they all settled in, pulling three benches into use—one against the iron railing overlooking the nearly deserted training hall, the other against the stone wall, and a third in the middle, which served as a makeshift table.

The girls sat, two on each side of Lorabelle, on the bench against the stone wall, leaving him the bench opposite, alone.

He felt like an ogre sitting down to dine with a band of faeries. Okay, one faery and four devils, he corrected. He didn't know what to do or say around his sisters—much less his bride, and he felt impossibly awkward. He didn't belong with them.

They unwrapped their pies and began to eat. Below, two squires had returned and were practicing their swordsmanship. Damon swallowed a bite of his meat pie to the clang of their clashing arms.

Gwyneth didn't stay seated long, but got up to lean over the iron railing, forgetting her pie, her eyes brightly fixed on the squires.

"Gwyneth, sit down and eat," he said, and she surprised him by obeying, seating herself near him now on the bench that backed up to the railing. He'd laid his sword down beside him, and it rested between himself and his boyish little sister, forming not nearly enough of a barrier to suit him.

He reached for the pitcher, intending to pour himself a cup of the watered-down ale that was served at the midday meal, and his hand connected accidentally with Lorabelle's as she took hold of it at the same time.

Was it his imagination that her breath quickened, that she responded involuntarily to his nearness, the way he responded to hers?

It was so slight, so elusive, so easily fantasized. And his fantasies were working too hard lately. He dreamed as often of her now as he did of Blanchefleur. After all, she was closer, just across the room. Just an arm's reach apart now. So near, so available, so *his*.

No doubt about it, the denial of her had only weakened him further instead of strengthening him.

He dropped his hold on the pitcher, surrendering it to her.

"Shall I pour a drink for you, my lord?" she said, and her voice was quite clear and strong, but she chewed at her lower lip in a nervous way and didn't meet his eyes and all he could do was stare, captivated by that lush mouth.

Here he was in a big, drafty room with the sound of swords clashing, surrounded by four children, and he couldn't stop thinking about bedding his wife. *Heaven help him.*

Unfortunately, he'd given up on heaven's help.

"Thank you," he said. He cast about for some safe topic of conversation. "How are lessons proceeding?"

"I'm too old for lessons," Elayna said in her surly, unflinching, make-me tone.

She had ribbons threaded through her hair—crimson ones that stood out against the thick, dark luster of her braided hair. Damon noticed from the corner of his eyes how one of the squires seemed to be parrying and thrusting and mooning at Elayna at the same time. A sense of protectiveness rose in his chest.

"You're still a child," Damon said grimly, hoping he was right, worrying that he wasn't, that his beautiful sister was blossoming way too fast for her own good.

"Elayna is a big help in the schoolroom," Lorabelle put in smoothly. "She's really my assistant more than my student. I don't know what I'd do without her help."

For a moment, the surly cast left Elayna's face, then she cocked her head and eyed her brother.

"Maybe I'll learn to be a great teacher," she said. "Lorabelle says that in the convents, all the teachers are women."

Damon frowned, knowing right away the implication his recalcitrant sister was going for. Elayna's sulky mouth curved in a devilish way. He couldn't figure out whether she was serious, or just seriously trying to annoy him.

"Lorabelle is helping us with our sewing," Lizbet put in. She'd finished her pie and was fingering the ribbon of bells around her neck. "Someday when I'm a falconer, I'll be able to knit wings back on my birds, and tend their tiny wounds." Her eyes lit again. "We're going to visit the mews this afternoon. The falconer told Lorabelle we could visit once a week and he would teach me to take care of the birds."

There was nothing devilish in Lizbet's expression at the moment, so he had to accept that she was quite sincere. He gave Lorabelle a questioning look, and she gazed back at him, her shuttered eyes unreadable but absolutely unapologetic.

Marigold had eaten half her pie and curled up on

the floor at Lorabelle's feet, resting her cheek against his bride's knee. Of course Marigold hadn't said a word to anyone.

"Has Marigold taken to her studies?" he asked.

Lorabelle put down her napkin, having finished her own pie, and patted Marigold gently on the head. The little girl's wild hair had been trained into a ribboned braid similar to Elayna's. As he looked at Marigold now, she picked up an end of Lorabelle's gown and held it up in front of her face, blocking him out. He felt suspiciously like an ogre again, but couldn't convince himself the feeling was undeserved. If he'd come home sooner, if he'd thought of his sisters more, maybe he would have been here before whatever had happened that had robbed Marigold of her will to speak.

Guilt wormed into his gut, familiar and dark.

"Marigold is doing wonderfully," Lorabelle said. "She's been practicing her letters, and she's very quick to learn. She's very smart."

Marigold peeked out from behind her scrap of skirt and gazed up at Lorabelle, her big eyes shiny and adoring.

His supposedly dead heart clenched and it shocked him to realize he wished Marigold would look at him that way, as if he were a hero, not an ogre.

He looked away, feeling more uncomfortable than ever. He suppressed the intense urge to flee.

"Can I hold it?"

He found Gwyneth stroking her finger along the vicious edge of his long-bladed great sword.

"Gwyneth!" He snatched her hand away, closing his much bigger one over her small one. "Take care.

That's very sharp. It could slice your finger open in a heartbeat. Never touch the edge of a sword."

"Can I hold it?" she repeated, determined.

Lorabelle watched him with a look of—hope? expectation? doubt?—in her eyes.

He wanted to say no, but knew he would feel that much more of an ogre if he did. And he realized with another clench to his chest that it wasn't just his sisters who he didn't want to have see him that way—it was his wife, too.

"It's heavy," he warned Gwyneth. He got up, came around her, and sat behind her to put his arms around hers to guide her grip.

He helped her lift the hefty weapon, feeling the slightness of her shoulders, her arms, her hands, and feeling protective again.

What was he doing showing his slender little sister how to lift a sword? he berated himself. How did Gwyneth—how did Lorabelle—engage him so easily in such nonsense?

A glance at Lorabelle showed that she watched intently, something inexplicable in her eyes. She bit her lip, smiled at him, and he didn't feel like an ogre in that moment. He felt . . . warm, and it had nothing to do with the blazing fire pits below. He felt himself falling into those smiling, sweet eyes of his bride. Falling, falling—

"I can do it!" Gwyneth protested loudly, shaking off his help. Without thinking, he let go. Gwyneth dropped the cumbersome sword with an immediate thunk to the bench, and he jerked his thoughts from—what? Insanity?

"No, you can't do it," he said to Gwyneth, more harshly than he intended though he refused to censor his tone. His wife and his sisters didn't belong here in the first place, and Gwyneth certainly had no business learning to heft a weapon. The bunch of them had his head turned upside down. "And you shouldn't be trying to do it, either," he went on ruthlessly, ignoring the disappointment that flared in Gwyneth's eyes, blotting out the look of excitement that had lit her features a moment before.

The hall was filling up again, squires and knights returning from the midday meal.

He squared his gaze on Lorabelle. The smile had disappeared from her eyes, and he told himself he didn't care.

"I have to get back to work," he said.

Lorabelle got up, took her cloak, and started gathering up the cloths the food had been wrapped in, packing them and the emptied pitcher and cups into the big basket the maid had left behind.

Stuffed full now, she started to pick up the basket and chivalry seized him. He reached for it, and the cascade of her hair as she leaned forward brushed his arm. She smelled like sweet rosewater and mint, and he wanted to kiss her right then, right there, in front of his sisters and his men.

She looked up at him, her mouth parted, her expression shaken, as if she, too, knew the same wild desire. His heartbeat pounded in his ears.

He straightened, and shoved the basket into her arms before his weaker side could take hold of him completely.

"Thank you," he said tensely. "It was quite"—annoying, frustrating, baffling, maddening?—"considerate of you to bring my meal here. But if I work through the midday meal, it's because I'm busy. It would be better if this didn't happen again."

He hated himself. He could see his sisters' faces stiffen, his bride's eyes darken. Then there was no expression at all. Lorabelle was good at banishing her emotions. What painful experiences had developed such a skill? The thought bothered him.

"Of course, my lord," Lorabelle said, not looking at him at all now. "Let's go, girls." She settled the basket against her hip and the five of them filed toward the tower steps, leaving him alone again. Alone with his soldiers and his swords and the only part of his life that made sense, that he could control.

He spent the rest of the afternoon unsettled, irritated, glancing up at the now-empty gallery, wishing for—what? He didn't know, yet he couldn't shake it off. Damnation.

" 'Maiden in the moor lay, maiden in the moor lay, seven nights and a day,' " the falconer crooned over and over to the falcon perched on his wrist in the darkened mews. " 'Seven nights full and a day.' "

The falconer had explained that the young tiercel had only recently had its hood removed and was still being trained to human touch. In another day, she would be exposed to pale dawn, then gradually accustomed to full daylight again. As the falconer sang softly and stroked the tiercel, he allowed Lizbet to feed tiny bits of chicken to the nervous bird, letting the girl share in an integral part of the routine at this stage.

He was an older man, grayed and grizzled, and while he'd been frustrated by Lizbet's constant prowling about the mews and her pilfering of his equipment in the past, he'd been amenable to Aurelie's request that they approach Lizbet's fascination with the birds in a supervised manner.

Aurelie had convinced the castle's hawk trainer that it would serve his own best interests to indulge Lizbet's infatuation with the birds just enough to keep her from sneaking in when he wasn't looking. He'd agreed to a weekly tutelage.

" 'What was her bower? What was her bower? The red rose and the lily flower,' " Lizbet picked up the song, singing in a sweet whisper as the bird ate from her hand. " 'The red rose and the lily flower.' "

Aurelie smiled through the darkness, enjoying the glow of happiness in Lizbet's eyes. The other girls looked on, almost as intrigued as Lizbet.

She tried to focus on the moment, wishing her mind would stop turning over the awkwardness of the hour they'd spent with Damon.

Had she made a mistake? She wasn't sure. He hadn't been glad to see them, but he'd acquiesced to their picnic, hadn't he? Yet when it was over he'd made it quite plain it wasn't something he wanted to repeat.

The image of him with his arms around Gwyneth, his huge form dwarfing her tiny one, wouldn't leave Aurelie's mind. Something about the scene had been so right. His sisters needed him, she was more sure of that than ever. Whenever she saw them with him, she saw something that touched her. Adoration. Sheer adoration. They looked up to him. It showed in their eyes, behind the sullen wariness, behind the sulky rebellion. Behind all the uncertainty. They wanted his attention—and yet still he pushed them away, even while she sensed he'd felt something, too.

But he didn't act on whatever it was he'd felt, except to send them away again. Aurelie felt irritated on behalf of the girls, and a good part of her wanted to stomp back to the training hall and demand he do—what? Her anger dissipated. His sisters weren't the only ones hurting. Damon hurt, too. Something shadowed his grim eyes, held him back, kept him so alone no matter how many people surrounded him— even his family.

Nothing was simple at Castle Wulfere, and she wondered if it was possible for her to heal Damon's sisters without also healing Damon.

As if he would let her heal him. As if she had that choice, even if it were a wise choice—which it certainly wasn't.

As if Damon would come anywhere close to her. He'd shoved that basket at her as if she carried the pestilence.

"Come, girls, let's go," she said abruptly, shoving away the awful thoughts because they hurt and because she was so close to losing her perspective completely and that frightened her. "Master Falconer has been kind and we don't want to overstay our welcome."

They left the mews, Lizbet looking over her shoulder woefully. Aurelie had to smile at that, amazed at the girl's affinity for the hawks.

"Where did you learn to love birds as you do?" she asked as they crossed the bailey toward the gate to the inner courtyard and keep. They were all huddled in their cloaks and hoods against the cold afternoon.

As they walked, Lizbet told her of how their father

had loved to hunt, until he'd grown too sick. The last hawk he'd trained himself he'd named Lizbet because it had been caught and brought to the castle the same day she was born. He used to take her to see the bird all the time when she was a very little girl, until he'd stopped leaving his bed, not long after their mother died.

Aurelie took Lizbet's hand, holding on to Marigold's with the other, and she noticed how Elayna took Gwyneth's, and they were quiet the rest of the way to the hall. She thought of how they must miss those days, and she wondered if Castle Wulfere would ever be a happy place again.

She determined that if she had anything to do with it, it would be, for them. And she vowed she would find a way to talk to Damon about his sisters—if it meant she had to hunt him down in the training hall again to do it.

Somehow, she would keep her wits about her, her perspective. It would be unbelievably hard—she knew that now. But for the girls' sake, she had to take the risk.

Tucking the girls into bed as was her habit now, Aurelie bent over to blow out the candle on the table by the bed in the main chamber. Elayna was allowed to keep a candle burning late in her connecting room so she could read the manuscripts of poetry that she loved. Through the partially open door to Elayna's room, Aurelie could see her writing on the parchment she'd asked Aurelie to get for her from the steward's office. Aurelie hadn't questioned her about why she wanted it, but she suspected the girl was composing poetry of her own.

The firelight flickered over the three younger girls' faces as they cuddled in their bed and Aurelie turned to tiptoe from the room, her lips curving at the sound of Lizbet's soft whispering, " 'Maiden in the moor lay, maiden in the moor lay,' " when she heard a little shriek and whirled back around.

Marigold sat straight up in the bed, where she slept between Gwyneth and Lizbet. She clapped her hand over her mouth, and tears welled up, shiny in her big eyes.

"What is it?" Aurelie rushed back to her.

"Her doll," Gwyneth said suddenly, sitting up, too. "It's her doll. She doesn't have her doll."

"It's in the schoolroom," Lizbet said. "She left it there before we went on our picnic. I remember she didn't have it in the training hall."

"I'll get it." Aurelie leaned over the bed and brushed Marigold's wild hair back from her cheeks, thumbing away the streak of moisture that squeezed down one soft cheek. "I'll bring it right back. Don't cry."

She carried a candle with her. The schoolroom was dark, the fire gone from the hearth now. They never used the schoolroom in the evenings, so the servants didn't keep it lit then.

The large chamber felt strange in the dark, alone. Ghostly, almost, and she thought of how the girls' mother would have spent happy hours there with her children in years past, and she felt a warmth, almost an acceptance for a moment, that was surely nothing but her imagination, but she knew she *was* doing something good for these girls—or at least, she was trying. And for once she didn't feel like a shameful interloper, a sinner, a wanton who'd taken another woman's life. She was going to make Lorabelle proud, and she took a deep breath and felt strong and not quite so ashamed.

The doll was nowhere to be seen, and it occurred to her that Marigold had had it in her hand when she'd crawled under the chair by the hearth, so she set her candle on the floor and peeked beneath. There was the doll. She pulled it out, tucked it in the crook of her arm, and was about to pick up her candle and go when she noticed the stack of slates on the hearth where she routinely had the girls set them down after they finished their work for the day. She always had them scrub them clean with a cloth first, but the one on top wasn't cleaned now.

She stared down at it, her blood chilling. Numbly, she reached for the candle behind her, brought it up to hold it over the slate to be sure, to know that her eyes weren't deceiving her.

Her hand shook, the candle fluttering in reaction, as she read the scrawled words again.

*Greetings, sweet Sister.*

# Sixteen

Aurelie's heart banged hard against the wall of her chest. *Greetings, sweet Sister.* Sir Santon's horrible, glittering eyes seared through her mind. *He'd found her. Somehow, he'd found her.*

She struggled to breathe past the ball of horror in her throat. *This can't be happening,* she thought desperately, trying to think over the roaring in her ears. It couldn't be Sir Santon. *Could it?*

She stared at the slate, forcing herself to breathe past the choking block in her throat.

*Think.*

She'd been disciplining Gwyneth and Lizbet about calling each other names. She'd been making them correct themselves using endearments, and one of them had simply left a note to the other, playful, teasing. That was all. That had to be all. Anything else was a product of her dark, dire imagination, a byblow of her sin and deception. She'd taken everything that didn't belong to her, and she expected to be found out any moment—and she would be, if she couldn't get control of this stupid panic.

She had to be cool, calm, collected. She couldn't lose it over such a silly thing as a note between Gwyneth and Lizbet.

Setting down her candle, almost tipping it into the rushes because her hands were shaking so much, she dropped Marigold's doll beside it. She grabbed one of the cloths the girls used to clean their slates and scrubbed at the chalked words.

Her fingers started hurting, and she realized she could stop scrubbing. The words were gone, long gone. She dropped the slate on top of the stack of other slates as if it were burning her hand, cast down the cloth, and picked up her candle and the doll. She backed away from the hearth.

*Breathe, breathe.* She took long, uneven breaths but her pulse wouldn't stop pounding. Her stomach hurt and she felt dizzy.

*Do you like that, sweet Sister?*

Sir Santon's leering, awful eyes smashed into her mind's eye again. *Stop it, stop it, stop it—*

But his eyes wouldn't go away.

*You will, sweet Sister. You will.*

A hand touched her shoulder. She let out a startled scream and whirled in the dark room.

"Milady! Forgive me!" Fayette, the young maid from the village who'd been assigned to serve the girls, stepped back, jerking her hand down.

Her eyes were huge in the flicker of the candle-light.

"Fayette. It's all right. I'm just . . . jumpy." Aurelie put out her hand to pat the maid on the arm, her own heart still in her throat, but realizing at the same time that she'd scared Fayette as much as Fayette had scared her.

The maid was very timid—and very young, only a year older than Elayna. Fayette had seemed excited to be brought to the castle as a lady's maid, and Aurelie knew she was fearful of displeasing.

"I'm so sorry, milady," Fayette repeated.

"It's not your fault." Aurelie took another harsh breath. She couldn't fall apart now, not in front of Fayette. *Not at all. She couldn't fall apart at all,* she told herself sternly. "Don't worry about it. What—what are you doing here?"

"I checked the girls' room, and Marigold was crying," Fayette explained. "I came to help ye look for the doll."

"Here it is." Aurelie handed the doll to the maid. "Would you please take it to Marigold?"

She couldn't face the girls right now. She needed to get herself together, get back in control.

Fayette took the doll.

"Wait," Aurelie said suddenly. "Do you—have you ever heard of a knight at Castle Wulfere named Santon?" She felt as if she died a thousand times while she waited for the maid to answer.

Fayette shook her head. "No, milady. I don't think so. Are ye looking for a knight named Santon? Would ye like me to—"

"No, no," Aurelie stopped her. She didn't want Fayette to do anything.

The last thing she needed was to have the girls' maid asking around for Sir Santon.

She would have to think about what to do on her own. Aurelie left Fayette in the passage, taking the opposite path to her own chamber. A tub of fragrant, warm water waited for her in front of the fire. It had become her custom to bathe every evening and Eglyntine had a tub sent up as a routine at this time now. Usually, Eglyntine waited for her, helping her to undress and wash her hair.

It was a luxury she enjoyed, feeling wicked at the same time. This was not her pleasure to take, and yet she took it, anyway. It scared her a little that guilt didn't stop her.

There was no pleasure in her bath tonight, and not because she was late and Eglyntine had already gone. Her head ached and her pulse pounded on. She couldn't stop thinking about the words on the slate. She couldn't let panic carry her away, and yet at the same time it would be foolish to ignore it.

One thing she could do was ask the girls if they'd left anything written on their slates. She'd question them about it in the morning—but there was always the chance the girls wouldn't even remember what or if they'd left anything on their slates.

It wasn't at all unusual for them to draw or scribble notes to each other on their slates at the end of lesson time.

If she could just make sure there was no one by the name of Santon at Castle Wulfere, then she could relax. And if there were—

The thought of running away from Castle Wulfere now brought a thick lump to her throat. She swallowed it down.

She couldn't get too attached to her life here. She'd always known that. *She was already attached.*

Slipping out of one of the many beautiful gowns that was hers and yet not hers at all, she carefully draped it over the chest. She needed to think—and didn't want to think—at the same time. Eglyntine had laid out her night rail on the bed.

There was a huge, thick bath sheet warming over

the chair closest to the fire, and she stepped into the tub, sinking to her chin. Thoughts whirled inside her mind, whether she wanted them or not.

Fayette hadn't known of a knight named Santon at Castle Wulfere. Fayette had lived in the little village of Fulbury outside the castle all her life.

But would Fayette know all the knights? Probably not, Aurelie had to concede. The villagers came and went through the castle gate every day, and she knew the knights entertained themselves in the village tavern and no doubt would attend the fair and games and all manner of activities in Fulbury through the year.

But Fayette was timid and wouldn't have spoken to any of these big, fearsome men.

Some of the men were recent arrivals, returning to England with Damon. Others had moved around as a result of the pestilence.

Even Damon might not know all the men-at-arms by name yet. He'd only recently returned himself.

There was only one person to ask, one person whose business it was to know every knight, every soldier, every watchman. Julian, Castle Wulfere's chief man-at-arms.

She shivered despite the comfortably heated water. Her eyes still squeezed closed, she plunged low in the tub, covering her head, fighting to stop the terrible track of her thoughts. Rising again, gasping for breath, she smeared her hands over her face, wiping back the water. She reached for the bar of rose petal soap in a dish on the table and began sudsing her hair.

The soap slipped out of her fingers into the tub. She opened her eyes to look for it, and the soapy water ran into her eyes, stinging them. She pressed her fingers to her eyes, which only made them sting more.

She squeezed her lids shut, leaning and reaching blindly for the pitcher on the nearby table that Eglyntine used to rinse her hair.

From across the room, she heard the door open and felt a brush of cooler air enter the room as Eglyntine returned. Her fingertips skimmed the empty pitcher, and knocked it off the table.

"Would you get that, please?" She rubbed at her eyes again, and wrapping her arms about her knees, she bent her head, waiting for Eglyntine.

There was no sound for a moment, then the hushed snick of the door closing, soft footfalls crossing the room.

Another long beat, and she heard the rustle of the rushes as the pitcher was taken up. She felt her hair being lifted by a strong hand, and the whoosh of the water as it was taken in then poured out of the pitcher, over the back of her head. Dip and pour, over and over, until her hair was clean and sweet with roses and the light touch of mint from the bathwater.

She surrendered to the sensation of warm water and kind hands, stroking her hair, squeezing the excess water out of it.

There was the scrape of the silver comb being taken from the table, then the comb sifting through her hair. It felt so good, this tender pull, this skimming caress of fingers against her neck, behind her ears, lifting and combing. She had been touched so little in her life and she savored this time, these baths, the simple, comforting service that demanded nothing of her, only gave. The wonderful, soothing touch slid down her neck, and stopped at the tight knots of tension there.

Aurelie moaned involuntarily, and the fingers probed, examined, found the painful knots. A sigh escaped her lips, and the bliss of touch continued. Kneading, pressing, pushing at her tension. She relaxed and sighed, then breathed in deeply.

She caught a scent of leather and man that made her think of her husband. His tunics hung nearby, on the pole by the chest, and she turned her head that way now, breathing in again, pulling in the lingering trace of *him*. Tension fingered down her spine, a different sort of tension, and she felt an ache in her chest.

Would she ever know this mysterious man she'd wed?

Or would she have to run away first, caught, disgraced, revealed?

Which was the more dangerous fate—to know her husband, or to be revealed?

She sighed again, a broken sigh, almost a sob, and she couldn't believe her weakness. The thickness was back in her throat, and the ache in her chest went deeper. She opened her eyes and shoved away the thoughts that only made her more confused.

It was late and she didn't want to keep Eglyntine so long. The hands fell away as she stood in the tub, turning toward the maid.

"Could you reach the bath sheet, Eg—"

She gasped, her words cutting off, her heart slamming, because it wasn't Eglyntine at all.

\* \* \*

He shouldn't be there. He shouldn't have touched her. He shouldn't have washed her hair or combed it or pressed his fingers into her sweet, tense flesh.

But how could he not? He'd found her, body hunched together like a lost faery, drenched and gorgeous and amazingly vulnerable and reaching out—to her maid, not to him. But he'd been there, and he'd wanted to touch her so badly, for so many long days and so many longer nights.

She hadn't been out of his mind for a single heartbeat since that silly picnic in the training hall. *Who brought a picnic to a training hall?* He couldn't figure her out, and maybe that was part of the reason he couldn't stop thinking about her.

He'd come back to the keep, to their chamber, earlier than had been his habit this past week, driven to see her, talk to her—about what, he didn't even know.

The last thing he'd expected had been to find her nude and reaching for him, even if she hadn't known it was him. Maybe if she had, she wouldn't have reached for him.

And he wouldn't have reached back. But she hadn't, and for a few awesome beats in time, he'd let himself do what he'd wanted to do for a sennight.

*Touch her.*

To her credit, she hadn't dived back into the tub. She stood there, with that jutted jaw of hers and those secret blue eyes, the flush staining her cheeks the only color on her pale face. Water drained down her arms, over the small, perfect peaks of her breasts, her flat belly and curved hips, dusky curls in between, her long legs disappearing into the water.

Time spun out between them, shocked and breathless.

Then he realized she was shivering and he snatched the warmed bath sheet from the chair by the fire. He thrust it toward her, training his eyes away from the exquisite body she refused to hide from him.

How he wanted her. And still nothing held him back. Nothing but himself, his own reason or pain or fear. He wasn't sure anymore.

"Thank you, my lord," she said, and she wrapped herself in the towel, looking away from him now, hiding those secret eyes and hot cheeks. "I didn't expect you."

"It's my room."

"Is it?" She stepped away from the tub and looked up at him, her expression carefully blank.

He watched her, wondering what she was thinking, longing to demand to know, to demand to know everything about her.

Almost he would have spoken, weak as he was in that moment, his will drained from touching her, seeing her, breathing in her sweet fragrance—the scent that came from the bath, he realized now, and mixed so intoxicatingly with the pure womanly essence that was hers alone and came from nothing but mystery.

But there was a knock on the door.

"Come in," Lorabelle called, holding his gaze with that empty look of hers that was driving him crazy because it hid something—what? Her cheeks were still red.

Eglyntine poked her head around the door. "I'm sorry, milady, I was distracted belowstairs helping one of the other maids. I'll have them come up now to get the tub if ye're finished."

"Thank you."

Eglyntine glanced at Damon and withdrew.

The spit of the fire filled the silence.

"Why—" she started, then her words broke off. She turned just slightly, looked toward the fire. "Why did you do that?"

She didn't specify what she was referring to, but he knew. He couldn't stop looking at her, like a man possessed. And perhaps he was.

Firelight gleamed on her bare shoulders. Her shiny gold hair dripped into the rushes around her.

"You asked for help," he said finally.

She pivoted. Her eyes blazed across the space between them.

"I didn't know it was you," she said evenly.

He experienced that flare of warning that came to him whenever he was with her.

"Would you have, if you'd known it was me?" He shouldn't be asking this question, following this line of conversation.

Yet he couldn't stop.

Her gaze on him was wary, steady, but that steadiness seemed fragile, encased in all that tension he knew was there. It pulled him to her as much as anything, as much as her sweet body and thick hair and mystery eyes, this pain pulled him.

Now, she was all pride and coolness, hiding that hurt. "No," she answered him.

Her haughtiness made him want to smile. Or kiss her. Or take her straight to that big bed that was waiting for them to share.

He most definitely shouldn't have come here tonight.

"Did you mind?" Why couldn't he stop, turn away, leave her, leave this dangerous conversation?

"Well, it was considerate of you," she said in that quiet little monotone of hers that told him nothing, "but since this is when I bathe every night, it would be better if you weren't here. It would be better if this didn't happen again."

It took him a few beats to realize she had repeated his own words when he'd dismissed her from the hall and told her not to come back.

Had he actually—hurt her?

The feeling was uncomfortable, and he knew suddenly what had been bothering him all day. He owed this sweet-proud bride of his an apology.

He wasn't used to making apologies. He wasn't used to her.

"I'm sorry if I seemed . . . harsh . . . earlier. You took me by surprise today," he said.

Her lips curved, and she surprised him again. He caught a glimpse of that sparkle in her eyes.

"It can't be easy to take you by surprise, my lord," she said, watching him with that half smile that bewitched him and irritated him at once.

"Did they teach you to be so meek in the convent?" He walked toward her, closing the space between them. She didn't back away, but held her ground with that vulnerable pride and shy strength that was uniquely hers and drew him desperately.

It was a perilous thing, this desire, nearly overwhelming him. He stopped short of her.

She didn't reply to his question, but answered with one of her own.

"Did you know how much your sisters admire you?" she inquired, her chin up, her eyes even—mystery and demand at once.

Now he laughed, a harsh sound, an unfamiliar sensation that hurt his chest.

"I'm the last person they would admire."

"You're wrong."

Firelight danced, shimmered, in the golden strands of her still-damp hair, casting a golden glow around her. Angel. Sorceress.

"Why does Gwyneth wear new boys' tunics?" he inquired, pushing the dangerous thoughts from him, controlling the desire, the need. *Need.* Could he still deny it? He didn't want to consider it. He drove whatever wedge he could between himself and this temptation, this craving, this urgency. "You had new clothes made for them—and you had boys' clothing made for Gwyneth."

"She has new kirtles. She refused to wear them." She tilted her head to regard him tensely, her arms crossed as they held the towel still wrapped around her. "She wants to be a knight, like you."

His chest tightened.

"And Lizbet wants to be a falconer," he said abruptly, his voice hard, controlled. "Is that why you're letting her have weekly lessons in the mews?"

"It makes her feel closer to the memory of her father," she told him.

He couldn't stand to stare into those demanding eyes of hers any longer. They wanted—what? He didn't know, he only knew he didn't have anything to give—to her, to his sisters.

"Gwyneth should dress properly, grow her hair," he stated. He moved past her, closer to the fire. "And

Lizbet needs to give up this foolishness about becoming a falconer." He looked back at her. "Elayna must accept her fate, her betrothal. And Marigold needs to speak again if she's to have a normal life."

Her color had risen again.

"Am I a miracle maker, my lord?" she asked quietly, though the heat in her voice, the flash in her eyes, told him she was not as cool as she appeared. "If I were, then you—"

She broke off, the color draining from her cheeks as quickly as it had risen.

*Then he what?*

His gaze dropped to her mouth, those full lips. He was still close to her, and he had only to shift slightly to find himself closer.

"They act out in different ways," she said into that tight awareness. "But they all want the same thing."

"And what is that?" He felt a simmer of anger himself, frustration that she knew what they needed and he didn't. Frustration that she seemed to expect . . . something . . . from him.

"Attention."

"And you want me to give it to them."

"Yes."

"I'm a knight." He didn't even know how to talk to his sisters. Just looking at them bothered him. He'd always felt invincible, as if he could do anything.

He'd learned he was wrong.

"I know nothing of children," he went on roughly. "Especially girls."

"You're their brother, their family." There was a long pull of time between them and she said softly, clearly, "They don't have to be alone, and neither do you."

It was more than a little alarming that she saw his detachment, defined it. He didn't want her to be close to him, under his skin, not in any emotional way.

But he couldn't stay angry with her.

Slowly, so slowly, he watched himself reach out and touch her face. Sweet, tempting, so very near. His.

A new tension came over her and he felt her breathe, the mere sensation alluring to him. She didn't shrink back, though he felt her tremble. Not from fear, he realized now. Desire.

She was as aware of him as he was of her.

"They need you," she whispered, low, and if he hadn't been so close, he never would have heard her. "And you—"

"What do I need, Lorabelle?" he prodded, unable to stop himself, too weak-willed in this instant. His physical frustration was painful, and would only get worse. He wanted to make love to her. But he didn't want it to matter.

Yet what he feared was that she mattered already.

"I said I was no miracle worker."

"What are you?"

Mystery. Temptation. Downfall.

He had to stop, turn away. This was too hard, not giving in to this desire, this woman who mattered.

She wasn't helping. She just stood there, almost as if she knew. As if she were daring him.

Her secret eyes didn't flinch.

"I'm your wife."

# Seventeen

The words came out of her mouth so easily.

She'd challenged him. As if she had the right. As if she were truly so bold.

*I'm your wife.*

She wanted to be his wife. She wanted to heal him, his sisters. And somehow if she could do that, maybe she could also heal herself. Make everything right.

Would she have the chance?

Aurelie, her breath trapped in her chest, gazed at Damon, a breath away through the flickering fireglow. She leaned into his touch, completely vulnerable to him, needing, wanting.

There was a knock at the door.

He dropped his hand from her face and turned. "Yes?"

Eglyntine entered with servants to remove the tub. She carried a tray with mulled wine, which she left every night on the table by the fire.

"Milady?" She looked questioningly at Aurelie.

"I'm fine, please," she said, working to steady her voice, her breathing. "You need your rest."

Eglyntine followed the servants, shutting the door softly, leaving them alone in this chamber that seemed huge suddenly, where it had seemed tiny a moment before.

Damon had moved in front of the fire again, giving her his back. He picked up the pitcher, poured a drink. "Would you like some?" he asked without looking at her.

She shook her head, then realized he couldn't see her. "No."

The moment was gone, shattered, along with her courage. She'd stood before him naked, brazen. But he had turned his back on her now. Remote.

And yet did his hand shake ever so slightly as he lifted that goblet?

She stood there for another long beat, wishing, remembering that penetrating link in his hard eyes, that unspoken something that told her he wanted her as much as she wanted him.

He wanted her. But he didn't take her. It didn't make sense, and it made her horribly uneasy. *Why?*

She changed into the night rail and climbed into bed. Blowing out the candle by the bed, she pulled the smooth sheet over her. Time magnified. She heard his breath, the soft clink of the goblet as he set it on the table. The spit of the fire. The sound of her heart beating.

She turned restlessly, thinking of Damon, the girls, the terrible panic of finding those words on the slate. Everything turned over and over in her mind.

Her head started to pound again.

*I charge thee by the Father, the Son, and the Holy Spirit, that if any of you know any cause why these persons may not be lawfully joined together in matrimony, he do now confess it.*

The priest's words at their wedding came back to

her, joining the mix of thoughts and feelings turning in her mind.

*She was standing before the chapel, that bitter wind taunting her as the priest spoke, as if the very elements of Nature knew her deception, sought to punish her. She looked up at the priest.*

*Sir Santon's glittering eyes met her from the priest's tonsured face. Shock stopped her heart. Slowly, agonizingly, she turned to look at her bridegroom.*

*Sir Santon's cruel eyes replaced Damon's harsh, pained ones.*

*She gasped, fear ripping through her as she found breath again. Whirling, her gaze swept over the crowd. Sir Santon was everywhere, his eyes blazing from every face. Those glittering, brutal eyes. She ran, up the hall steps, inside the castle keep, through the cavernous hall to her room, safety— but she couldn't find it. Passages opened up, everywhere, and she was lost. Echoing down the long, dark corridors came a voice.*

*Greetings, sweet Sister. Greetings, sweet Sister. Greetings—*

Damon came awake abruptly, a blaze of images— ugly, dark—breaking apart. Seconds beat by as he adjusted, realizing what had shaken him from the black grip of his sleep. Choked cries came from the bed. He bolted from his chair and crossed the room.

In the dim flicker of the lowering fire, she writhed and twisted in the bedsheets, her hair wild, her arms fighting—what?

He got down on the bed beside her, took hold of those flailing arms.

"Lorabelle, Lorabelle," he called, urgent.

She jolted upright, pushing at him. "Stop!" she

rasped, lashing out with agitated swings of her arms, stronger than the fragile way she felt to him, shaking free of his grip.

He tried to grab hold of her again and she caught him with one of those punches straight on the nose. Seizing her wrists, he held her tighter, yet still she fought. He was on top of her now, rolling over her, pinning her with his body.

Her eyelids fluttered open and she stared straight up at him, glassy, wild-eyed. Comprehending.

"Oh, I'm sorry," she cried. "I'm sorry—"

"No," he soothed, brushing at the sweat-damp hair flying into her face, her eyes. She was shivering and sweating and crying all at once. "It's all right. Nobody's going to hurt you here. I promise. Nobody's going to hurt you."

"I was so frightened," she whispered brokenly.

"I know." He knew more than she could understand. He knew nightmares. Knew their power. Their relentless pursuit.

She shook her head in the darkness. "No, you can't know. You can't—" Her words ended on a hitch.

"You can't forget the attack at Briermeade," he said quietly, moving slightly to take his weight off her now but staying close. Holding her. "It comes to you at night. Dreams. Nightmares. Torment."

"You have nightmares, too."

"Yes."

"And they frighten you?"

She sounded dubious, as if she couldn't imagine that anything could scare him. He almost laughed. Thank God it was so dark. Somehow it freed him.

"Oh, yes," he said at last, slowly. "They frighten me."

Admitting any weakness to her was danger. She was his greatest weakness of all. But there was this penetrating thing, this closeness, that compelled him to a measure of honesty he didn't want.

"How do you make them go away? The nightmares?" Her eyes searched his in the blackness, shiny and hurt and unshuttered in this tenuous moment.

"I don't know," he said, and he'd never felt so inadequate in his whole life.

She was silent for a long time. Always, she was so strong, so proud, and he sensed the tension in her body, the struggle.

"Oh," she said at last, and suddenly she began to cry. Her slender-strong body began to shake and he cradled her close as she wound her arms around his neck. It was the wrong moment for lust, though telling himself that didn't stop the need, the physical reaction of his body.

"Don't leave me tonight."

Every nerve end in his big body tensed. The scent of her filled his nostrils. She was soft where he was rough, curved where he was hard. His jaw clenched, and the ache of need deep inside intensified.

It was one thing to sleep across the room and not touch her. This was another thing altogether. This was torment.

Misery.

He couldn't leave her.

"No," he promised. "I won't leave you."

Morning filtered into the room through the thick glass windows. Aurelie opened her eyes, dazed. It took a long stretch for her to realize she wasn't at the convent. Lorabelle was dead. They were all dead.

She was the lady of Wulfere.

She'd spent the night in her husband's arms.

*Or had it all been a dream?*

She sat straight up. The nightmare, familiar now and horrible, smashed into her mind.

Then Damon, holding her. Damon, brushing her face, cradling her close, comforting her. Her stone-cold knight of a husband, soothing her.

Suddenly she remembered more, those nights she'd slept through, semiconscious, when she'd first arrived at Castle Wulfere. Damon. He'd been there, those nights. Those fragmented memories were real.

What manner of man was this fearsome knight? Cold, harsh? Gentle, tender?

She realized abruptly that she'd overslept, and she remembered the words on the slate. She threw off her bedcovers.

Dressing quickly, she knew the girls would already be gone. She'd probably missed morning prayers completely.

No one had woken her. Damon had left without disturbing her. Even Eglyntine had let her be. She wondered if her gentle-harsh husband had instructed the maid to let her sleep in. That this harsh knight could also be thoughtful and caring and tender no longer seemed impossible.

*Don't start thinking about him again,* she warned herself. When she thought of him, she felt weak, wobbly, and alive, so alive. It was bewildering.

This morning, she had to put her mind to other matters. Despite how much the prospect scared her.

The castle bustled with activity. Servants went

about their business. Knights broke their fast and hurried off to their day of tilting and fencing or standing watches. House maids carried reeds and rushes through the hall for plaiting into baskets while kitchen staff carted in loads of wood for carving new spoons, platters, and bowls.

Damon's sisters sat at the high table by themselves. They saw her, and Gwyneth and Lizbet waved to her. She waved back.

As it happened, she didn't have to seek out Sir Julian. She ran into him at the foot of the stairs.

"My lady," he said, and his mirrorlike gaze fixed on her.

He stopped, one booted foot resting on the bottom step, his arm positioned casually against the hand-rail—blocking her passage. She stood on that bottom step, eye-level with her husband's cousin. He wore a particolored tunic, black and red. She was struck again by how extraordinarily handsome he was, and how much he resembled her husband—and yet was nothing like him at all.

He continued, "You're looking well this morn. You must be quite recovered by this time."

"Yes, I'm very well, thank you."

"Your memories," he said easily. "Have they returned?"

"In part," she said, assuming an innocent air that cost her in terms of her churning stomach muscles. He'd played into her hands, though, and she took full advantage of his conversation. "But not entirely. Things come to me in bits. In fact, just yesterday, I saw a knight and could have sworn I knew him. It wasn't until later that it hit me."

He arched a brow and waited. He still hadn't moved, still blocked her path.

"There was a boy, a page, at Sperling Castle. His name was Santon. We—" She swallowed the lump in her throat, panic rising at the voicing of Santon's name. "We used to play together. I thought this knight looked like him, but I'm not sure. I wouldn't want to approach him if I were wrong. Is there a knight here named Santon?"

She was taking a fearful risk to ask this question, and she felt light-headed, waiting for his answer. But she had to know. She couldn't take the time to wait it out, to wait for Santon to come to her. If he was here, she had to know now. Before it was too late to flee.

No flicker of recognition crossed Julian's face. "Santon?" he repeated the name slowly. "No, there is no one here by that name."

Not collapsing was a feat, she was so relieved.

"Ah," she said, shocked by how calm she sounded. "I see. I was afraid I was wrong."

"Yes," he said. "Quite wrong."

She stood there a beat longer.

"Well," he said, "I must attend my duties."

He moved his arm, proffering his hand in a gallant fashion that she wished desperately to refuse but couldn't. She took it, taking the last step. He let go, and she moved past him.

She felt his eyes on her back, her skin prickling at her nape. She held her head high as she maneuvered between tables to the girls.

When she had the courage to glance back, he was gone.

\* \* \*

The girls couldn't remember if they'd left anything written on their slates. Aurelie questioned them, carefully, but their blank looks and confused responses told her nothing. But what other solution could there be? There was no one at Castle Wulfere named Sir Santon.

The uneasiness didn't leave her. This, she told herself, was the price of her deception. She would live with bouts of fear and panic for the rest of her life.

Midmorning, she knew she had to get out of the castle. She needed fresh air, sunshine—even cold, gray sunshine.

"Let's put away our lesson and get our cloaks," she said, and the girls looked up in surprise. "It's a beautiful day, and Christmas is coming. How would you like to gather greens to decorate the hall?"

The girls' faces lit up at once. Aurelie warmed, and felt excitement fill her as well. For years, she'd listened to Lorabelle's wondrous, enchanted stories of Christmas festivities at Sperling Castle, before she'd come to Briermeade. The convent celebrated the solemn, religious side of the season, but Aurelie had always dreamed of the splendor of a real Christmas. It was only days till Christmas Eve, yet she thought now of how there'd been no sign that the season would be properly celebrated at Castle Wulfere.

As lady of the castle, it was up to her, she realized.

"We're going to celebrate Christmas?" Elayna asked, the ever-mutinous set of her mouth softening.

"Like when Mama was here?" Gwyneth whispered. Marigold watched, her eyes huge.

Aurelie nodded. "That's right. You'll have to help me." She looked at Elayna, knowing she would recall best of all how the Yule season would have been celebrated at Castle Wulfere in the past. She hoped it would be good for the girl, too—help take her mind off her own troubles for a time.

Quickly, the girls put away their slates. They gathered their cloaks and gloves, and went down to the kitchen to fetch baskets to carry the greens.

Aurelie informed the burly cook that they would be celebrating a proper Christmas and ordered him to prepare a feast.

"We'll want gingerbread and plum pudding—" Aurelie started.

"And posset," Elayna put in.

"And frumenty," Gwyneth added. "And Yule dolls."

Aurelie was surprised when the beefy cook's face broke into a smile. "All right, miladies," he boomed. "We'll do it!"

He looked, she thought, almost as excited as the girls.

There were almond cakes cooling on the racks on the big worktable. "Wait," he said, when they started to take their baskets and go. He cut up one of the cakes, wrapped the pieces in a cloth, and stuffed them in Aurelie's basket.

She was, Aurelie thought with a sense of warmth, winning over the castle staff. Slowly.

In the cold passage between the kitchen and the great hall, Gwyneth all but danced, walking backward, reeling off the names of games she remembered playing in years gone by. At ten, she could remember them better than Lizbet, and Marigold would never have known a real Christmas at all. Gwyneth and Elayna traded off calling out games.

"Hunt the slipper."

"Bee in the middle."

"How do you play that?" Lizbet asked.

Gwyneth stopped in front of them and started explaining. "Everyone sits in a circle—"

Aurelie watched, glad she was wearing her cloak already. It was cold in the passage. They'd stopped in front of the corridor leading down to the storage basement and the river dock.

Gwyneth carried on, while Lizbet listened avidly. Elayna put in corrections, recalling the game better than Gwyneth.

Only Marigold didn't seem to be interested. Her back was to Aurelie in the tight confines of the passage. She faced the corridor to the river dock and was backing, slowly, one step at a time, away from it. She bumped into Aurelie and let out a tiny cry.

Aurelie put her arms around her, and was shocked to find the girl shaking uncontrollably. More than she would shake from cold alone.

"Marigold?" She hugged the trembling girl and reached for her face, tucking her fingers up under her chin so that the little girl had to meet her eyes. "What is it? What's wrong?"

Marigold buried her face in Aurelie's cloak.

Her sisters had stopped talking and just stood there, staring now.

"Come on," Aurelie said, frustrated. Pain, torment, secrets. What was going on here? She handed the basket she was holding to Elayna and picked up Marigold. "Let's get out of here. Christmas is coming. We have evergreens to gather."

She tried to sound cheerful, but the mood had changed and she had no idea why.

\* \* \*

"Where was he found?"

Damon frowned down at the dead body of a knight he didn't know. Blood covered the front of the man's tunic. He'd been moved into the infirmary at the rear of the soldier's quarters.

"In the passage between the soldier's dormitory and the training hall," Kenric answered.

The passage allowed a shortcut from the dormitory to the gatehouse, and was used frequently. Damon had been locked away with Eudo, reviewing the steward's accounts again. The death fines had been returned, and he was satisfied on that count now. It had been Rorke who'd found him and had informed him of the gruesome discovery.

"He couldn't have been there long," Damon said. "No one saw anything?"

Rorke shook his head. "We're questioning the men, but so far—nothing."

"Who is he?" Damon asked, anger burning in his chest that a man under his command, his guardianship, would be murdered within the walls of Castle Wulfere. Anger—and prickling apprehension.

The murderer was still here, somewhere, among them.

"His name was Prewitt. He has a brother here, Stephen," Rorke told him, his startling blue eyes locked with Damon's. "That's all I've found out so far."

Damon stared down at the man. He'd been stabbed only once.

Once had been enough.

"I want every man questioned," he said. "Every

servant. Find out who came through the castle gates this morning."

"He said something, before he died," Kenric said.

The younger knight's eyes held Damon's for a long stretch. He was still young, but Damon had come to know and trust Kenric in France, almost as much as he knew and trusted Rorke. Kenric was worried, and about more than the dead body stretched in front of them.

"What did he say?"

Kenric glanced at Rorke. It was Rorke who answered.

"He wanted to talk to you. He was rambling, struggling to speak at all. He said something about your sisters. 'Find her, she's in danger,' he kept saying, but he was choking, coughing. I could hardly understand him."

"Her? My sisters? Which sister?"

Rorke shook his head. "Not your sisters. That's what didn't make sense. The name he kept repeating. It wasn't one of your sisters."

"Who was it?"

"Lorabelle."

# *Eighteen*

A misty pewter sky hung over Castle Wulfere, ominous, waiting. Darker clouds streaked the horizon far beyond the river and woods, promising more snow to come. But for now, the air was crisp and fresh, and the walk down the sloped approach to the gatehouse seemed to cheer her little group, Aurelie noticed. Even she felt better, renewed, her worries evaporating.

The snow had melted over the past few days, leaving patches of white drifts and cold earth dotted with dead leaves of autumn and nuts and fallen sticks. Their boots crunched over the winter ground as the three younger girls skipped, swinging their baskets. Lizbet's bird bells, always hanging around her neck, tinkled in the fresh air.

Sir Beldon trudged along behind them, the only dour note on their expedition. Her husband's knights were ever present. It was rare that she could so much as leave the schoolroom without attracting their watchful eyes.

The young knight had preferred to fetch mounts from the stables, but Aurelie had explained that they intended only to walk to the rim of the dark, thick woods to cut greens. It wasn't far, only a brisk march away. They skirted the village, where men could be seen repairing the banks of the millpond while boys ran back and forth across the frozen meadow with a ball, kicking and throwing and yelling to one another.

They hiked the perimeter of the meadow, Beldon grudgingly following behind. Gwyneth cast numerous longing glances at the boys playing ball. They were at the far end of the meadow when the ball sailed over their heads, almost to the edge of the woods. Gwyneth dropped her basket and chased after it.

"You, lad, this way!" called one of the village boys. He held up his arms for her to toss the ball back at him.

Gwyneth darted a look at Aurelie. The villagers thought she was a boy with her short hair and tunic, and it was no surprise that this turn of events was entirely appealing to Gwyneth.

"Please," she said, her eyes huge and bright as she clutched the ball, what looked to be a stuffed pig's bladder, to her chest. "Can I see if they'll let me play?"

Elayna rolled her eyes.

Beldon huffed up to join them where they'd stopped. Disapproval marked his features.

"Please, Lorabelle!" Gwyneth pleaded, tipping up and down on her toes in her excitement.

Aurelie had to grin at her enthusiasm. What could it hurt? "Yes," she said. "Go ahead. We'll be here, gathering greens, when you're done. Don't go out of sight, all right?"

Gwyneth nodded, and impulsively threw her arms

around Aurelie's waist before she ran off to join the village boys in their game.

Aurelie led the other girls to the fringe of the forest. The earth was soft with fallen pine needles. The air was colder in the shadow of the trees, but sweet, woodsy, winter-fresh. Aurelie shoved Gwyneth's basket at Beldon.

"Good thing you're here," she said, snapping a smile at the dour knight. "We could use an extra hand."

Beldon stared down at the basket, looking exceedingly unenthusiastic. Aurelie figured he'd much rather be practicing his swordsmanship in the training hall.

She handed Lizbet and Elayna small blades for cutting, and instructed Marigold to pick up what she could find already on the ground—twigs to add structure to the evergreen bunches they would tie together with ribbons later when they returned to the keep.

"I hope we find some mistletoe," Lizbet said. "Then we can make a kissing bush!"

"Mama always hung a kissing bush in the doorway of the keep," Elayna told Aurelie. "Papa would kiss her there on Christmas Day." She looked wistful as she stared down at her basket.

"Then we'll hang a kissing bush there, too," Aurelie said firmly. Would Damon kiss her beneath it on Christmas Day? She looked at Elayna. "You miss your mother a great deal, don't you?"

Elayna nodded. Together, they began cutting branches from a small evergreen while Lizbet searched for mistletoe and Marigold picked twigs and pinecones from the forest floor.

"Everything changed," Elayna said, surprising Aurelie by continuing the conversation. "Damon left right before Mama died, and then Papa got sick."

"And you took care of your sisters," Aurelie guessed.

Elayna shrugged, fiddling with the branch she'd cut. "Not very well. Not like Mama."

"I think you've taken care of them more than very well," Aurelie told her, locking gazes with the young girl. She could see the vulnerability behind Elayna's proud, jutted chin. "They're healthy, strong. They're amazing girls. I'm proud of you." She wondered what would have happened to the three younger girls without their older sister. As neglected a state as they'd been in when she'd arrived at Castle Wulfere, it could have been much worse. Elayna would have been younger than Gwyneth when their mother died. It had been a big responsibility at a very young age.

Elayna's cheeks heated a little at the compliment. "People think we're strange."

"People are wrong," Aurelie said. "Gwyneth and Lizbet are who they are, and so are you. Don't ever be afraid to be different. It makes you interesting." She remembered how the nuns had chastized her for being different, for dreaming.

"Marigold is more than different," Elayna whispered.

There was a damp shine to her eyes. Aurelie watched her closely. "Why doesn't Marigold speak?

Elayna shook her head and stared down at her basket. "I don't know," she admitted, and Aurelie realized from the raspy sound of her voice that the older girl felt guilty. Whatever had happened to Marigold had happened on Elayna's watch. And somehow, she wasn't certain Elayna was telling her everything.

"It's not your fault," Aurelie told her. Elayna looked up at her.

"I don't have to take care of them anymore," the girl said suddenly, and she wiped at her eyes, brushing away the dampness before it could turn into tears. "I'm going to do what I want now. I'm not going to marry. Ever. No matter what Damon says, or the king. Maybe I'll join a convent. Or I'll run away again. I don't know yet. But I'm not marrying Lord Harrimore. He's old. He's—" She stopped. "I don't love him."

Aurelie set down her basket and reached out and touched Elayna's arm. She could hear the cries of the children playing ball in the meadow, the soft chatter of Lizbet and Marigold and the crunches of Sir Beldon's footfalls as he traipsed around after them.

"You don't know him yet, remember?" she reminded Elayna gently. "Maybe he could arrange for you to meet Lord Harrimore. We'll think of something. But you're going to have to tell Damon how you feel."

"I have told Damon how I feel!" Elayna cried.

"Running away isn't the same as talking it out with him and looking for answers together," Aurelie pointed out.

"I can't talk to him," Elayna said stubbornly. "And he wouldn't listen, anyway."

"Try," Aurelie persisted. "He'll listen."

She hoped she was right, but when she thought of the tender man who'd held her, soothed her through the night, she couldn't believe she was wrong. He was kind, this big, strong, hard knight of hers.

Why did he hide it so? She couldn't stop thinking about him, wondering about him. It was unwise and weak and impossible to deny.

She was falling for this tough-gentle man, and that scared her more than anything. She'd fallen already for the girls, and hard. So much for not forming attachments, keeping her perspective.

*What perspective?* she thought darkly. It was all gone. If she ever had to leave this strange castle, these uncommon girls, and this puzzling husband, it would kill her.

Elayna had begun to saw her blade at a slender branch again, giving no response but a silent shrug.

They continued to work until every basket was filled to overflowing with pine boughs. They stopped, and Lizbet placed her slender arms akimbo, her basket between her feet on the ground, and looked annoyed.

"We didn't find any mistletoe," she said. "We can't have a kissing bush without it."

Aurelie wasn't sure whether she was relieved or not. Maybe it would be easier not to have a kissing bush. That was one Christmas custom that would make for an awkward moment if Damon didn't want to use it and his sisters insisted.

She turned her attention to inspecting Marigold's basket. The little girl had collected an array of oddly shaped and twisted twigs. Aurelie had noticed in the schoolroom when she played in spare moments with her slate that Marigold had an artistic eye.

"These are wonderful," she praised the little girl and started to hug her but Marigold pulled at her arm. "What is it?"

Marigold pointed into the woods and pulled at her arm again.

"Tell me," Aurelie said, holding her ground, wondering if there was any way Marigold might want to show her whatever she was pointing at badly enough that she would speak.

Marigold shook her head.

"Why not, sweetling?" Aurelie pressed. She bent to touch Marigold's soft cheek. The girl's flyaway wild hair and rosy cheeks made her look like some kind of forest sprite. "I want to hear your pretty voice," Aurelie urged softly.

Marigold's dark eyes filled, and Aurelie felt crushed. Maybe it was wrong to push the little girl. She didn't know. She just knew Marigold used to talk, and no accident or illness had precipitated this sudden curtailment of her speech.

"Oh, Marigold." She sighed, and hugged her close, then pulled back to smooth the wild hair out of the little girl's face. "I wish you could tell me why you won't talk. Maybe if you told me, I could make it better." She smiled ruefully then. "But you would have to talk to tell me that, so I'm just being silly, aren't I?" Marigold smiled back at that, and Aurelie ruffled her hair and took her hand. "All right, show me."

She let Marigold lead her several steps into the woods, and then she saw it.

"Mistletoe!" Lizbet cried, dancing up beside them. Marigold beamed proudly.

Just then, Gwyneth came running up with the ball, her cheeks flushed, her eyes glowing.

"They had to go in," she said breathlessly. "But

they said I could keep the ball. Want to play camp-ball with me?" She glanced eagerly at her sisters.

Elayna frowned. "I don't think so. I'm not messing up my hair." She'd fixed her hair in an intricate braid, two different colors of ribbons running through it, and she was looking down her nose at her boyish sister.

Lizbet hesitated. "I don't know. I'm hungry," she added.

Beldon's expression perked up at the mention of food. The sun was high above them and Aurelie knew it would be time for the midday meal. In fact, that was probably why the village boys had run inside their thatched cottages. The men at the millpond had vanished, too.

"Please!" Gwyneth cried. "I can't play at the castle with the pages anymore. The pages get in trouble if they let me join in."

Aurelie had to laugh. Poor Gwyneth. She set her basket down. "I'll play," she announced.

Gwyneth's mouth wreathed into a big smile. "Really? Oh, thank you, Lorabelle!"

"We need teams," Aurelie said. She hadn't the slightest idea how to play camp-ball, actually, but she'd noticed that was how the villagers were playing. "Come on, girls. Gwyneth, you pick first."

"Lizbet," Gwyneth said right away.

"Marigold," Aurelie selected, aiming to see Marigold's eyes light up.

"Sir Beldon," Gwyneth chose next. The knight blinked, startled.

Aurelie didn't give him time to argue. "Elayna."

The older girl's mouth dropped open. "Lorabelle—"

Aurelie didn't give her time to argue, either. She grabbed the ball from Gwyneth. "So, what do we do now?"

There were no witnesses. Every man who bunked in the rear soldier's dormitory was examined. Damon left Rorke, Kenric, and Julian, widening the circle of questioning to the soldiers who berthed in the twin gatehouse towers and might have either heard something or seen someone behaving suspiciously as they came from the area between the training hall and dormitory.

Either Sir Prewitt had been murdered by a phantom, Damon thought tensely, or someone was hiding something. Why? No motive for murdering the seemingly pleasant, if colorless, Prewitt had surfaced.

But more pressing now was to find Lorabelle and his sisters and bring them back to the castle. He'd sent Kenric immediately to verify their safety, assuming them to be within the keep, most likely still at lessons in the schoolroom, as he believed was their habit in the mornings.

It had taken Kenric over an hour to return, with the uncomfortable news that according to the cook, to whose kitchen Kenric had eventually traced Lorabelle and his sisters, they had left with baskets for the forest.

Damon was relieved to discover from the watchmen at the gatehouse that Beldon had been with them. Still, he wanted to see Lorabelle and his sisters for himself, to know for himself that they were safe. If anything happened to any of them—he couldn't stand the mere thought.

Something was wrong at Castle Wulfere, and the dead man's last words had been his wife's name. The sick slamming hadn't left his chest since Rorke had told him of Prewitt's dying moments.

Why would this unknown knight, new to Castle Wulfere since he'd left for France, cry out his bride's name as he died? It made no sense, as Rorke had said.

And what had Prewitt been trying to say about his sisters?

Damon's horse's hooves pounded the frozen ground as he left the castle at a gallop, racing down the sloped bank toward the village. Smoke curled from the cluster of roofs. The forest beyond was still, dark with shadows and pines.

Skirting the village, he bent over his horse's neck, urging his huge destrier on, then reared back, pulling on the reins as he came around the village to the wide, open meadow. He trained his mount away from the children kicking, screaming, running with a ball. He barely glanced at them, looking over their heads, scanning the forest's rim.

Damnation, where was Lorabelle and his sisters and Beldon?

His gaze roved over the figures chasing the ball again, and he realized with a shock that they weren't children, not all of them.

Lorabelle? Elayna? Beldon? He wasn't surprised to see his younger sisters at this wild game. But his bride? And the haughty, lovely, blossoming Elayna? And his knight?

He was struck dumb for a startled beat as he stood there, pulling in long breaths of frozen air. Beldon saw him first.

"My lord," he puffed. He'd thrown off his cloak, and his tunic was spattered with mud and small twigs were stuck in his hose. Distracted, Beldon found himself hit smack in the side of the head with the pig bladder.

Gwyneth clapped her hand over her mouth, to hide her . . . dismay or laughter, Damon wasn't sure.

Lorabelle turned, saw him. Her beautiful face, expressive, striking, froze. He stared at her, his breath catching in his throat.

Like Beldon, she'd thrown off her cloak and was splashed and spattered with pieces of dried leaves and bits of twigs and plops of mud. A woodland faery now, all breathless and alive, her nose and cheeks red, her chest heaving, and he was so hot suddenly, and hard, and all he could think of was how he'd held her all night and how he should have made love to her.

In this instant, he wouldn't have any control at all if they were alone. He would take her now, under this clear blue sky and damn the consequences.

Thank God they weren't alone.

He dismounted and charged across the meadow toward them, frustrated—with himself, with his beautiful faery-temptation. And relieved, damnably relieved, that she was safe, they were all safe. Whatever threat hovered over Castle Wulfere, his family was safe.

An intense coiling *something* gripped his chest, and he wanted to . . . What? Embrace them, kiss them, tell them how much they mattered? Because they did matter, all of them. So much. Lorabelle in a way that he'd tried to deny, and his sisters in a way he hadn't wanted to think about because, like Lorabelle, they tore at the heart he didn't want to acknowledge.

He scowled, feeling vulnerable and confused, and dealt with it all by roaring at them.

"What do you think you're doing?" he demanded with every bit of the bewildered frustration pounding inside him. He stomped right up to Lorabelle.

They needed keepers, all of them. And apparently, Beldon wasn't up to the task. Here was his bride, romping in the muck with a pig bladder and his sisters and one of his knights.

"I was hoping you would turn my little sisters into ladies," he grated, "not that my little sisters would turn you into a barbarian."

Lorabelle lifted that damned chin of hers. "We're playing camp-ball." Her sparkly eyes defied him. Marigold ran to hide behind her skirts.

His irritation mounted. "You're encouraging them to act like hellions!"

"I'm encouraging them to act like children," she countered.

She leaned down and picked up the ball where it had dropped after smacking Beldon in the head. Gwyneth and Lizbet stood back, staring at him. From the corner of his eyes, he noticed Elayna, ribbons askew in her amazingly untidy hair, standing in her mutinous way, arms crossed, as if she were just waiting for him to lop off all their heads.

*Damn, damn, damn again.* "Get back to the castle," he ordered. He didn't want to explain the danger that had arisen, not in front of his sisters. He would shield his sisters from the news if he could.

"We're not finished," Lorabelle said, not moving an inch.

He noticed Beldon rubbing his temple. "Take my horse," he said without taking his gaze off Lorabelle. "I'll walk back with the camp-ball team," he said dryly.

Beldon didn't need a second invitation. He was out of there.

"My lady," Damon began again, watching his bride's defiant face, and thinking of nothing but how she had looked naked, rising from the tub. The image smacked him in the head like that ball had smacked Beldon, robbing him of his ability to think straight or continue.

"We're tied," she said. "We can't leave until we break it. We have a bet."

Damon focused, trying to figure out what she was talking about. "Tied?"

"Camp-ball," she said. "Don't you know how to play?"

"I was a child once, believe it or not," he pointed out, annoyed.

"I don't," she said, and suddenly she smiled at him, that breathtaking, brilliant smile that wiped his head clean of coherent thought for another heartbeat. "Believe you were ever a child," she clarified, and he realized he must look as insensible as he felt at the moment. "You're going to have to prove it."

She wasn't as bold as her confident words would have him believe. He could see the doubt in her eyes, but she tip-tilted her chin and stared at him, waiting for him—to bark at them again. It was the same way Elayna was looking at him, and all of his sisters.

"What's the bet?" He couldn't believe he was asking this question. He had troubles enough back at the castle. This was more trouble. She was more trouble.

Lorabelle was watching him with narrowed eyes, mystery blue light mixed with dark shadow. Doubt. "Whichever team loses has to carry all the baskets back—and they're heavy. You can take Sir Beldon's place. I'll even let your side have the ball first."

He blinked as the ball in question was suddenly rammed at his chest and barely managed to catch it.

"Watch out," she added. "We don't play fair."

This statement didn't surprise him. His sweet, amazing bride hadn't been playing fair with him from the start. He tried for a whole second or two to make himself order her back to the castle again, to refuse to participate in this nonsense.

But the truth was, he wanted to be right here, with her, under this winter-mist bowl of sky, pretending to be the young, hopeful man he'd once been.

It was silly, and yet suddenly it seemed very important.

"Fine," he said. "Who's on my team?"

There was a collective gasp, then smiles. His sisters' smiles made his chest band with something tight and warm.

"Me!" Gwyneth piped up.

"And me!" Lizbet chimed in.

Lorabelle explained where the goals were on each side of the meadow. Village boys had been playing earlier, and they had heavy sticks set up to form goal boundaries.

"All right." His heart pumped, and his mouth twitched. He shoved his cloak off. He ran back, stopped, and kicked the pig bladder high in the air and across the field. Gwyneth and Lizbet tore after it, with his bride and her team close behind.

Elayna dived at Gwyneth's ankles as she caught it, pulling her down. Gwyneth passed to Lizbet, who threw it over Marigold's head—straight toward Lorabelle.

His bride almost had it, but it skimmed the tip of her fingers and landed straight in his hands. She almost tripped, but righted herself and took off after him. His sisters shouted for him from across the field. He had to run sideways to escape Elayna, giving Lorabelle time to catch up to him. He couldn't believe it when Marigold made a beeline straight for him, with Elayna and Lorabelle blocking him on both sides. He pulled up short, panting, laughing, and realized he'd made a terrible mistake when Elayna hurtled straight at him where he'd stopped.

He grabbed the ball to his chest. Gwyneth and Lizbet were shouting at him again, but he couldn't possibly pass. Lorabelle tackled him and he was down this time, his cheek smacking cold dirt.

"We'll take that ball now," she demanded breathlessly. She was sprawled over his back, laughing, and smelling incredible—like winter pine and spring roses combined. Her soft breasts were squashed against his back, her legs straddling him.

Gwyneth and Lizbet plowed atop Lorabelle and Elayna, and Marigold jumped in, and their weight suddenly caused a strange pop and Damon yelled for mercy.

"You're killing me," he groaned. He could feel the pebbly peas the bladder had been stuffed with spilling out beneath him, but it was the soft warmth of

Lorabelle that held his focus. "The ball burst. You girls are as heavy as warhorses."

"Oh, bloody saints," Gwyneth moaned, "then nobody wins the bet." She rolled off, along with his other sisters. Elayna started picking meticulously at her clothes, as if suddenly remembering her appearance.

She was the only one who seemed to care.

Damon didn't have the heart to chastize Gwyneth for her language. Lorabelle rolled off in the other direction, and he turned over and stared up at the sky, which was turning slightly darker now as clouds moved in more thickly.

Lorabelle leaned over him.

"Are you all right?" she asked, her incredible eyes fretful on him.

It was freezing, but his heart jumped and he felt warm and aroused and amazingly happy. He'd forgotten what that felt like. He was still smiling, he realized.

"Why are you looking at me like that?" she asked, and her voice was thick with something—emotion, panic?

He felt the same way. Emotional, and panicked.

It was as if they were alone. Nothing but hard, cold ground, stormy sky, Lorabelle, and his wildly beating heart.

The heart that wouldn't die, no matter how much he'd wanted it to.

"I don't know," he admitted honestly, not censoring himself, not caring in that moment. "You're beautiful. Have I told you that?"

He saw her swallow, and she whispered, breathless as he, "No."

There was something tentative in her eyes, as if she were afraid to believe he meant it. And it struck him that all these nights he'd denied himself the bliss of her, she must have felt rejected. It pained him to think that he had done that to her.

"Then I've been remiss," he said ashamedly, and he reached up and touched her sweet face, feeling her heat. She made him heady, and he slid his hand behind her neck, into that glorious, tangled hair. "Because you are beautiful," he whispered. "Very beautiful. Belle."

She gave him that brittle look again, the one that hurt him the most. "What did you say?"

"Belle," he said. "I called you Belle. It suits you." He wasn't sure what he would have said next, or what he would have done, if they'd been alone. If Gwyneth hadn't bounced back down beside him.

"You *do* know how to play," she said, her voice excited, amazed.

Lorabelle shifted slightly, and he dropped his hand, reluctantly, as she sat back. Her gaze still held his, and he watched the shadows play across her face, uncertainty and something else—happiness?—warring for precedence.

Gwyneth went on, "Do you know any other games? Will you teach me? Will you tell Julian not to make the pages do extra laps around the bailey for letting me play with them?"

He struggled to focus on his rambunctious sister and her parade of questions. "I know plenty of games," he said. "I'll have to think about whether I should teach them to you." He glanced at Lorabelle. She smiled at him encouragingly. "And I don't think you need to be playing with the pages. But I'll think about it. Deal?"

He couldn't believe what he was hearing coming out of his own mouth. He was indulging Gwyneth in this folly of hers. It was Lorabelle, turning him soft. Turning his head.

But he liked the way Gwyneth was smiling at him right now, and how it made him feel. How Lorabelle made him feel. He'd been afraid of allowing these feelings, and he realized now that he'd not only blocked the horror—but also the pleasure—of living life to the fullest. He'd lived a half life, if it could even be called that.

He was tired of that half life. Lorabelle had shown him what he was missing, what his secret soul longed to claim again, and the realization was as terrifying as it was tantalizing.

Lizbet had taken a bundle of almond cakes from the basket and he sat up as she started passing them out. "I'm hungry," she said. "Are you?"

"Yes," he said, and he glanced at Lorabelle again. "Very." She cast her gaze away from his, but she was aware—as aware as he, wasn't she? He saw her fingers shake slightly as she took an almond cake from Lizbet. She didn't look at him as she ate it. The girls munched and chattered, still excited from their game.

Gwyneth devoured her almond cake. "Okay," she said between bites, picking up the previous discussion where they'd left off. "Deal."

He noticed Elayna watching him curiously, then she looked away, too. But there was something somehow not so mutinous in her expression now, something different. He wasn't sure what was going on, but he felt different, too.

Purposefully, he drove the puzzling thoughts from his mind, temporarily banishing all his concerns. He was enjoying this moment, and he didn't want to think about all the reasons it couldn't last, only two of which were that there were dark clouds threatening more snow on the horizon and there was a dead man at Castle Wulfere.

# *Nineteen*

Inside the keep, Fayette waited to bring the girls to their room, to change them into clean, warm clothes, and make up for the meal they'd missed. Servants came to fetch their baskets to the schoolroom where the evergreens would be fashioned into Christmas decorations.

They'd brought back the broken pig bladder, and Gwyneth hadn't been satisfied until Damon had ordered it taken to the seamstresses for repairs, to be returned to the village boys later. Gwyneth didn't want to risk offending her new friends.

Eglyntine followed Aurelie and Damon to their chamber with a tray of food. She left as soon as she set the meal down. Damon stoked the fire with fresh wood that had been left stacked by the hearth.

Aurelie leaned against the base of one of the windowsills. She should change her clothes, but she waited, wondering what her husband would do if she stripped down, right now, before him.

She'd seen a side of him today that amazed her, and she watched him now, thinking of it.

The feared lord of Wulfere, with his face of Hell, as she'd heard the servants whisper, had played a child's game, had laughed, had let his sisters knock him down and tumble over him. He'd eaten almond cakes in the thin sun, sitting on the ground in the fragrant winter meadow while bits of leaves dotted his tunic.

He'd called her Belle, and it had almost made her cry because in that moment she'd felt reborn in some way. Not the wanton Aurelie or the false Lorabelle—someone new. Belle.

The girls had picked it up, and they were all calling her Belle now. Hope—that she could live a true life here, a life of her own—squeezed her chest.

He stood away from the hearth now, and half turned toward her. He wasn't smiling, and still she felt that sizzling awareness, that fantastic intensity that was him. And she felt something not finished. He scanned her face with his darkened gaze and she was helpless to look away, or even move.

She wanted to finish it, what they'd started in that meadow. What they'd started the first moment he'd held her in his arms in the chapel of Briermeade. It had all begun then. It wasn't the need to bind him to her, to make herself his wife in deed, though that was always in the back of her mind—that uneasiness, that fear. But it wasn't what drove her now. This was a different kind of need altogether, one that spun curls of longing inside her, heat between her legs, wildness in her heart. He did all of that to her, with just his look.

He came toward her and her pulse accelerated.

"Hungry?" He indicated the meal Eglyntine had left.

She shook her head, her stomach in such knots she could barely breathe much less eat.

He stopped very near to her and seemed to study

her curiously. "What manner of convent was this at Briermeade," he began, "where they produce such ladies as you?"

"I'm not much of a lady," she answered, her heart pounding against the wall of her chest. The way he was looking at her—it stole her breath, weakened her knees. "The nuns despaired over me."

"I can imagine," he said with a half smile.

*I was hoping you'd turn my little sisters into ladies, not that my little sisters would turn you into a barbarian.*

"Forgive me," she said, turning away to stare at the storm-shrouded window. "I'll try to do better. I—"

"I wasn't criticizing."

His voice was so very close. She could feel his warm breath beside her cheek. Then he touched her, just lightly, on the back.

She turned.

"You made me laugh," he said, his voice low, grave, and bemused at once. "You made me feel like a boy again. I want to find fault with that, but I can't."

"It meant a great deal to your sisters," she said carefully, uncertain where this was leading, what he was thinking. "They needed that. They needed—"

"What do *you* need?" he interrupted, his expression grim, strange, almost impatient.

She swallowed thickly. "Me?"

He laughed, a low, husky sound that surprised her because it was so very rare from him. "Yes, you. Belle." He moved his hand to her face, gentle, exploring, a skim, a caress. She closed her eyes, reveling in the earthiness of his scent, the warmth of his breath, the heat of this *thing* that pulled so hard when he was near. Afraid to answer his question.

There was nothing else, just this man, suddenly holding her in his arms, breathing into her hair. She felt the hard lines of his body pressing against her soft curves, that hot and thrilling part of him against her stomach.

"Tell me, Belle," he whispered against her brow. "Tell me what you need. I love that you care so much about my sisters, that their needs are so important to you. But I want to know what you want, what you need."

*You,* her heart whispered, and she opened her eyes, looking straight into his dark gaze that gleamed with something raw and oddly vulnerable. *I need you.*

The words stuck in her throat.

"Why?" she prevaricated, and she thrust her chin out unthinkingly, so afraid to be honest with him about anything and longing for it at the same time.

"Because I can't stop thinking about you," he said, holding her gaze. "Because I'm training my men, and I'm thinking of the silkiness of your hair." He curled a lock of her hair around one of his fingers. "And I'm judging disputes between my villagers and dreaming of your sweet brow." He released the lock of hair to trace his touch over her forehead. "And I'm pacing the ramparts in the icy cold air and imagining your warm lips." He rubbed his fingertip over her mouth, along her jaw.

His dark eyes burned into her, oh so close, and she felt giddy and confused and afraid to believe him.

"You're not a sentimental man," she said, reminding him of his own hard words to her before they wed, trying so hard to keep her perspective. "Perhaps you're missing too many meals in the hall, and it's making your head swim."

He shook his head and laughed softly. "I don't think that's it. I don't know what it is. I don't know what to make of you. I'm not a sentimental man, you're right. I didn't expect this to happen. I didn't expect you to make me feel anything. But you do, Belle. You make me feel. I wanted to hate you for that at first, but now—"

"What now?"

"I don't know," he said again. "Today, when I rode out of the castle . . ." His fingers touched her neck, pushing away her hair. Then he held her close suddenly. "I thought if I didn't find you, I would go mad."

There was something stark in his voice. A sensation of dread crept up her spine, dread that had no name, no reason.

"I was afraid I wouldn't find you," he said so softly, his voice a breath against her ear.

She drew back and looked into his face.

"Why?" she asked, her heart drumming hard against the wall of her chest. She had no idea what she expected him to say.

"A man was killed today in the passage between the training hall and the soldier's dormitory. He was murdered."

She blinked, her mind going blank at his words. One of his men-at-arms, killed. She waited for him to continue, confused, wondering what this incident could possibly have to do with her.

"His name was Prewitt. Did you know a man named Prewitt? He came to serve here several years ago, after I left for France, with his brother—Stephen."

He examined her, so very near, so very serious, his gaze taut, the awareness still tight between them, sim-

mering beneath this revelation—pushed aside for
now, but unfinished. She didn't know if she felt so
dizzy from his nearness, from the awareness he'd ac-
knowledged for the first time, or from this strange
case of murder he was detailing.

"No," she answered. "At least, not that I can remember." Had Lorabelle ever mentioned a man
named Prewitt? Should she know a man named
Prewitt? It was unsettling and confusing and horrible.
She hated more than ever that she had to lie to this
man she was starting to care for so much. "How was
he killed?"

"He was stabbed. He wasn't dead when he was
found, but close to it. He had time for a few last
words."

"What were they?" she asked, her heart in her
throat.

She had a feeling she was about to find out why
he was watching her this way, why this strange
knight's death was in some way connected to her.

"Your name. Over and over."

"My name?"

"Lorabelle."

What had she thought? *Aurelie.* She'd been so
scared he would say *Aurelie.* She was losing it again,
letting panic take over. Even now, as he held her and
called her Belle, the panic was still there, simmering,
waiting to claim her. She hated it.

She struggled to push it back down.

"And something about my sisters," he went on. "I
don't know which sister. They couldn't understand
him. He was rambling, raving. There was only one
thing that was clear—your name," he said again. "Do
you have any idea why?"

She shook her head. "I can't imagine," she whispered, and she wanted to believe this man's death had nothing to do with her. How could it? She'd never heard of him, and Lorabelle had spent the past eleven years of her life at Briermeade. If she'd known a knight named Prewitt, Aurelie would have known about it.

But her logic didn't reassure her. Instead, it terrified her. She'd known for a long time that something was wrong at Castle Wulfere. Now that *something* was connected to her.

Damon would have given anything not to have put that look in Lorabelle's eyes. He'd terrified her. He hadn't wanted to tell her about Prewitt, but he'd had no choice. For her own safety, he had to find out if she knew anything about the man.

But he couldn't stand what it was costing her.

"I'm sorry, Belle," he said gently, cupping her face as tenderly as his huge, suddenly clumsy hands could. He touched her sweet mouth lightly with his and held her. Just held her. "I'm so sorry," he whispered against her cheek. "I didn't want to tell you that. You've been through too much, after what happened at Briermeade. The last thing I want is to give you more nightmares."

"I know," she said thickly, and he could see emotion shining in her eyes. "Thank you. For caring," she added, and there was something almost formal, almost distancing, in her voice, and he felt again that tentativeness in her that he'd seen in the meadow when he'd told her she was beautiful, and most of all when he'd called her Belle.

This tentativeness was his fault. He'd hurt her—by

neglecting her, ignoring her, slamming home to her that their marriage was nothing but a business arrangement, treating her like a damned governess. All to shield himself from these terrible-wonderful feelings, feelings she just might share if he was right about the hurt that hid behind that proud jut of her chin.

He didn't want to shield himself anymore—whether it was crazy or stupid or just plain dangerous. It didn't matter. What mattered was her, that he was hurting her.

"Belle—" he began, only to be stopped by a sudden pounding on the door.

Frustration streaked through him. He wanted to ignore the pounding. He didn't know what it was that he wanted to say to her right now, he just knew he had to face down these feelings. He was a fighter—and for too long, he'd run from this slip of a faery-woman, and most of all from himself.

It was time to stop running. But the world had other ideas, and the pounding didn't cease.

"Lady Wulfere!" Now there were cries, too. "Milady, please!"

"It's Fayette," Belle said, her hurt-clouded eyes wide and dark. "It could be something about the girls."

His blood chilled as she tore away from him and ran to the door.

It took agonizing moments to understand Fayette. The young maid was overwrought, wringing her hands, crying, so terrified of displeasing in any way.

Aurelie thought for an instant that the timid girl would faint dead away when Damon came up behind her and demanded she get hold of herself and tell them what was happening. Fayette was among the many maids who barely had the courage to look the lord of Wulfere in the face, much less speak directly to him.

It amazed Aurelie, now that she had come to see another side of her husband, that he was so feared by his servants. She'd never seen him display cruelty toward any of them.

It was his scar, she knew. And the hardened reputation that had followed him home from France.

"Fayette, please." Aurelie took hold of the maid's hands to stop their wringing and stared the girl straight in the eyes, fixing Fayette's attention on her. "Tell me what's wrong."

Fayette gulped and seemed to grip her wits. "Milady," she started, stopped, and took another choked breath. Her thick strawberry-red hair flew over her pale cheeks, escaping the confines of her simple net and veil. " 'Tis Marigold."

"What about Marigold?" Aurelie prompted, forcing calm into her voice, still holding Fayette steady with her hands and her gaze.

"She's missing again," Fayette whispered brokenly. "And this time, we can't find her."

There were a thousand places for a child to hide in the massive, towering maze that was Castle Wulfere. Aurelie had been there long enough to discover three of them: the turret room in the north tower, which she'd learned had been their mother's spinning room; behind the thick drapes in the deep window bays of the schoolroom; and in the wardrobe chamber—where Marigold would camouflage herself amidst the innumerable piles of beautiful fabrics and watch the seamstresses work.

She was nowhere to be found.

"Where else could she be?" Aurelie asked Elayna, feeling desperate and trying not to show it. The girls were in the schoolroom, working with ribbons and twine to create Christmas decorations out of the evergreens they'd brought back from the forest. They all looked frightened and upset. It wasn't unusual for Marigold to disappear—she'd been disappearing for months, hiding away by herself. What was different this time was that no one could find her.

"I don't know," Elayna said, her dark eyes huge. She looked like the child she was, stripped of the petulance and rebellion that sometimes made her seem older.

Damon was still searching, assisted by Kenric and Rorke now. The anguish he held so grimly within himself shone in his eyes, and she'd never seen his love for his sisters so clearly before. Never again would she question that he was capable of love. Her heart tore for him, but she knew nothing would comfort him but finding his tiny sister.

The servants had been alerted. If Marigold was within the castle, she would be found.

But as one candlemark passed and then another, Aurelie couldn't stop thinking of the full-fledged winter storm now raging outside. She worried that Marigold might have, for some reason, left the shelter of the keep.

"Elayna, if there's anything you're not telling me, anything you've kept secret—"

Elayna's eyes filled and she pressed her hand over

her mouth. Gwyneth and Lizbet stared, the looks on their faces unreadable to Aurelie. There was still so much she didn't understand. It was always as if something smoldered just beneath the surface of Castle Wulfere, something terrible, something unsaid.

Aurelie slipped her arm around Elayna. "Elayna—"

The door of the schoolroom burst open.

"Marigold!" Aurelie ran across the room to Damon, where he stood holding Marigold in his arms.

The girl was shaking, her teeth chattering, her clothes damp, her lips blue. Her doll was clutched to her chest.

"They found her near the kitchen," he said grimly. "We don't know where she's been—outside somewhere." Snow flaked the girl's hair. Her face was so white. She'd been outside, in this awful storm—without her cloak—for saints knew how long. Aurelie's heart constricted. Marigold opened her eyes—they were bigger than ever against her colorless skin—and reached for Aurelie.

Aurelie reached back. "Sweetling," she whispered thickly, and for an endless moment she stood there, she and Damon embracing the little girl together.

Aurelie pressed a kiss to Marigold's still-cold brow. "Close your eyes, sweetling," she whispered. "I'm right here." Marigold didn't shut her eyes. Aurelie glanced back at Fayette. "Go back to the schoolroom," she told the maid. She'd left Eglyntine there while she'd taken Marigold back to the girls' room. Fayette had helped strip the child of her icy, wet clothes, stoked the fire and fetched warm soup and cider from the kitchen while Aurelie remained close to Marigold.

The little girl seemed to panic every time she so much as left her to cross the room, so she stayed, feeding her the warm soup, stroking her hair.

A page had come for Damon moments after he'd appeared in the schoolroom doorway with Marigold. Damon had given over precious hours of his demanding day to her and to his sisters, and his responsibilities had returned to claim him.

He hadn't let the page speak, had interrupted him before the boy could finish his sentence, and Aurelie had sensed that the situation that required his attention had something to do with the murder. Damon didn't want his sisters to hear about the killing, at least not this way.

They would have to be told, Aurelie knew. It was no doubt the talk of the castle by now. But he would protect them as long as he could, especially after the ordeal they'd just been through with Marigold's disappearance.

Damon had instructed Fayette to have the girls' evening meal brought to the schoolroom. His gaze had shown a torment of unspoken thoughts as he'd passed Marigold into Aurelie's arms.

*In the morning,* he'd said quietly, his gaze locked with hers. How she'd ever seen his eyes as harsh, she couldn't imagine now. *We'll talk to them together in the morning.*

Then he reached out and touched her cheek so tenderly she'd felt her knees shake from it. *You and I will talk tonight,* he'd promised. *We didn't finish our conversation.*

A mix of emotions struggled within Aurelie's breast

as she sat by Marigold's side, tucking in the blankets. The fire burned hot across the room, heating the bed. Marigold's face flushed as color returned, and Aurelie felt the knot start to uncoil in her stomach. Marigold was going to be all right.

Fayette left, shutting the door quietly behind her, and Marigold shot up from the bed.

Aurelie wrapped her arms around her. "Marigold, sweetling, stop, you have to rest. You need to—"

Marigold pushed at her, shaking her head. Her fragile child's body was surprisingly strong, but Aurelie held on to her.

"What is it?" she cried.

Marigold reached over her shoulder, pointed across the room at the pile of clothes Fayette had left to dry near the fire. Her doll was there, too, damp, left to warm at the hearth.

Aurelie let the little girl down and Marigold ran across the room on her bare feet, her clean white chemise flapping at her ankles. She pulled her doll into her arms, looked back at the door, almost nervously it seemed to Aurelie, then she tore quickly at the strings that closed the pouch that hung on the doll's braided belt. The seamstresses had taken to Marigold after they'd found her so many times hiding in the wardrobe room, and they'd created several fantastically detailed outfits for the doll—including such accessories as tiny velvet boots, and the belt and pouch.

Fire glinted off the gleaming blur Marigold withdrew from the pouch and enclosed quickly inside her hand.

Aurelie knelt beside her. The lavender scent of the

rushes struck her as she crushed them beneath her knees and the spit of the fire filled the room.

"What is it, Marigold?"

The little girl looked up at her and slowly, slowly, she uncurled her fingers. Inside her palm rested a stunning gold brooch, the vivid blue of azurite beaming from its center.


Aurelie paced back and forth, alone in her own chamber, her mind churning. *What was Marigold trying to tell her?*

There was no doubt in her mind that Marigold was trying to tell her *something*, and that if she could figure it out, it could be the clue to everything that was wrong at Castle Wulfere.

*I wish you could tell me why you won't talk. Maybe if you told me, I could make it better.*

The weight of the promise she'd made to Marigold in the forest pressed down upon her. Now, somehow, Marigold had found a way to tell her what was wrong, why she wouldn't talk, she was sure of it. Marigold had risked her life, disappeared somewhere into the awful stormy cold, and brought back this curious brooch—and waited until she was alone with Aurelie to bring it out.

Aurelie's instinctive response was to take it to Damon, but Marigold had become nearly hysterical at the prospect. The little girl had needed no words to make it abundantly plain to Aurelie that she, and she alone, had been entrusted with whatever it was she was trying to say.

Finally, the girl had slept, seeming to relax now that she'd given Aurelie the brooch and Aurelie had promised to keep the strange treasure to herself. Fayette had returned later with the girls, and Aurelie had left them all tucked snug in bed with Fayette sleeping on a pallet by the fire. Eglyntine had had her tub prepared, and she'd bathed and slipped into her night rail to wait for Damon and the conversation they hadn't finished.

Nerves prickled her stomach. She still wanted to show him the brooch, but the trust she'd spent these careful weeks building with Marigold hung in the balance. She didn't want to betray the little girl, but to keep it from Damon felt like a betrayal, too.

She stopped pacing, sat down on the edge of her bed, and stared down at the beautiful brooch. It was the sort of thing one would use to clip a cape together, a brooch that would belong only to someone of noble class, or perhaps a wealthy merchant. Where would Marigold have gotten it? She'd never seen such a brooch amongst Damon's mother's things, or in the girls' room, and there were no other ladies at Castle Wulfere who could possess such a luxurious item.

No one knew where Marigold had been tonight, and when she'd pressed Marigold and asked her if she would take her there in the morning, Marigold had shook her head almost violently and pushed the brooch at her.

For several long beats, Aurelie continued to stare down at the brooch, her puzzlement no less than when Marigold had pulled it out of the doll's pouch.

She pushed off the bed and crossed the room to kneel down at the chest by the wall. She lifted the lid and jammed aside the wealth of gowns folded up inside, and carefully placed the brooch deep in the bottom corner, pulled the clothes back over it, and shut the lid.

It was late, and Damon hadn't returned. She curled up on the bed to wait, not expecting to sleep. She stared up at the draped top of the bed and couldn't stop thinking.

She had no idea how much time had passed when she woke, unsure what had startled her. Wind battered at the thick glass of the windows, the storm otherwise muffled by the thick stone walls of the keep. The latches creaked against the onslaught, but held fast.

It wasn't winter's fury that had woken her, she realized then. A low groan came from across the room, and she sat up. Through the opening in the bedcurtains, she saw Damon, wrapped loosely in a blanket before the hearth, thrashing and moaning.

She dashed from the bed and knelt down beside him. "Damon," she called softly, leaning back to barely escape a stray blow. He was, she realized with a shock, completely naked. Sweat slicked his shoulders, gleaming in the flickering light. "Wake up," she called again, and risked bending over him to grip his strong, warm upper arms and shake him, her heart breaking at the torment on his face.

"Angelette," he rasped harshly in his sleep.

She released him and fell back, not from a blow but from the pain that suddenly flashed through her. It was the name he always called out in these horrible bouts.

Suddenly, he opened his eyes and stared straight at her. Long heartbeats pulsed as comprehension dawned in his gaze. His breaths came in fierce gasps. He sat up abruptly, seemingly unaware of how the blanket pooled at his hips, revealing the tight expanse of his stomach.

She stared back at him, her heart thundering in her ears. "Are you all right?"

He said nothing, his eyes so dark and raw with some hurt she knew nothing about but that was no longer shrouded behind that hard mask he showed the world. There was nothing between them but the scrap of blanket and these painful breaths and one word, a name.

"Who," she whispered into the tautness of the room, "is Angelette?"

# *Twenty*

"It doesn't matter. She's dead. Angelette is dead."
He felt strangely helpless, compelled to bring to the
surface a name trapped inside his ruined heart for
so long. A name made of darkness, ugliness now.

He didn't want to taint Belle with that ugliness. He
wanted to protect her, from everything. From himself.

But she wasn't going to let it go that easily. "It
matters to me," Belle said, and there was pain in her
eyes. Pain he'd caused, he realized. "It matters to me
that my husband cries out her name in the night.
Tell me who she is. I want to know. I need to know."

Her words shattered him. He'd asked her what she
needed, and now she was telling him. He reached
out, cupped her face in his hand, felt her warmth,
her tension, her sweet, soft hurt.

She was his wife, and she was caught in this hell of
his own making with him now. Taut beats passed, and
she dropped her gaze, hiding those expressive eyes,
the strain, the hurt, and something else—was it fear?

"Belle." He put his hands on her shoulders and
wouldn't let her go. "Sweet Belle, don't run away.
Don't be afraid. I can't stand it if you're afraid of me
now, tonight."

She stopped resisting, put her head on his chest, and let him hold her close. The scent of her enveloped him. He could feel the tension of her body.

"I'm not afraid of you," she breathed against the bare flesh of his chest, as if she couldn't speak these words if she looked at him. "That's not it."

"Then what is it, Belle?"

She pulled back, but kept her gaze from him. She was drawing inward as he watched. His heart constricted painfully because it was his fault.

"I shouldn't have asked you about Angelette," she said quietly. "I have no right. I—"

"You have every right," he said in a terrible voice, ashamed, understanding too well now how deeply the distance he'd placed between them had cut her. "If you think I don't care about you, it's only because I've been trying so hard not to."

She looked up at him, and the look in her eyes bound his chest even tighter. He reached out and took her hand. It was his responsibility to protect her, yet he knew he had to tell her something.

The last thing he wanted was to tell her everything.

"You have every right to know about Angelette," he told her again. "Every right."

"Did you love her?"

He almost laughed at that because it was the easiest question she could have asked. "No," he answered. He gazed down at their two hands together. His large, rough. Hers small, soft. "No," he repeated, and he realized it wasn't enough. She deserved so much more.

She deserved to know the truth.

\* \* \*

"Angelette was the daughter of a French lord."

He didn't look at her as he spoke, his gaze connecting with something over her shoulder and far away. The past, France. His depthless eyes were luminous with that hidden fire of his, for all appearances the master of his emotions. But he wasn't unemotional at all, she knew now. He secreted his emotions behind an armor of detachment—but inside, they were still painful, still deep, still unmastered.

The warm, calloused skin of his hand pressing against hers tightened. She waited for him to speak, ashamed at how relieved she felt to know that he hadn't loved Angelette. The black pit of Damon's pain was still beyond her ken, and that was what mattered and she struggled to focus on him.

"Her father, the lord of Saville, had let her travel to visit her sister," he went on in a hard, distant tone, "who had just given birth to twins, and she was caught in a siege led by my foster lord, Wilfred of Penlogan. The castle was taken, and we occupied it—and Rorke fell in love with Angelette. In time, Angelette was returned to Saville, to Chateau Blanchefleur, as part of one of the truces negotiated constantly over castles and villages and lands. She had to go back.

"There was no way the two could marry, no chance that her father would ever allow it. He hated the English, and he hated Rorke even more. Saville's lands were still free of English power, and he would never give his treasured, youngest daughter to Rorke, or any Englishman for that matter.

"But Angelette loved Rorke as much as he loved her. She went back to Saville, but she didn't want to stay. Rorke had already asked her to marry him, and she concocted a plan to escape her father. She would switch clothes with her maid, and she would simply walk out the gates of her father's castle—and wait in the village for Rorke. She chose a place no one would notice her, but that was also terribly dangerous."

"Where?"

"An alley behind a tavern, where whores were known to loiter. Rorke was desperately worried—but there was no way to get word back to Angelette that the plan was too dangerous. Rorke made arrangements to depart the Continent at once and take Angelette home, to Valmond Castle.

"The first part of the plan worked—Angelette escaped Chateau Blanchefleur and made it to the village, to the dark alley behind the tavern where they were to meet. It was Rorke who didn't make it—he'd participated in a joust that day, at the request of the king himself. There is no man who could best Rorke, but that day his mind was wracked with thoughts of Angelette and the risk she was taking to be with him. He was seriously injured, nearly killed, on the field. There was no way to get a message to Angelette, so he sent me in his stead, to meet her and explain what had happened, that their departure would have to be delayed. She would have to sneak back into her father's castle and wait until Rorke was recovered and they could try again."

"What happened?"

"It was too late," he said grimly. "I was too late. I was alone, traveling through a dangerous area—dark, forested, known for its bands of disenfranchised soldiers—and I was attacked. There were so many French soldiers scattered, separated from their lords, roaming lawlessly—no lords to command them, no homes to which they could return. I was robbed—I didn't have much—a pouch with some coins, my sword. There were a dozen of them, and I didn't have a chance. They came down from the trees, pulling me from my horse. I killed one of them, the first one, but not before he slashed my face."

*The scar. That awful scar.* Unthinkingly, she pulled her hand away from his and reached up to touch that ghastly thin slice that devastated one side of his face.

He met her eyes then, and he looked drained already, as if revealing so much of himself exhausted him, but he went on: "I was surrounded. They were disgusted when they found how little I had, and I don't know why they didn't kill me. They took my sword, and the pouch and they left me there. I was bleeding but I couldn't go back. Angelette was out there, waiting for Rorke—for me now. But by the time I got there—"

Her heart climbed higher in her throat. "What happened to Angelette?" She waited, transfixed, for him to answer.

"She was alive when I got there. She was behind the tavern, waiting—but I wasn't the first one to reach her. Someone else had been there first. She'd been beaten, raped. Brutalized. It was as if an animal had been there, but it was no animal, it was a man. She opened her eyes, and I knew she was trying to tell me something, but she could barely speak—her throat was horribly bruised. She'd been nearly strangled. 'Help me,' she whispered over and over, brokenly, crying.

"There was no choice. I could hardly take her into the tavern with its whores and drunken men. It was the middle of the night. The safest place, the only place where I knew she could get help, was her father's castle. It stood on a rise above the village, and it took mere moments on horseback to ride to the gate—but still she was dead before I reached them."

He stared into the fire now as if in a trance, his face more remote than ever.

"I spent the next twelve months shackled in the dungeon beneath Chateau Blanchefleur. Diplomatic efforts to gain my release were fruitless. Saville believed I was the one who had killed his daughter. And sometimes he almost made *me* believe I'd killed his daughter. Rorke was relentless in seeking my release, trying to track the real murderer of Angelette."

Aurelie listened, appalled. This vital, powerful man had been trapped in shackles, month after month. It was unimaginable.

"Did they ever find him?" she whispered thickly.

He turned his head and looked at her again. "Saville never accepted that anyone was responsible for Angelette's death but me, not until they found proof that it was someone else.

"But Rorke never gave up. He had to know who had killed Angelette. He was consumed by guilt—for Angelette, for me. He worked relentlessly to find the killer, questioning every villager, nobleman, soldier in an ever-widening circle around Blanchefleur, risking his own life. It wasn't safe to be an Englishman on Saville's lands. It became Rorke's obsession. He did nothing else. Kenric and his brother Ranulf joined him. Without these men, I would be dead."

She understood now the close bond she saw between Damon and the men who had returned from France with him. It had been forged in more than war. It had been forged in Hell—a Hell they'd been to together.

"Always, they would come back to the village, to the place where Angelette had died," he went on in his strained voice. "Rorke was convinced someone had to have seen something, but was afraid to come forward. Saville terrorized his people, and they feared that their lord would blame them if he knew they'd seen something, could possibly have prevented Angelette's death. Finally, one of the village wardens confessed. It was Ranulf who found the man, pressed him, went back over and over until he admitted the truth. He'd been at the tavern that night and he'd accompanied a whore to the rear alley. He found Angelette, and he saw a man with his hands around her neck, shaking her, and he saw his face. It's probably because he interrupted him that he left without finishing off Angelette on the spot."

"Who was it?" For some reason, she had a terrible foreboding that she didn't want to know this answer.

The look on Damon's face now was tight, rigid. "It was an Englishman. Saville was right about that—he just had the wrong Englishman. It was Wilfred of Penlogan. My neighbor. My foster lord. The man who had raised me to knighthood. He had been in love with Angelette—we had all known that. He was much older than she—old enough to be her father. But there was never any question. She loved Rorke. No one knew that he seethed with such jealousy, that it would drive him to such lengths."

"He left you there, in that dungeon, for twelve months—for his crime?" she asked in disbelief, fury and horror for him rising inside her.

"Saville's men seized him within the day," Damon said. "Wilfred was out hunting, unaware he'd been revealed. He was easy prey for Saville. He was brought to Blanchefleur, and he confessed immediately. Saville executed him."

"And you? You were released?"

He made a sound that could have been a laugh but wasn't. "Saville told me I would be released, but he changed his mind."

She frowned. "Why? Once he knew you were innocent—"

"Saville was irrational. Insane, I came to believe. He—" He stopped, jaw clenched, closing his eyes against some deep, secret agony. He opened them again, staring off into that distant time. "He had taken on the role of achieving my confession personally, and he'd taken his failure personally, too."

"What did he do?" She was afraid to ask, a terrible apprehension crawling up her spine.

"We were alone, together, in the dungeon. The guards had been dismissed suddenly and I don't believe he knew that they had already released my bonds. My hands were free—but still behind me. He'd arrived abruptly, as the guard was unlocking the manacles. When Saville ordered a man to move, he moved.

"The guards were gone in the blink of an eye. Looking back, perhaps they knew what I would do. Perhaps it was what they hoped I would do."

He was silent for so long, she wasn't sure if he would continue.

"Saville had a certain way of . . . encouraging confession," he said finally. "He intended to encourage me again. He insisted that I must have known about Wilfred's crime and that I had been protecting my foster lord all this time. I believe Saville would have killed me that day, though I don't know that with any certainty. I only know what I believed, and what I did."

She'd thought she wanted to know everything, but she didn't. Suddenly, she didn't. She wasn't sure she could bear to know more. The more he spoke, the more detached he became and that scared her.

"What did you do?" she whispered.

His gaze moved abruptly, from that distant time to now. He looked straight into her eyes. "I killed him," he said. "With my bare hands, like an animal. Like the animal that killed Angelette. Like the animal I had become after twelve months shackled in a black hole."

His gaze was hard on hers, and she saw something oddly vulnerable within that hardness, and she realized with a small shock that he expected her to be disgusted, or afraid, repulsed by him and what he had done, what he had become.

"I put on his clothes, his cloak and hood, and I walked out of the dungeon, out of the keep, out of the castle gates. No one stopped me. No one would dare speak to Saville, or waylay him. He was that feared. I found Rorke, Kenric, and Ranulf, luckily, where they'd been waiting outside the village for word of my release.

"That was six months ago. I found out that my father was dead when I came out, and I returned home as soon as I could. Kenric and Rorke came back with me, and Ranulf—he'd been honored with Wilfred's castle and title as a token of the king's gratitude for discovering the truth."

It might have been six months ago, but it had only been a few moments since he'd been to Blanchefleur in his dreams, Aurelie guessed. She understood the.

relentless power of his nightmares now, the darkness that pulled him down again and again.

He still looked at her, searchingly, then he glanced away and she thought of how much he'd told her, and of that awful pain he'd hidden so long.

"You did what you had to do," she whispered, touching his arm.

"Did I?" he asked, and there was that detachment again, that part of him she couldn't touch, might never be able to touch.

"This is what you dream," she whispered. "All of it. The dungeon, Saville. Angelette."

"If I say Angelette's name, it's because she's always there, in those dreams," he whispered back, his guilt thick in his voice. "I hear her choked voice begging me to help her, and I fail. Every time, I fail. She dies before I can get her home."

"You didn't fail." She touched his face again, tenderly, tracing the line of that awful scar. "You tried to save her. You spent twelve months in a dungeon because you tried to save her."

"I was too late for her. If I'd arrived sooner—I was reckless, riding off alone to meet her. I should have taken Kenric with me, at the very least. I knew there were bands of marauding soldiers in the area—and I knew I would be entering enemy lands. I was too late for her because I had left myself open to attack. And I was too late for my sisters, and even for you, Belle. It all goes back to that one judgment call, that night, when I rode away from Rorke alone to meet Angelette. I thought I was invincible. I was arrogant. And so I was too late."

"You weren't too late for me," she argued, and she felt hot tears sting her eyes, scorch her cheeks. "You saved me. "There was so much more truth to that than he knew, than she could tell him.

He wiped her cheeks with his fingers, his touch cool against her hot skin. When her eyes met his, confusion and pain connecting, he took her into his arms. "When I came to Briermeade," he whispered against her hair, "and you were there and I thought you were dead, it was like the nightmare was starting all over again. But you were alive, and from the start you made me feel. I didn't want that. I couldn't bear that. Those months at Blanchefleur—"

He pulled back enough to look into her face again, as if he had to see her to know he was here, at Castle Wulfere, as if she anchored him in this reality.

"You survived. You did what you had to do." She understood so much more than she could explain to him.

"No, I didn't," he said, his voice devoid of inflection. "I didn't survive."

She saw it now, what the hard darkness of his eyes hid, but deep inside, there was that life burning from within, alive and refusing to die no matter how much he'd tried to let it, no matter how deep he'd pushed it.

"Yes, you did," she insisted softly. "You have a heart, alive and beating. You survived."

He was so close, his mouth a breath from hers, and he kissed her lips gently, briefly, then simply pressed his cheek against hers.

"Sometimes," he murmured, "when I'm with you, I think that could be true."

There was no sound but their breathing, the hiss of the fire, and the beating of their two hearts. He kissed her forehead, her temple, her eyelids, her mouth again. She sighed unevenly, hardly able to bear the tenderness.

His tongue parted her lips then, and she felt his need, hunger, as he claimed her with sweet fury. He filled his hands with her, stroking, caressing, thrilling. She was beneath him without realizing how she got there, the blanket he'd been lying on softening the floor beneath her, and his body—huge and naked and beside her.

He kissed her again with heated lingering. "I want you," he murmured against her mouth. "I need you."

She kissed him back, just as hungrily, just as needily, tasting warmth and man and salt, and she wasn't sure if they were her tears or his. Her arms curled around his neck, and the sensual sensation of his body against hers was unbelievable. Suddenly, this thing she had never done before felt as natural as breathing.

"Damon"—she gasped when he released her mouth—"I need you, too."

His mouth trailed shivery kisses down her throat, to the neck of her chemise, and she felt his hands move down her body, cup the fullness of her breast through her chemise. She arched against him, her heart drumming, a driving rhythm deep within blinding her.

He fisted her chemise in his hands and pushed it up on one side. Impatient, she tore at the strings that bound it at the neck, then shifted to allow him to pull it over her head, then she was naked and breathless and very aware that he was naked, too.

She shivered in the fire's heat, conscious only of his eyes, his heat, and yet cold at the same time. She was a virgin, and her boldness fell away as quickly as it had seized her. Then he was there again, blanketing that chill, that virgin's fear, sending new firebursts through her veins. His bare body came down upon her, searing heat. He claimed her mouth again and there was this shaking heat and him and nothing else again.

In her dreams, there had been nothing that had prepared her for this. She let her body tremble and sigh as she closed her eyes and absorbed the bliss of it, of his mouth on her lips, her throat, and then lower. His tongue blistered her nipples with fiery sensation, exploring with restless hands and desperate lips all of her untouched places. She explored back, feeling his powerful shoulders in her hands, tearing at the thick, dark hair at his nape, nibbling his ears, kissing his neck and chest. She felt smoothness broken by scars, the marks of a warrior. The muscles of his shoulders bunched beneath her touch, and she slipped her arms around his back, wanting more of him, pleasuring in the feel of his body beneath her hands. The skin of his back under her fingers felt different, not smooth but ridged, grooved, patterned with something not natural. Confused, she splayed her hands, trying to understand, but she gasped as he reached between their bodies, rubbing her softly in that most secret of places. He moved, gently, in and out with his fingers, stroking and caressing.

She knew what was coming, and yet her heart pumped with sudden panic.

"Damon," she cried softly even as he plunged his finger deeper still, his mouth hot and intimate against hers as he captured her cry and spent timeless beats building the sweetest of aches within her, and then stopped. "Please," she whispered, almost sobbing. "Please don't stop."

He pressed that rigid heat of his against her again, and this time she parted her thighs, pushing against him instinctively. He buried that hard, throbbing part of him inside her, stretching her open. Stinging pain struck her, sharp and extraordinary.

Her eyes flashed open and she looked straight into those dark depths of his.

"Are you all right?" he asked her, breathless.

"Yes. No." She swallowed thickly, her entire body humming with passion even as the stinging pain of him filling her increased. "Don't stop," she whispered again, and she laughed—embarrassed and free at the same time.

He smiled down at her. "Oh, my sweet Belle," he said huskily, "thank God. Because it would surely be the death of me if you asked me to stop now." He kissed her jaw, her lips, her eyelids, and then slowly, so very slowly, her big, strong knight moved inside her again, whispering soothing words in her ears and kissing her face until the sting receded and her body accepted him completely.

Now her hips twisted to meet his rhythm, learning him, loving him, needing him so much more than she could have ever imagined. He consumed her, and the stinging pain transformed into something else. Flame.

A cry of surprise, pleasure, slipped out of her, setting off a reaction in him. He rocked harder, and she rocked with him, following some natural dance, as inevitable as sky and stars and sun. The passion in his body radiated into hers, each sweet jolt releasing something wild inside her, something uncontainable, primal.

She hadn't expected this. She didn't know what she'd expected, but it hadn't been this. . . . This glorious, aching, fierce pressure that built and built. It was like a tiny, throbbing firestorm between her legs that left all thought of pain far behind.

The first tremor shocked her, even scared her a little. The second took her breath. The third made her cry, soul-deep, profound; she had never known anything like it before—as if her body shattered from the inside out.

She became aware that he'd stilled over her, and she clung to him. "I'm fine," she said thickly, seeing the distress in his eyes. "I'm more than fine," she whispered. He held her and kissed her, and it was as if she couldn't tell where she ended and he began. They were one. He moved inside her several more times, escalating to one last push that crashed over her with white heat and wonder. He collapsed over her, carefully supporting his weight with his hands at her sides to keep from crushing her.

They remained joined for a long time, both of them uneager to end the moment, but finally she slid away from him, and he snuggled beside her, tugging the edges of the thick blanket over them both to make a cozy bed by the fire. Beneath the covers, she slipped her arm onto his waist, curving lightly around his back.

She felt again those raised places, those grooves. Those places that didn't feel as they should. The blanket fell back as she shifted onto her elbow, leaning around to see—

Scores of marks slashed his flesh, intersecting, converging, crossing, mutilating his skin.

She drew in a sharp, shocked breath, and the last piece of the puzzle clicked into place. He hadn't just been imprisoned in that black dungeon. He'd been tortured. That had been Saville's encouragement. The whip.

Agonized, she jerked her gaze to meet his. He stared up at her, that detachment coming back, already, and she hated it. She reached out, needing somehow to hold him here, with her, to keep him from descending into that dark place where his soul hid.

"Saville wanted a confession," he said simply. "I refused to give him one. He didn't stop asking. I didn't stop refusing."

She touched the vicious scar on his face now, the one that now seemed beautiful, courageous, and noble and honorable, everything that Damon was to her. She leaned over him, pressed her lips to that terrible scar.

*How do you make them go away? The nightmares?*
*I don't know.*

"Take me again," she begged against his cheek. "Make love to me. Let me make love to you."

She felt him beneath her, already growing aroused, his breath shaking. There was so much darkness inside him, but there was also light.

Tomorrow was a mystery. She might never be able to heal all that was wounded inside him. But for now, for tonight, there was light and she held him there as long as she could.

\* \* \*

She came awake slowly. There was a brightness, and she thought at first it was the sun beaming through the windows, then she realized it was the fire. They'd slept here, before the hearth. She sat up abruptly, blinking.

It was day. Pale dawn misted the windows. Damon was gone.

Again, he'd let her sleep. Her lips curved at the thought of him, of the memory of what they'd done in the night, together, on this blanket by the fire— again and again. The sweet ache between her legs was a tangible reminder. She felt sensuous and warm and as if she could fall back to sleep like a lazy cat.

She should have been ashamed, she thought, and part of her was. But she didn't regret what had happened between them.

*She loved him.* The rush of emotion hit her out of nowhere, and it frightened her. How deeply she had fallen into this life that wasn't hers.

Desperately, she tried to focus her thoughts, fearful of letting emotion take her away. There was yet danger here. Mystery, murder, and more. What?

The terrible thoughts cut through the tender haze of the night before. She pulled the blanket around her and moved across the room to the chest. She lifted the lid and poked deep inside to retrieve the brooch.

Sitting back down, the blanket pooled around her, she stared down at the mysterious object Marigold had brought back to her . . . from where? If she could uncover that, perhaps she could uncover what was wrong at Castle Wulfere. And perhaps the girls would be safe. And Damon. And even her.

Suddenly, she wanted this life so desperately. She

would do anything to protect it, and to protect the ones she loved.

She held the brooch in her fist, her mind running in circles. Marigold, missing, for hours. Snow on her hair. Freezing. *They found her near the kitchen.*

Another memory struck her. She and the girls, in the corridor outside the kitchen. Gwyneth explaining to Lizbet how to play a Christmas game. Marigold backing, backing, backing away until she crashed into Aurelie. Marigold shaking, afraid—why?

*They found her near the kitchen.*

There were any number of places she could have been outside. The kitchen garden was the most likely place. She could have sneaked unobserved through the scullery, back and forth. But why would she have been in the winter-barren kitchen garden, hiding in the freezing cold?

Aurelie's mind came back again and again to the storage dock that Julian hadn't wanted her to see.

Had Marigold been down those winding stone steps to the storage dock? Marigold had been afraid of that place, of that Aurelie was certain. Why was she afraid? Would she have braved that fear to bring Aurelie back something, a clue?

She threw off the blanket and dressed quickly. Damon and his sisters would be at prayers. She should wait for Damon, show him the brooch. But she was too impatient. She donned her cloak and took her gloves. The corridor outside her room was empty. She slipped down the back stairs, easily familiar now with the circuitous passages of this part of the castle. She came out behind the screens and slipped down the kitchen passage.

The draft that blew up the winding steps from the

storage dock alerted her well before she reached the passage. She was alone, though she had passed a few maids rushing platters of bread up to the hall for those who would be breaking their fast soon.

They had paid her no heed, busy about their duties, their steps rushed, their eyes on the loads in their arms.

Aurelie pulled her cloak tight around her, tugging up her hood. She tied it securely, fighting an intense instinct to flee, to forget she'd ever seen that brooch. All of the innocent curiosity she'd once held for this storage dock evaporated.

What was she thinking?

What if there was something down there, something terrible, something that had frightened Marigold so deeply she hadn't spoken for three months?

Who was she, Aurelie, to believe she could conquer whatever evil might lurk there? She didn't want to know what was down there now. She didn't want to know what was wrong at Castle Wulfere.

But she took the first step down, anyway.

# *Twenty-one*

The walls were ice-slick, the draft harsh. Aurelie pulled her hood closer to her face and steeled herself to go on. She slipped on her gloves as she took the next step.

Above her, from the kitchen corridor, she heard footsteps. More maids bearing food for the tables in the great hall, she thought.

But the footsteps stopped. She stood there, just a few steps within the passage. There was no sound now, nothing but her own shaky breathing.

She shook herself. What was she doing? She was going mad. Like as not, this was nothing but a wild-goose chase. Footsteps sounded again, voices. Maids. Of course. What had she thought? She'd unnerved herself. She could be wrong about everything—the brooch could be nothing more than something Marigold had found lying about in some forgotten corner of the castle.

Just like the message on the slate was nothing but a game between Lizbet and Gwyneth.

*But a man was dead.* She couldn't forget that. *A man who'd died with the name Lorabelle on his lips.*

Still, how could any of these strange things be connected? None of it made sense.

She continued down the spiraling steps, deeper and deeper. The full force of winter hit her as she rounded the last curve.

Instinctively, she stopped there, her body flattened against the wall, her dark cloak blending in with the shadows, not yet entering the light.

She saw knights, two of them, pacing out their watch along the cliff. The storage dock seemed to have been fashioned from Nature herself—a nearly flat, narrow expanse of rock dropping off to what she knew was the river below. A rope ladder was drawn up one side, allowing access to the river below but preventing approach unless lowered—protecting Castle Wulfere from unwelcome intrusion from this its only other aperture aside from the huge gate-house that overlooked the village.

The knights huddled in their cloaks, arms wrapped about themselves, as they paced. Aurelie waited, there in the shadows. There wasn't a solid reason not to show herself, and yet she didn't. If—and it was a big if—Marigold had come down to this icy storage dock last night, she had come down here in secret. No one had seen her. Aurelie tried to think as Marigold would have thought, to see the dock as Marigold would have seen it.

She could just see a row of stacked barrels near the entrance to the passage, and when the opportunity arose, if she was quick enough, she could slip down the last few steps and duck behind them. She felt silly suddenly, and told herself the worst thing that could happen to her down here was that she would be caught hiding behind barrels. How would she explain that?

The knights tromped past each other, then briefly,

both of their backs were turned from the steps. Aurelie sprinted down the last steps and stopped behind
the barrels. Her breath came in misty pants and she
felt just as silly as she'd expected to feel.

Now what? She turned to look between the barrels
where she could see the knights continuing to pace.
She flipped back around and studied the storage area
now revealed to her. Small, cavelike stone cellars were
situated on either side of the steps, built beneath the
entire domestic range of the castle. The cellars were
covered by iron grills, and she could see into them
and pick out various household items, mostly kitchen
implements or supplies. In one she could see large
cauldrons, tongs, iron pot rests, fire fenders, and
kitchen shovels. In another she spied kitchen furniture and even a dismantled bed that might have been
used for travel purposes, and rugs. In yet another,
stacks and stacks of earthen vessels were stored.

She crept over the icy stone, using the stacked barrels as a shield. Her body felt so cold now, she was
practically numb. She wondered how the knights
could stand it, especially those who paced out the
night watch on all the freezing ramparts of the castle.
No wonder they huddled about the huge hearths of
the great hall whenever they were off duty.

Bundles and barrels and jars filled another one of
the cellars. She couldn't see what was inside, and she
pressed the grilled door with her gloved hands. It
yielded to her light touch and she slipped quickly
inside. The cellar was deeper than she expected, and
she crept toward the back, out of sight of the knights.
It was shadowed, but enough light came in for her
to examine the contents—sugar, rice, almonds, all of
which would have been purchased in towns or at fairs

and transported back to the castle by boat. Boulting cloths for the kitchen, and steel knives and assorted pewter cooking tools rounded out the stored items.

No curious brooches, or anything to even suggest such an article would have ever been stored here. She had to have been wrong. It was her imagination again. She'd let it carry her away, and here she was, scrounging around in the dark cellars of a frozen storage dock on Christmas Eve morning instead of hurrying to join her family at prayers.

*Her family.* Her throat tightened up. They were her family now—Damon, Elayna, Gwyneth, Lizbet, and Marigold. She loved them all. The chapel was where she belonged, with her family.

She shut the grilled door behind her quickly and gazed through the cracks between the barrels. The knights weren't looking this way. She looked back over her shoulder at the cellars one last time and noticed there was one more iron-grilled cellar. A chain with a lock held it fast.

None of the other cellars was locked. A prickle crept down her spine. She stared unblinkingly at the locked grilled door of the last cellar.

*Go. Go back to your family. This locked door means nothing.*

She experienced the same throat-choking, sickening feeling she'd known when she'd first stepped into the spiraling passage down to the storage dock. She didn't want to know what was inside that locked cellar. She didn't want to know what was wrong at Castle Wulfere.

She had to know, though. She had to find out. Perhaps it was nothing more than imagination. Perhaps that cellar wasn't even used. She crept closer so that she could see inside.

The cellar was arranged haphazardly. Bags and bundles were shoved together toward the back. She couldn't see anything that was within them.

She looked over her shoulder again. The knights had stopped; they were talking together, staring out over the cliff.

Aurelie examined the lock. She couldn't budge it. It was old, rusted, but secure. Marigold wouldn't have been able to open this door. For a second, she felt relief. She almost turned away again when her gaze fastened on the grill. The iron bars were close enough together that she couldn't possibly fit through, but Marigold could.

Tiny Marigold could have easily slipped sideways through the bars. These dark cellars would appeal to the little girl's penchant for hiding in secret places, especially this one locked cellar. But it was so very cold here, even within the recesses of the cellars.

*The mite stopped speaking about three months ago, 'tis all I know. She's turned skittish, runs away before anyone can take hold of her. She lets her sisters touch her, that's it.*

Eglyntine's words when Aurelie had questioned her about Marigold came back to her. Whatever had happened to frighten Marigold, to cause her to stop speaking, had happened three months ago. In October, the weather would have been comfortable, she thought.

Had something in that cellar terrified Marigold? Or was she leaping to conclusions?

Her heart pumped and she hardly felt the cold now. How could she get inside that locked cellar? She could go back upstairs, ask Mistress Betha or the steward, Eudo, for keys.

Damon. She should go to Damon, she thought, as she should have done before and she almost turned away again when she thought—*the keys,* and a sense of startlement stopped her. She pushed her hand inside her cloak and felt the chatelaine chain she always wore about her hips. They were old keys, unused for years, forgotten.

Could one of Damon's mother's keys fit this lock?

She unhooked the metal ring from the chain and drew it out from beneath her cloak. She was here, so she would see, just see, if they fit. Kneeling, furtive, she tried first one then another, her heart beating so fast, so hard, it was like thunder in her ears. Finally, the second-to-last key turned the lock and the cellar door fell open.

It made a small creak and she gasped, pivoting to check on the knights. They were pacing out their watch, unaware of her, the wind buffeting them on that open promontory.

She slipped inside, tucking the keys back inside her cloak and onto the chatelaine chain. The cellar was dark and deep, like the others, and she crept to the back. To the bundles and packs and bags. She pulled the first bundle open. It was a huge, leaning canvas sack, and what she saw inside stopped her heart.

It was a pitcher, ceremonial and rich, engraved with the image of a griffin. She lifted it out and stared down at it for a frozen beat, then put it down and looked back inside the canvas sack. There were gold footed wine cups, silver plates, and something soft, very soft. Fur. She could pull the sack open enough to see what looked to be a fur-trimmed robe.

She tore open the next bundle. Medallions, brooches, fillets, rings encrusted with lapis lazuli, marcasite, and all manner of jewels beyond her ken. It was dark in the cellar, but the dim light that reached her glinted off the stones and precious metals. Her mind spun. Where had all of this come from? Why was it kept locked inside this household cellar?

Who had put it all here?

The next bundle and the next were more of the same. Ivory combs, gem-studded belts and girdles, rich furs, painted cordovan leather shoes, and boxes.

Here, in this cellar, was where Marigold had found that brooch, Aurelie thought with a sense of confusion and nameless dread. Here, in this cellar, the little girl must have hidden months ago, having slipped between the iron grill bars, and then she'd gotten curious and opened the sacks and bundles to peek inside. Then what? Someone had found her. Someone had terrified her. Why? And then last night she had come back and retrieved that brooch as a clue. Had she been trapped down here, afraid the knights would see her sneak back out? Was this where Marigold had huddled for hours, a freezing storm wreaking havoc just outside?

A noise broke through her anxiety. A breath, a footstep, what?

Panic clawed at her nape. Aurelie whirled. She couldn't even see the knights from this deep inside the cellar. She was too anxious to feel relieved that she was still unnoticed, still alone.

She didn't want to be alone. She wanted to get out

of this cellar, away from this dock. She wanted Damon.

Quickly, she packed the bags and bundles back how she'd found them. In setting one larger bundle against the wall again, she overturned a smaller one. The contents spilled out onto the icy stone. The clatter of it coiled her stomach muscles tighter, then she forgot to care about the sound. Forgot everything but what fell onto the floor at her feet.

Silver chalices, brass candlesticks, engraved mazers. And a precious gold box. She couldn't feel herself pick it up, could see her hand take it as if it were someone else's hand and she were watching from far away. The lid made a too-familiar squeak as it opened. Without realizing it, she squeezed her eyes shut, not wanting to see what was inside, not wanting to face this horror. In her mind's eye, she saw it clearly—the small chip of bone resting inside on dark blue velvet.

"No, no," she whispered hoarsely and she opened her eyes.

*There was the small chip of bone, on its blue velvet couch.*

It looked no different from how it had appeared any one of the countless times she'd opened this same box and gazed with fascination at this same chip of bone that had once been part of the body of John the Baptist . . . and which had been kept for years in a place of honor in the chapel of Briermeade.

Nothing was real—not the cold, not Marigold's brooch, not the knights pacing out their watch on the cold cliff. Nothing but this sacred relic that had been stolen, along with everything else spilling out of the sack at her feet.

*What was the stolen treasure of Briermeade doing at Castle Wulfere?*

"Greetings, sweet Sister."

She stood there, heart pummeling madly, not sure for an endless moment whether that voice came from her nightmares or from within this very cellar.

Slowly, agonizingly, she turned.

# Twenty-two

Aurelie stared at Sir Santon in disbelief. He seemed gigantic in the low-ceilinged cellar, something more than human, towering over her like a monster from legends. He looked different—clean-shaven now—but she knew him, knew those eyes from her nightmares.

She couldn't think or move for shocked pulsebeats, but through the haze of horror she remembered the knights, the watchmen, and she began to scream for help.

Santon whipped his arm out, viciously slapping her hard on the mouth, spinning her around with such force that she stumbled, her hood flying off her head as she fell hard, sideways, against the wall of the cellar. Before she could even try to rise, he jerked her to her feet by her hair, gripping it so hard she had no choice but to tip her head back at a brutal angle. Her neck felt as if it might snap in two at any moment.

He stroked something cold across her cheek, and from the periphery of her vision she saw that it was a knife.

"You're still a fighter," he said, close and hot, blowing the words across her frozen cheek, "but don't waste your precious voice. Do you think we let men pace the watch down here who are not with us?"

She felt something warm trickle onto the corner of her mouth and she realized it was blood, her blood. Her lip was bleeding from her face smacking the stone wall.

"With you?" she choked out. What was he talking about? She had to think. She had to get away from him. But she could barely breathe or focus on anything but the knife and those glittering eyes that had terrorized her every night since Briermeade.

"It won't be long," he said, not responding to her question, "not long until we have everything. And you're going to help us. You're one of us now. You're just like us, aren't you sweet, pious Sister?"

"No." She felt cold, so very cold, and so very frightened. Nothing made sense. How could Sir Santon be here, at Castle Wulfere? How had the treasure of Briermeade come to be concealed here? And what of the rest of the booty? How long had he—and how many other men, this mysterious *we* of whom he spoke—been roaming the countryside, stealing, secreting the goods away here? Her thoughts reeled, unable to put it together.

She didn't even want to put it together. She wanted out of this cellar, nothing more than that. Escape. Damon.

"What are you doing here?" she demanded, fighting not to panic. Her wits were the only tool she had, and she could not let fear overtake them. "Lord Wulfere has been searching for you. When he finds you—when he finds out about this plunder you've hidden down here in this cellar—you'll be thrown in the dungeon."

He laughed, a cold, evil sound that had her heart hammering up into her throat.

"I'm a knight of this castle. I serve your lord husband."

"There is no knight named Santon at Castle Wulfere."

That cold laugh again. "Do you think you are the only one with more than one name, sweet Sister? My name here is Stephen."

Stephen. Her mind spun dizzily as she made a horrifying connection. "Prewitt. Philip—"

"Clever girl," he murmured, shifting, moving even closer. She couldn't move. She thought about kicking him, pushing at him with her arms, but the knife stopped her.

He'd moved the blade so that it rested hard against her throat. She couldn't swallow without feeling as if the knife was cutting into her flesh.

"It was you," she said, and she felt sick. "You murdered him. You murdered your own brother—" And Philip had died with Lorabelle's name on his lips, trying—to warn her?

"He had a soft spot for you," Santon said. "It was the death of him."

"He was your brother."

"He was a fool. Not like you, sweet Sister Aurelie. Or should I say Lady Lorabelle?" He looked at her thoughtfully. "I had no idea you were so quick-witted, so daring. I would never have left you for dead at Briermeade if I'd known you were so extraordinarily gifted."

"It's not what you think."

"Oh, what is it then, *Lady Lorabelle?*" he spit the name and title at her with sarcasm.

*Love, it's love.* But she wouldn't tell him that, she wouldn't let him corrupt what was the only true thing in her life. "You wouldn't understand."

His fingers tightened on her hair and she let out an involuntary cry. Without warning, he twisted her around and slammed her face against the stone wall, bearing down behind her.

"I wouldn't understand, would I? Well, you understand this, Sister. I know who you are. You're mine. I own you. You're one of us now."

"I know who you are, too. You're a murderer, a thief—"

He whipped her back to face him, cutting off her words. She felt light-headed, and she tasted more blood in her mouth.

"Your lord husband has not long to rule this castle," he responded. "He will soon be dead—and the true lord of Wulfere will take his rightful place. And when he does, you will either be the widow . . . or the imposter."

His threats against her meant nothing now, but he couldn't know that. *Dead, dead, dead. He was going to kill Damon.* It was all she could think for one horrified instant.

Santon's horrible eyes continued to blaze down at her, so close, so full of hate. His mouth came closer until his lips brushed hers, and she couldn't help it. She twisted her head away from his horrible kiss.

Viciously, he pushed her hard against the wall, releasing his grip on her hair, at the same time yanking both her wrists into one fist and forcing her arms over her head. He pressed his knee against her body, pinning her. The knife remained at her throat.

"It was my idea," he murmured, "to use you. All mine."

"Tell me what you want from me," she said, feeling as if ice had taken over her body. There was only one way out of this cellar. She would have to convince Santon she was as vile as he.

There was triumph in his eyes now. "Clever, clever girl."

His vicious grip on her wrists finally relaxed and he let her arms drop. They fell useless, numb, at her sides. He drew the knife along her cheek and then stepped back. For the first time, she could breathe without feeling as if she drew him into her lungs at the same time.

"What do you plan?"

He shook his head. "Don't try to be too clever, sweet Sister." He grabbed her arm and propelled her toward the grilled door. "The lord of Wulfere must be informed of your desire to cooperate. He will be pleased."

Someone else was calling the shots, she realized. The *true* lord of Wulfere of whom he spoke. And she had taken them by surprise—stumbling upon them before they were ready to come to her.

Santon's hold on her arm intensified as they neared the entrance to the cellar. She felt his breath hot on her hair near her ear.

"Hear me well, sweet Sister, and know I speak you true," he whispered savagely. "It's him or you. Remember that we are watching." He pushed her out of the cellar.

The knights pacing out their watch didn't turn.

She fled toward the winding steps, toward the life that wasn't hers, the life now destroyed, and burst into the kitchen corridor, behind the screens, up the back tower stairs, passing servants and knights, all of them a blur. Sir Santon's voice playing over and over in her head, the fetid taste of him clogging her throat. *We are watching. We are watching. We are watching.*

She barely made it to her room before she was sick.

She splashed her face with the cool water Eglyntine brought. The maid had been the one to find her, thank God, not Damon. She was trembling still, but she'd washed from her mouth the taste of Santon's breath and the sickness it had wrought.

There was no washing the horror from her mind.

She heard the door open.

"Belle."

She put down the towel she held and turned to see Damon crossing the room toward her. He closed the space between them and she felt dizzy suddenly, overcome by all that had changed so drastically, so unbearably, since the last time she'd looked at his dear face.

"You're bleeding," he said, frowning, lifting his concerned gaze to her eyes. He put his hands on her shoulders. "And you're shaking. Belle, what's wrong?"

Oh God, she had to find the strength to tell him. She opened her mouth, not sure how she would do it, only that she had no choice, when a knock sounded on the door.

"Damon!"

It was Beldon's voice.

Damon stared hard into her eyes and she cringed

with the horror of everything that stood between them now.

He strode to the door, and spoke briefly in an undertone with the knight. When he came back, his look was even more concerned.

"I'm needed elsewhere." He touched her face again. "But first—what happened to you?" he asked again gently.

She could still see Beldon beyond him, waiting in the doorway. "I—I fell out of bed," she blurted. Stupid, she thought immediately when he drew his brows together in an odd look. She hadn't slept in the bed. He knew that. She was so worried about saving him that she couldn't think straight about anything else. "I'm fine," she said quickly. "Truly. Did you—did you still plan to speak to the girls this morning, before you go? We should hasten."

He nodded, though he watched her with a sense of puzzlement that destroyed her a little more with every passing instant.

But he didn't press her. She could see that his mind was full of worries that went beyond her, and he simply put his hand beneath her arm and escorted her to the schoolroom.

His meeting with the girls was blessedly brief. She was awed by his tenderness as he told them that a man had been murdered. When he was satisfied that they knew they were safe despite the events that had occurred so close to their keep, he left them.

"I may not see you again until tonight," he said. "There will be men guarding you and the girls all day." He touched her shoulder in reassurance, and she realized he sensed her fear and believed it due to a cause completely different from the true one.

She watched him walk away, and she looked at the two knights standing on both ends of the corridor outside the schoolroom.

*We are watching.*

She'd waited up for him.

Damon shut the door quietly, his exhausted body coming to life simply at the sight of her. Belle, with her vibrant gold hair and her sweet features—hiding her surprisingly bold spirit and her molten-hot sensuality. His chest filled and he was aroused, and for a moment he just stood there, gazing down on her, letting himself feel the sensations that she wrought within him. Joy. Pure joy.

When had he last felt such unadulterated happiness? And when had he ever felt this way in combination with such powerful desire? He hadn't even known such a thing was possible.

He had expected her to change nothing, and she had changed everything. She had done the impossible. She'd made him live again.

Setting down the small box he'd brought back with him, he leaned over to brush a kiss on her brow. She wore her night rail, thin and gossamer and enticing. He stroked her face to gently wake her. Fire lit the room with low flickerings, and he frowned as his hand moved over her cheek, feeling something slightly swollen. He studied her more closely and saw a dusky darkness there, almost like a . . . bruise.

Her cut lip sprang to his mind. He'd felt something wrong then, and he felt it even stronger now. She'd said she'd fallen from bed. But they'd spent the night together on the blanket by the fire.

Why would she lie to him? What was she hiding?

"Belle?" he murmured, and he shook her shoulders.

She opened her eyes and blinked, registering confusion. Something fragile and fearful filled her eyes, stunningly painful.

"Belle, it's me. It's Damon. Are you all right?"

She looked so lost, so afraid, as if awoken from another terrible dream. He moved his hands firmly down her shoulders, over her arms, and she gasped. Not fear, he realized at that. It was a sound that was sharp, physical.

He took in the darkness on her cheek, and he tore at the strings of her chemise too quickly for her to stop him and pulled it apart, pressing it open to reveal her shoulders. Bruises circled one of her upper arms. She made a choked sound, pulled at the material, and tried to tear away from him but he wouldn't let her go. He took hold of her hands and the sound she made then caused him to slice his gaze down to her wrists. More bruises manacled the tender flesh there.

"My God, Belle, what's happened to you?" Anger shook his voice. Who had dared touch her, hurt her this way? And why had she hidden it from him? "Don't tell me this happened when you fell out of bed," he said harshly.

"No," she whispered. "No."

He scooped her up and carried her to the bed. What else had happened to her? What else didn't he know? Someone had attacked her—"Who hurt you?" He sat her gently on the bed. "Did they—" He could hardly bring himself to ask her the terrible question. "Did someone force himself upon you, Belle?"

"No," she cried, and buried her face in her hands, drawing inside herself, shutting him out.

He stood there, bereft and baffled.

"Belle—"

She lifted her face then and he broke off at the sight of it—drenched with tears, hurting. Her voice when she spoke was rough and broken and he scarcely recognized it.

"Don't call me that anymore."

# Twenty-three

He reached for her as she tried to push past him, off the bed, away from him. Away from those intense eyes, that heart—barely opening again—that she didn't want to destroy. She'd betrayed him, and after what she knew of his past, she understood how deeply she was about to hurt him.

His hands on her were tender, but his voice was fierce. "What's wrong?" he demanded, holding her.

She winced involuntarily at his touch on her bruised flesh, and he let go of her instantly, guilt flaring in his anguished eyes.

"I didn't mean to hurt you." Body taut, jaw flexed, he stood back as if he were afraid to touch her.

*He* was afraid of hurting *her.*

She couldn't bear it.

"Tell me," he said again darkly. "Tell me what's wrong."

*Everything,* was all she could think. Everything was wrong, and would never be right again. But she had to try to do the only right thing that was left for her. She had to tell Damon the truth.

She walked to the window, leaned her brow against the thick glass for a long beat, feeling its cold kiss against her skin, leaning on its strength for a moment before she straightened, but she didn't turn. If she looked at Damon now, she wasn't sure she could do what she knew she must.

"There were two girls at Briermeade." She could feel him come up behind her, knew he was near. She felt that tense pull between them, that connection that had been there from the start.

What she did now would sever it forever.

She stopped, swallowed thickly, blinking back the sting of fresh emotion. Damon said nothing. She felt his presence behind her, but he didn't move, didn't even seem to breathe.

"They were as different as two girls could be," she continued flatly. It was cold by the window, but she could feel nothing past the roar of her own blood and the heavy beat of her heart.

"One was rich—the cherished only child of one of the most prosperous lords of the realm. The other was poor—abandoned at the convent gate when she was but a babe. She never knew her parents, where she came from. Never had so much as a name to call her own. The sisters named her, but always she wondered who she really was, what she might have been—what she could be."

Her gaze still fixed on the window glass, she almost felt as if she were telling a story. Briermeade seemed long ago and far away. The ache in her chest as she spoke was the only thing that made it real.

"But as much as they were different, they were also the same. They were of an age, and with their golden hair and blue eyes, they were like sisters. They loved to dream, imagining all the things they could be and do when they left Briermeade. When one of them would marry, she would bring her dear friend with her . . . to Castle Wulfere," she ended on a whisper.

She focused on a tiny imperfection in the thick glass of the window until she was quite certain she wasn't going to cry again.

Damon touched her arm, pulled her around toward him, and she didn't have the strength to resist.

"But it wasn't meant to be," she said, staring beyond him, unable to bear meeting the tortured bewilderment in his eyes for more than an instant.

"What happened?"

"One of them died. Only one of them made it to Castle Wulfere."

"Lorabelle—"

"No," she said firmly, softly, forcing herself to speak over the awful horror in her throat. "Not Lorabelle." She looked into his eyes one last time, and knew it would never be the same. She'd always dreamed of finding love; how ironic that she finally had, with a man who would never want her again. She took a deep breath. "Aurelie."

Damon's mind reeled with incredulity. *Not Lorabelle. Aurelie.* He stared at the woman he thought he'd come to know. The woman he realized now he didn't know at all. Bravely, she met his gaze. Color spotted her cheeks. Her devastated, tear-ravaged face tore at him, but he wouldn't let her into his heart. Not now.

He was devastated, too.

"Your name is Aurelie," he repeated, yet feeling dazed, angry, needing to comprehend this thing that seemed beyond comprehension—that this woman who had become so important to him was a fraud. That everything between them was a fraud, too.

"Yes," she said in that low voice of hers.

"Lorabelle . . . is dead." The finality of that was hard to believe. *She* was Lorabelle—and yet she was not.

She was a stranger.

"Yes," she said again.

She was the orphan of Briermeade, the orphan of her story. The girl with no family, no name, no home.

"Lorabelle died of the pestilence," she said softly. "Months ago, and I—"

"And you simply took her life," he said ruthlessly, almost glad when she cringed at his cruel tone. Immediately his throat constricted and he felt only pain. His pain, her pain. And looking at her, he suddenly realized that whatever she'd done, he couldn't inflict more pain on her than she had already inflicted on herself. She was in agony and it killed him to even look at her because he refused to comfort her, refused to forgive her.

She had betrayed him, lied to him, deceived him. He wanted to hate her.

"I didn't do it on purpose," she said, the spots of color heightening. "When you found me at Briermeade, I was wearing your ring. The ring Lorabelle pressed into my hand on the day she died. I never meant this to happen," she whispered, her voice small and genuinely full of remorse. "But when it did—"

"You didn't stop it."

Her shoulders, held so straight and tense till now, dropped. "No. I didn't stop it. I was afraid—the nuns were all gone. Lorabelle was gone. And when you told me the abbess was dead—" She broke off at a terrible hitch in her voice, taking time to drag in a ragged breath.

He thought of how she'd been so alone and so desperate, and again he fought compassion, pushing his anger to the fore.

"Is that your excuse?" he said harshly. "You were alone, afraid? So you took another woman's life. Another woman's husband. Why didn't you ask me for help?"

Her eyes filled with an apology he couldn't accept. Regret he couldn't acquit.

"I make no excuses. What I did was wrong. But I fell in love with your sisters, and—"

She stopped, casting her too-bright eyes away from his. He wanted to shake her, demand to know what she'd left unsaid, but he didn't. He wasn't sure he wanted to know, wasn't sure he could bear to know. It was over, whatever might have been between them.

It was better if he didn't know what she would have said.

"Why are you telling me this now?" He advanced on her, closing the small bit of space between them, struggling not to care that her scent wrapped him in remembrance, that the warmth of her skin as he jerked her jaw up and forced her to face him made him want to do nothing but kiss her. "Tell me why."

"Because," she said simply, "you're in danger."

He stared at her, taking in the last thing he'd expected her to say.

"What are you talking about?"

"They're going to kill you."

"Who?"

"I don't know."

"When? How?"

"I don't know," she said again, her voice quaking slightly.

Was she mad? he had to wonder suddenly, and it struck him then that it was what he had wondered about her in the beginning. It was just one more of her lies—those lost memories. There had never been any lost memories. For an instant, he felt almost dizzy, lost in the tangle of truth and lie that seemed impossible to sort out.

He took her hands now, forcibly detaching himself from their enchanting softness, and turned them over to the fresh bruises there. He couldn't detach himself from the sickening spear of emotion that looking at her savaged skin shot through him.

"Who did this to you?" He lifted his gaze to meet hers demandingly. He wanted to kill whoever had done this to her, still. No matter what she'd done, she didn't deserve to be treated with abuse.

"His name is Santon. Sir Santon and his brother, Sir Philip, are the ones who robbed Briermeade. Santon is the one who beat me there, who left me for dead."

Of course, he thought dully. She'd always known their names. She hadn't told him because it would have endangered her deception.

"They knew my name," she said, almost as if she'd read his thoughts. "They knew who I truly was. They were the only ones. I never thought I'd see them again—they were criminals. But they weren't gone—they were here, all along. Knights of Castle Wulfere."

Damon's body went rigid. "What?"

"They aren't known as Santon and Philip here."

He waited, and somehow, in some strange way, he wasn't surprised when she finished.

"They're known here as Stephen and Prewitt."

New rage rose inside him, and he would have turned away from her and taken his rage out on the one living beast who had attacked Briermeade, but something in her tormented eyes held him back. She wasn't finished. There was more, and as much as he suddenly knew he didn't want to hear it, he knew he had to.

"Tell me everything."

She began with the brooch. She took it out of the chest and showed it to him and the story came out in low, pained words and when she was finished, he wanted to crash his fist into the face of the man who had hurt her at Briermeade and again in that locked cellar beneath Castle Wulfere.

But he knew he could not.

He had to uncover the so-called true lord of Wulfere. He had to find out who was behind the robberies and murders he'd discovered when he'd first searched for the men who'd attacked Briermeade. The man who was behind so much more than that, he knew now—the man behind this dire scheme to seize control of this castle, to murder him.

Only he was afraid he already knew who that man would be. He just didn't want to believe it, couldn't completely accept it.

"Julian," he said grimly, and walked away to glare at the fire, away from her hurting eyes. He was almost relieved to face this new pain, anything that drew his attention away from this shattering of everything between them.

So many things fit into place. Julian was behind

this band of thieves—which would explain his strange absences, his preoccupation. His loathing.

"I don't know," she said, her voice low and seeming so far away suddenly. "I surprised them by discovering what was in that cellar. They don't trust me enough to tell me everything—not yet, at least. They'll come to me, he said. But they have to think I'm one of them." She was silent for a heartrending beat. "They have to believe that you don't know, that nothing has changed."

*They have to believe that nothing has changed.* His heart clenched.

"I don't want you to do this. It's too dangerous." It was also too painful, but he forced his mind away from emotion.

"I have to do it. You need me."

*You need me.* She didn't know the truth of her words. He would learn to not need her in time, but for now she was right about this one thing—without her, he could seize Sir Santon, seize that treasure in the cellar, and return those things to those from whom they'd been stolen, but that was all. He would never be able to prove that Julian was behind the scheme, or know who else was involved. The thought that countless knights at Castle Wulfere could be embroiled in this plot, and that not only he but his sisters—*his sisters*—could be desperately endangered, made his blood run cold.

He understood now that it probably hadn't been his sisters that Prewitt had meant in his last gasping words—but Aurelie instead. She'd explained that Santon and Philip had believed her to be a holy nun. Still, his sisters wouldn't be safe at Castle Wulfere if he were dead. The danger swirled around them all—

and in the center of that boiling darkness was the woman who gazed so bravely at him now. *You need me.*

She'd lied to him about everything. And for all he knew, she was still lying. She could be faking every bit of the hurt he saw in her eyes, heard in her voice. Her confession could be part of the plot.

And yet now he had to trust her with his life.

# Twenty-four

"It's Christmas!" Lizbet announced at daybreak.

Standing behind her, Elayna looked as if she were trying to appear indifferent, but her eyes glowed, giving her away. Even Marigold was smiling, dancing from foot to foot eagerly, clutching her doll.

All four girls had come, still dressed in their nightgowns, to beat upon their brother's chamber door.

"I'm so sorry about their waking ye, milord," Fayette apologized, coming up the corridor after them. "They are wild with excitement this morn."

Damon shook his head, and the sad smile with which he greeted his sisters' prancing enthusiasm set up a throbbing ache in Aurelie's chest. He'd had little sleep, she knew—she'd had even less, alone in the huge bed without him.

"It's all right, Fayette," he said gently. "You may go. We'll send them back when they're ready to be dressed."

"Wait." Aurelie rushed to the chest, her night rail whispering at her ankles. She dug a bundle from beneath a pile of clothes. "We have something for you."

The maid flushed prettily, her cheeks nearly as red as her strawberry-colored hair as Aurelie handed her the package wrapped in soft linen, tied with twine, and decorated with a sprig of pine. Fayette unfolded it to reveal long lengths of sky blue, forest green, and ivory hair ribbons the girls had selected for her with much argument and decision-making from the wardrobe room.

"Oh, thank ye, milady," Fayette cried, almost teary, and she hugged Aurelie and all the girls. She cast a shy glance at Damon. "Thank ye, milord," she said, and Aurelie thought she didn't look quite as afraid of him as she had before.

Damon nodded his acknowledgement and Fayette ran out with her ribbons. He shut the door behind her.

The girls stood all in a row, the younger ones tipping up and down on their toes, Elayna still trying very hard to be mature while the excited grin that kept breaking out on her face ruined the picture.

"We have something for you, Damon," Elayna said.

"We all do," Lizbet explained.

Aurelie hung back, her heart full, watching these four girls who wouldn't even look at their brother a few weeks ago now interacting with him so easily.

Damon focused on his sisters as they stepped forward one by one.

Elayna went first. "My present isn't really a present," she said. "It's a promise. I promise I will not run away again"—she took a breath and qualified her promise—"if you'll arrange for me to meet Lord Harrimore face-to-face before the wedding. Then if I still don't want to marry him, the promise is off." There was that rebellious lift to her chin coming through now. "But I won't try to run away till then, not without giving him a chance."

Damon studied her for a long moment, his mouth

quirking slightly at the compromise. "Thank you," he said in all seriousness, "for the reprieve. I'll send word to Lord Harrimore as soon as possible to arrange a meeting."

Elayna stepped back and Gwyneth came forward, her arms behind her back. She moved to hold out her gift. It was a sword stick. Damon took it, raising a brow.

"It's a sword stick of your own," she said cheerfully. "So you can practice swords with me. Until I can lift a real one."

He shook his head, smiling. "All right," he said. "And I pray you are never strong enough to lift a real sword."

Gwyneth's face settled in a stubborn expression, her eyes gleaming. "I will be," she swore. "You watch."

"That's what I'm afraid of," Damon replied under his breath.

Now was Lizbet's turn.

"You know that Master Falconer has been letting me help to tame the new tiercel," she began, her earnest face glowing as she launched into her favorite subject. "It's to be yours when it's fully trained, and the present I would like to give you is to train it for you." Lizbet gazed up at him optimistically.

"You're already helping Master Falconer in the mews," Damon pointed out.

"I want to go into the field!" Lizbet said excitedly, then she bit her lip and slowed down. "Master Falconer says it takes great patience to train a falcon, and I think it will help me to be a fine lady someday because ladies need to be patient, you know."

Damon laughed. "That's a good argument," he

said, and Lizbet threw her arms around his waist impulsively.

"Can I have a bird, a bird of my own?" she asked eagerly.

He patted her back. "We'll see," was all he'd say, but Aurelie knew it was only a matter of time.

Her big, fierce knight had a soft, tender center. Her heart clenched as Marigold stepped forward. Damon leaned down, waiting, and she knew the one thing he would wish most would be that Marigold would speak to him.

They hadn't spoken to Marigold about the cellar. Damon was worried about his family, about what would happen next, and she knew he would wait, until it was over, until he knew they were safe, before he spoke of this to any of his sisters.

Marigold tipped up on her toes and very, very softly, she placed a kiss on Damon's cheek. Then she stepped back, blushing, her bright eyes cast down at her tiny feet.

It was a small thing, but Aurelie knew how important it was. Marigold wasn't afraid of her brother anymore.

"Thank you," he said.

Marigold looked up at him and smiled.

Aurelie could see the shimmer of emotion in Damon's eyes, and she stepped into the sweet tension. "We have something very special for all of you," she said.

"Wait!" Elayna interrupted. "We have something for you. Something from all of us."

Elayna unfolded a soft square of cloth to reveal a meticulously sewn satchel embroidered with a circle made up of their names, each one connecting to the next in a never-ending chain: Damon, Belle, Elayna, Gwyneth, Lizbet, and Marigold. Inside the circle were tiny hearts and flowers made of intricate knots of cross stitches—clearly the work of Elayna, who'd been taught by her mother to embroider this well.

The small satchel released the soft fragrance of dried tansies and violets.

"I made it in my room at night," Elayna said now, "and everyone stitched their own name there—except for you and Damon, of course. So it's from all of us. It's filled with sweet dried flowers to put in your wardrobe chest and make your clothes smell pretty."

Aurelie forced herself to speak over the huge lump of grief in her throat. "Thank you so much," she said huskily, and she didn't look at Damon, just stared down at the precious circle of names, a circle that was already broken.

She folded the cloth back up and used the excuse of putting it away to swipe secretly at her eyes and take deep breaths. She pulled herself together and drew a bundle from beneath the bed.

"Skates," she said, presenting each of the girls with a pair of specially made bone ice skates fashioned by a craftsman in the village. With Damon's permission and Eglyntine's help, she'd arranged to have the skates made, but what Damon didn't know was that she'd also had a pair made not only for her, but for him as well.

She handed him the last, largest pair. He looked at her with an unreadable expression as he took the skates.

"Now we can go skating," Gwyneth cried happily. "The whole family."

Damon's face hardened at his sister's words, and

Aurelie felt her heart breaking again because they weren't a family at all—at least, not a family that included her.

"Go back to your room and dress, girls," Damon said in a soft but grim voice. "We'll talk about skating later. It's Christmas, and our first duty is to our prayers—on this day especially. Now go." He shooed them out.

A tense silence followed their departure. Damon spun toward the fire, scraping a hand through his hair.

"When this is over," he said without looking back at her, his voice toneless, "I will dower your way into the abbey. You will be safe there, and comfortable."

She felt her insides rip apart and she hugged her arms tightly around herself, fighting to hold it all together.

"I never wanted to hurt the girls," she whispered. "Or you."

She almost wondered if he'd heard her, he took so long to respond. Finally he turned, and he said, "I know." His eyes were dark and hollow, and she longed to reach out to him, but knew better.

It was impossible now.

There was to be no more discussion of this painful thing, she understood. When he spoke next, it was as if the conversation they'd just had had never happened.

"I have a gift for you as well." He went to the table and opened the small, carved wooden box she hadn't noticed before. It hadn't been there yesterday, so she realized he had to have brought it with him when he'd returned to the keep last night.

Inside, she saw a leather sheath, and from that he withdrew a small dagger.

"I carry the like in my boot," he said, "and it has served me well."

There was something in his voice now, something not so flat, not so unemotional, but then it was gone and she knew she had to have imagined it simply because she wanted to hear it.

He replaced the dagger in the sheath and left it on the table. Aurelie's heart thumped painfully.

"Thank you," she said, thinking of wearing that dagger in her boot. Thinking of using that dagger.

She watched as Damon grabbed his sword belt and mantle off the hooks where he'd left them. He was already dressed. He'd never *un*dressed last night.

"After we've said prayers and broken our fast, we'll take the girls skating, as they wish."

She nodded, but he wasn't looking at her and she didn't bother to say anything aloud. There wasn't time. He was already gone.


It was torture from the start, before they even left the keep. The girls and Aurelie had festooned the hall with Christmas decorations, the joyous atmosphere a mockery to his mood now. Greenery decked the walls, windows, and tables, and beneath the wide main entrance, a kissing bush of evergreen boughs and sprigs of mistletoe hung from a slender chain.

He would have walked straight past it. He wouldn't have even noticed it, but Gwyneth stopped him in his tracks by running in front of him and planting herself determinedly there.

"You have to kiss Belle!" she demanded, pointing over their heads.

He followed the track of her gloved fingers, then looked back at Belle. *Aurelie,* he corrected himself.

It was impossible to still think of her as his Belle. And impossible not to.

She stood there, stunned, her cheeks burning, her eyes pain-bright. He felt his ruined heart crack a little, and he deliberately hardened it, focused on the betrayal twisting inside him.

He had no choice about kissing her. But he had a choice about whether he let himself care.

It was the merest of touches, a connection of soft, giving lips, and yet it was too much because it was dizzying and as necessary as air. Despite everything he knew, he wanted her.

He forced himself to break the contact, to push away the hopeless need. He strode out into the harsh, cold morning, his so-called bride at his side. His sisters spread out around them, dancing more than walking as they headed for the frozen village pond, the click of the bone skates they carried breaking the wintry stillness.

That, and the heavy beating of his supposedly ruined heart.


Night fell on Castle Wulfere, and the great hall teemed with Damon's people—peasants and castle folk, knights and maids. Friends and enemies.

The festivities swirled around him, and he sat at the high table in the midst of it and apart from it at the same time, working to maintain the thin wall of detachment that had carried him through the difficult day. Watching Belle with his sisters today, teaching them so patiently to skate and beaming with pride when they succeeded, had shaken his confidence in the decision he had made to send her away.

How much damage would the separation cause to his sisters?

But what would the alternative do to him?

He took in the conversation, the cheers, the toasting and revelry, and gave every appearance of joining in. He smiled down at his sisters as they devoured the special gingerbread figures—the Yule dolls—the cook had prepared just for them, and the frumenty and posset and other treats.

They left the table as the games began. His sisters clustered together with village children as their mothers led them in a round of bee in the middle. The one in the center wore the special mask made to give the appearance of antennae and feelers.

The children roared with laughter as the "bee" tried to sting them.

Through the shifting crowd of his people he saw his cousin watching him from across the hall. Damon purposefully kept his own gaze blank, flat, as he met Julian's.

Then Julian's gaze moved past him, to where Belle stood. Slowly, he inclined his head, almost as if to signal someone in the thick press of people.

Damon felt his senses sharpen, clarity kicking in. He turned to reach for Belle, but he was too late. She was gone.

# Twenty-five

"It's time, sweet Sister. Time to prove you are one of us."

Aurelie lifted her chin, assuming a bravado she didn't feel as she faced Santon in the dark corridor to the rear of the screens where he had pulled her. One minute, she had been standing beside Damon, and the next a cruel grip had taken her. No one had noticed, not even Damon. But then, Damon could hardly look at her now, had hardly looked at her all day as they had gone through the motions of family life.

She was relieved that the sham would be over now, relieved that they had come for her.

"Soon," Santon said, his breath hot against her cheek as he moved to come around behind her. He spoke close against her ear, his breath on her cheek. "Soon everything we desire will be ours. You will have position—the grieving widow of Wulfere. I will be the invaluable second-in-command to the new lord." He ran his hand over her shoulder, down her arm. "After a respectable period of time, we will wed. Our fortune is assured, downstairs in that cellar. No one will know," he whispered hotly, "our secrets."

"Someone will know," she pointed out in a surprisingly even voice. "The new lord of Wulfere will know."

He circled around her till he was in front of her again, his eyes intense and near, his touch trailing around her back, her waist, now on her other arm, then crushing one of her hands in both of his. "Ah, sweet Sister Aurelie, but we will know his secrets as well, will we not?"

Blackmail. He planned to blackmail Julian.

"You are wicked, sir knight." She managed to make her words sound flattering, and was rewarded with Santon's evil smile, a smile that made her shiver in the chilly passage. "And so is our new lord. Who is he?" She held her breath.

"Soon," he promised. "But not now, sweet Sister mine." He narrowed his eyes on her and she knew that he wasn't going to tell her what she wanted to know. "Soon," he said again.

"I can hardly wait," she said, despair choking her throat.

He let go of her hand and it took her a moment to realize he'd pressed something into it.

She looked down to find a small glass vial in her hand. The glass was thick, greenish.

"A small amount will make him sick," Santon said. "More will kill him." His voice turned low and harsh. "You will give him more."

She tore her gaze from the vial to Santon, remembering to play her part. "But there will be talk, a healthy man suddenly dies—"

Santon shook his head. "There will be no talk," he said, that terrible smile returning. "Poor Damon of Wulfere, afflicted with the same disorder that took his father's life so slowly—and took the son so fast."

Aurelie's throat worked. She couldn't speak. Poison. They'd poisoned Damon's father, and now they wanted her to poison Damon.

"There is wine on the table in your chamber." Santon's voice turned sly. "It will be a simple task for one as clever as you to pour your lord husband a goblet and add the contents of this vial. First he will be cold, painfully cold, as his body becomes weak. He will have difficulty breathing, and his limbs will become as if too heavy for him to lift. You have nothing to fear; he will be completely incapacitated—and then he will be dead.

"There will be a new lord of Wulfere by dawn," he finished, "or you, my lady imposter, will be revealed."

Aurelie's fingers tightened around the vial and she suppressed a shudder.

"Go now, sweet Sister. Fare thee well."

She felt his eyes on her back as she walked away. She made it to the back stairs to the tower, and fled up them. She burst into her chamber, blood roaring in her ears.

The wine was on the table, just as he had said it would be.

The door crashed open behind her, but before she could fully register it and turn, there were hard, warm arms around her, desperate arms. Damon's arms.

"Thank God," he rasped against her hair. "Thank God." He turned her in his arms so that she faced him, only a breath apart. His eyes were deep and aching. "When you disappeared from the hall—"

The way he was looking at her, as if he still cared— She couldn't stand it. "I'm all right. What of the girls?" she changed the subject. "Are they all right? Are they—"

"They are with Fayette. I asked Rorke and Kenric to watch over them. They are in the safest place they could be—a hall filled with people."

Then, as if he just realized that she, too, had been in that hall surrounded by people, he held her tighter. "I should have had someone watching over you. *I* should have been watching over you."

"No," she argued. "No. It's not your fault. I wanted them to come for me. They were supposed to come for me—it's what we planned." She pushed out of his arms, needing to distance herself from his concern, his kindness. "Santon gave me this." She held out the vial to him. "But he would tell me nothing more. I don't know who else is involved, how many men. And still he doesn't mention Julian. I don't think they'll tell me more until—"

"Until?"

"Until you're dead," she whispered. "I'm sorry. I failed you."

Damon took the vial from her and put it on the table.

"No," he said forcefully. "You didn't fail me. You did more than you should have done. You put yourself in danger for me. You could have walked away from all of this, saved yourself. But you didn't. Why?"

"Because you need me," she said softly, but that was only half the truth.

Damon didn't move. For an instant, she wasn't sure he was still breathing. Then he touched the side of her face, and she closed her eyes, leaning into his palm, daring to pray that what she'd said was true, that he needed her.

"So that's why you're still here," he whispered, "because I need you."

She closed her eyes to escape his intense gaze, but she couldn't escape the truth. She couldn't lie to him. "No," she admitted finally, opening her eyes. "I'm here because *I* need *you.*"

He kissed her suddenly, sweetly, tormentingly, his body brushing against her as he folded her into his arms. There was no mistaking his desire—it was real, not a dream. It was physical need, she knew, not the soul hunger that welled up from deep within her. But it didn't matter. She loved him, and she wanted him—and all she had was tonight.

She felt him lift her up and he carried her to the bed. He dispensed quickly with the tangible barriers between them—her clothing, her hose, her boots. It was as if he couldn't wait, as if he would explode if he had to, and she felt the same way. In an instant it seemed his clothes were gone, too. He loomed over her, his hands braced on either side of her head as he trailed his incredible mouth down her throat, to her chest, his fingers slipping deftly between her legs, urgent, demanding, and she wrapped her legs around him, needing fulfillment, impatient for it. She clenched her fingers in his hair as he penetrated her so deeply she could hardly breathe. Her muscles tensed with shock, and then pure pleasure, the pain disappearing rapidly this time.

There was no Julian, no Santon, no band of men determined to overthrow him, murder him, seize all that was his by right. There was only this one pure thing that was meant to be.

The tension in her body built to an aching pitch. "Now," she pleaded, tightening her legs around him.

"I don't want this to end," he whispered back, and she was aware of a tiny seed of hope springing to life inside her.

*He didn't want this to end.* At that moment, anything seemed possible. She was aware of only his heat, his pounding heart, and the sensation of surrendering to the moment, overwhelmed, as they went up in liquid fire together.

Damon slowly became aware of the soft hissing sounds of the fire, and the steady breathing of Belle. She smiled drowsily up at him, and he moved off her, realizing he must be crushing her. She shifted to snuggle into his shoulder, and as quickly as that, she was asleep.

He gazed down at her, at the hand she curled over his chest. Over his heart.

They should never have been together at all, and yet he couldn't regret a single day she'd spent at Castle Wulfere—or a single instant she'd spent in his arms. Only a miracle of circumstances could have brought her to him, and he was suddenly humbled by a sense of destiny that seemed larger than the two of them, larger than the pain and betrayal.

But to accept the miracle meant to forgive the lies.

His chest felt tight and sore, and he was more confused than ever. He didn't know if he could forgive her. And he didn't know if he could take her to the abbey at Worcester and simply walk away.

He didn't even know if he would live long enough to make the choice.

\* \* \*

It was his absence that woke her. How quickly he had become so basic a part of her. She sat up in the bed, blinking into awareness, looking for him. He sat by the fire, dressed again, holding the vial and gazing into the flames, his back to her.

The sounds of revelry from the hall continued, muted, and she knew she hadn't slept long.

He'd made love to her so thoroughly, so tenderly, she could almost have convinced herself that he cared for her. But she knew better. The brief hope she'd spun while they'd made love unraveled from the harsh pull of reality.

Quietly she donned her clothes again then sat down in the chair beside him. The fire cast a golden glow over his hard profile, then he turned and she ached at the fatigue on his face. His eyes were rimmed with red, and his hair looked as if he'd scraped his hands through it a thousand times.

He held the vial in his hand.

"Do you know what this is?" His voice was plain, unemotional. Anyone who heard them speaking now would not think they had just made love.

She shook her head, pushing back the hurt. She remembered what Santon had said about Damon's father, and that she hadn't had a chance to tell him about that earlier. "He said that a little would make you sick, and that more would kill you—and he told me to pour the entire contents of the vial in your drink. He said that people would believe your life had been taken so fast by the same disorder that had slowly taken your father's."

Damon met her eyes for a harsh beat. "My God," he said and stood and began to pace back and forth as he spoke. "My mother died in childbed, after Marigold's birth. I was already in France, and I knew my father was unwell then, but I thought it was the grief. I thought it would pass. Over time, I received word that he continued to be ill. But Julian was with him, attending him, seeing to the castle. I was comforted by that, and still certain my father would recover. My father always sounded confident when he wrote—he had spells, he called them. He would feel better for a time, then suffer more spells. Small spells that built over time, weakening him, until the final one that killed him."

He stopped pacing and stared at her across the firelit space, pain savaging his features.

"Julian wasn't glad to see me return. He must have hoped I would die in France. He killed my father, slowly, and when I didn't accommodate him by dying in that dungeon beneath Blanchefleur, he decided to kill me the same way he killed my father. Only he's not as patient as he was then."

"What now?" Aurelie asked, chilled already by the knowledge they'd uncovered, afraid to hear what he would say next.

"Now," he said, "I die."

# Twenty-six

The fire hissed and sputtered as she threw the contents of the vial and the flagon of wine onto the flames. Aurelie turned, feeling as if she were in a dream—a nightmare—from which she could not wake.

Her feet were heavy and she had to push herself to walk across the room to the curtained bed. There was a candelabra on the table near the bed, all its candles unlit.

The only source of light in the chamber was the fire in the hearth and a torch on the far wall.

She pushed back the closed curtain, and found Damon stretched out on the bed, the covers pulled up to his waist. His arms were crossed over his chest.

His face was drawn with fatigue. He didn't move, and for a hollow instant she knew how it would feel if he were truly dead.

He opened his eyes and turned his head toward her. "Are you ready?"

*No*, her heart screamed. *No*. But she said, "Yes." She wanted to tell him this plan was too dangerous, that he left himself too vulnerable with it, that too many things could go wrong.

But she knew it was useless, that he knew all of that and went forward, anyway. This was the way it had to be. Damon had been too close to Julian as a boy to let this end any other way. He had to hear the truth from Julian's own lips. And that meant that Julian had to believe he had succeeded.

He met her gaze, and she wondered what he was thinking. Did he fear she would betray him in some final way? The fact that he was putting his very life into her hands at this moment overwhelmed her, and she could not allow herself to believe it meant anything more than that he was desperate.

She sat on the bed beside him for an aching moment, delaying what could not be long delayed.

"Belle," he began, then whatever he would have said was lost as he slipped his other arm around her and pulled her into his embrace in a searing, urgent kiss that was so sweet, so familiar. She wanted to stay in his arms forever.

But she could not. She broke the kiss. His gaze revealed his conflicted feelings. For once he wasn't trying to hide his emotions from her, or himself. But his conflicted feelings didn't make her feel better. He could never forgive her; the fact that he might *wish* that he could didn't change anything.

"You're a fine kisser for a dead man." She forced a crooked smile.

He didn't return it.

"I'm scared for you," she said then, voicing the only honest thought she could allow herself in this moment.

"People see what they expect to see." His eyes changed, shuttered.

What was she thinking? How he had walked out of

Blanchefleur as Saville, or how she had walked into Castle Wulfere as Lorabelle?

Her throat tightened with regret, and tears stung her eyes but she held them back. She would not surrender to tears, not tonight. All that mattered in this moment was what she had to do next.

She stood, the dream sensation returning as she pulled the curtain back. It was time.

The corridor outside their chamber was strangely dark. The torches had been doused, she realized. There were always knights nearby, standing watch over their lord. But tonight the corridor was empty. *Someone had sent the guards away.*

From the great hall, sounds of revelry continued unabated. She stepped in that direction, hugging her arms about herself. "Sir Santon?" she whispered. She knew if she was gone too long, Damon would worry. Their plan would be ruined if he came after her.

She had expected them to be ready, waiting upon her this night. *Them.* Santon, Julian. Who else?

There was a turn in the corridor, and a glow of light in one direction where it led to the main stairs down into the great hall. The noise of the celebration grew, mixing with other, ghostly, sounds, confusing her.

She whirled; there was no one behind her. Her heart throbbed into her throat.

"Good eve to you, my lady," came a mellow, familiar voice that froze her pulse.

From the shadows to her right stepped Damon's cousin. He was alone. His black tunic and dark hair contrasted with his clear, colorless eyes.

She made no reply, smothered by emotions. Finally, he had revealed himself to her. He took her arm. His grip was too tight, but she allowed it and did not fight against him. He kept her close to him as they walked around the corner, back up the darkened corridor.

"How fares my dear cousin?" he asked her, his voice as passive as if they were enjoying a conversation across the high table.

She fought back a shiver of revulsion, focusing on the outline of the door where they'd stopped, the door to Damon's chamber. Light rimmed beneath it.

"My lord is not well, I'm afraid."

"It is done."

It was more statement than question. His grip on her arm tensed, though, as he awaited her confirmation.

"It is done," she repeated after him. "Shall we call for maids, his staff, his knights? There cannot be suspicion—"

"Leave it to me." He pushed the door open and took her inside. "He died quite suddenly, in a violent fit of illness. You panicked, and came upon me in the corridor. I quite naturally came to your aid and comfort. We don't wish to alarm the castle in the midst of a Christmas celebration. 'Tis not, of course, what Damon would want. Think of his sisters. The shock of it. We must have a care, my lady. Leave it to me. You do as I say now, and henceforth."

He shoved the door closed, roughly releasing her to march across the room to the curtained bed. She followed, anxiety roiling within her for this crucial moment as he whipped back the drape to reveal the man stretched out there upon the bed, lifeless.

Julian looked back at her briefly, a severe almost-smile flickering at the edges of his hard mouth. "Well done, my lady. Well done. You will have your reward."

She forced herself to play her part. Hers was so much easier than Damon's, she reminded herself, and the knowledge of what he was going through at this moment gave her strength to go on as well. He was enduring another betrayal from someone close to him, and he was placing his own life in danger to find the truth. What she did, to stand here and pretend to be his cousin's accomplice, was nothing compared to that.

"I hope so," she said steadily, tipping her chin at the vile man before her. "I pray we all receive our due for this night's work."

Julian did smile now, a truly evil smile, then pivoted to more closely observe the body of his cousin again with narrowed eyes. Aurelie's skin prickled at the intense scrutiny with which Julian perused Damon's prostrate form. If he suspected anything, so much as a breath from Damon's chest—

Damon detached himself from the emotions threatening to pull him apart inside—betrayal, pain, anger. His body burned on full alert as he sensed his cousin draw near and lean over him. With the abilities he'd honed in battle, he controlled his breathing, his pulse, his physical body, and his mind tuning together.

"So sad," he heard his cousin murmur in a voice

that was not sad at all, "to follow a celebration with grief. But such is the fate of men who love the wrong women."

"What do you mean, the wrong women?" he heard Belle inquire in her soft, even voice. She was so strong. But he didn't want her to be strong now. He wanted her across the room, as far away from Julian as possible. When the moment came, when he moved, he didn't want any risk to Belle. He had made it clear to her that her role stopped the moment Julian entered the room. But she was determined to help him reveal the truth, and he couldn't do anything to stop her now from continuing to probe his cousin.

"Damon died ensnared by the woman he loved, much the way his father died because of the woman he loved." Julian's voice moved away from the bed. "Or perhaps I should say, the woman he once loved and then forsook."

There was a moment of silence. Belle didn't speak, and Damon almost felt as if his heartbeat and hers connected in the strained air. Clarity flashed through him and he realized that Julian spoke at least one truth. Damon loved Belle. It didn't matter who she was, or how she'd come into his life. He loved her.

It was his pride that had made him tell her he would send her to the abbey. His terrible pride, and his pain. But she felt pain, too. And for all she had taken that wasn't hers, she had given, too. She had healed his sisters.

She had healed him.

And there, on his deathbed, behind the darkness of his shuttered lids, he glimpsed a tiny flicker of his

future—the future he could have with Belle, if he
forgave her. If he put away his pride and embraced
life instead of pain.

"We were raised as brothers, did you know that?"
Julian's voice broke into Damon's thoughts. He was
still near Belle.

"Yes," Belle replied.

"We looked as brothers, too," Julian continued,
and his tone hardened, vivid resentment and hatred
seeping through. "So alike. And yet so different. He,
the honored son of the lord of the castle. I, the pen-
niless relation."

"You were treated as equals, were you not?"

"I was never his equal. I was his better!"

There was something haunting in Julian's tone now,
something almost mad. Damon's heart pounded
within him as he controlled his mental energies, forcing himself to remain still.

"His father seduced my mother while she was betrothed to his own brother." Footsteps crunched on
rushes as Julian's voice grew nearer the bed. "He was
pledged to another, to Damon's mother—with her
family's wealth and lands to come with her. My
mother had nothing—but her virgin's blood, which
he spilled and then left her with a babe. Oh, she
passed it off as her husband's child—the younger
brother of Damon's father. They were wed soon af-
terward, and no one ever suspected anything but that
I was his true child. But when he died, my mother
brought me here, to his—*our*—father. But he refused
to recognize me, to recognize her for bearing me.
He chose instead the riches that would come from
wedding another.

"It killed her," Julian snarled, his voice whipping

the air. "She never recovered. She was forced to watch another woman bear him a son that would be raised as the heir to Wulfere instead of the one she had borne. She wasted away from grief. She told me the truth as she lay dying. I approached our father many times to acknowledge me, but he would not. He said my mother was out of her mind—but he was the one who lost his mind, lost everything by the time I was finished with him. I killed him—slowly, day by day, week by week, just the way he killed my mother."

He was on the bed. His weight dipped the mattress and Damon felt Julian's hot breath over him.

"You were supposed to die in France," Julian said over him savagely. "You could have died a thousand times in battle but you didn't—and when we finally received word you had been imprisoned at Blanchefleur, I thought your end had come. But you survived, returned. I have waited all this time for what is rightfully mine. It is I who has commanded this demesne while our father decayed in this very bed for years, and I who have assured its future with the fortune that will allow me to lead it into the future you couldn't even envision. And it was I who was born first. Now, finally, it's my turn."

Damon had heard enough of his insanity. Whether what Julian said bore truth or not, he might never know, but he knew one thing—Julian had killed his father, and that was enough to fuel so much anger that he knew he would be sore pressed to keep from killing Julian in return.

He took advantage of the element of surprise as he rose sharply, pushing the covers away with one hand while he jammed the other fist straight into Julian's face.

The other man reeled backward from the force of the blow, off the bed, stumbling as he barely kept his feet. Julian regained his wits quickly, roaring curses, pulling his knife out of his boot and slashing out at Damon, catching him on the shoulder, slicing through his tunic and flesh.

Damon heard Belle's gasp but he couldn't even feel the pain. It didn't matter in this moment.

"You're supposed to be dead!" Julian hissed.

"Are you willing to kill me man to man, *brother?*" Damon ground out as the two men circled each other warily, both holding daggers.

From the edge of Damon's vision he saw Belle take a involuntary step toward him, her gaze captured by the blood seeping into his tunic. Julian never moved his gaze, but the flicker in his eyes warned him. "Belle—" Damon was too late as Julian backhanded Belle, sending her flying onto the floor behind him.

He turned to shout at her to get up, run, and realized he'd played straight into Julian's hands as the man lunged at him, knocking his dagger out of his hand. Julian came at him again, and he spun out of the way.

"Don't leave, my lady," Julian said with icy pleasantness. "You distract him. Stay here and watch him die."

"You can't explain my death now," Damon pointed out, holding his ground for a moment, daring the other man, determined to hold his attention and give Belle time to escape. "You're caught, Julian. Deceived, the way you deceived me."

"I'll think of something," Julian said, his voice eerily calm, low, and menacing as he advanced on Damon. "I'll explain it somehow. You'll be dead, and your treacherous bride will be in the dungeon. You'll pay for this, you lying bitch," he roared at Belle without turning. "You know what she is," he said now to Damon. "A nun. Can you believe it? A holy sister in your bed."

"She's not a nun."

"Is that what she told you?" Julian inquired. "Oh, you are more foolish than I even knew. You've forgiven her, haven't you? Forgiven her lies, her treachery." He cocked his head. "Would you not also forgive me, my brother?"

"Do you ask my forgiveness?" Damon asked, his gaze trained on Julian even as he was aware of Belle struggling to her feet, retrieving his dagger.

Julian grinned. "No. But how touching of you to consider it."

Belle tossed the dagger low across the floor, and Damon knelt to grab it, fast, but not fast enough. Julian took the opportunity to kick him in the head. Pain, sharp and blinding, crashed through him. He went down, but he took Julian with him. Somehow, he held on to the other man's leg, and they came down hard together on the rush-covered stone floor. He met the virulent loathing in his cousin's eyes as Julian moved to press a knife to his throat at the same time Damon kneed him, hard, in the groin. Julian rolled away, groaning, giving Damon just enough time to make it back to his feet. He'd lost his dagger again, and now Julian was on his feet, too.

"Get out of here, Belle!" Damon ordered.

"I'm not leaving you. He's going to kill you."

"Get help!"

"There's no time!"

"She's right, brother, there's no time," Julian snarled, savagery flickering in his dead eyes.

The horrible, insane look in Julian's eyes left no doubt in Damon's mind. Julian had the upper hand, and he wouldn't hesitate to use it to the death. Damon would have to defend himself with his bare hands, and hope he lived long enough for Belle to come back with help.

But if he didn't live long enough, he wanted Belle to live. He wanted her out of this room.

"Run, Belle!"


Aurelie wasn't going anywhere. Instead, she grabbed the only thing there was at hand, a stool by the wardrobe chest, and crashed it with all her might over Julian's head. With a grunt, the man slumped to his feet and rolled onto the rushes.

She stood there, shocked for an endless heartbeat that she'd actually hit him hard enough to fell him, then she realized Damon's sleeve was saturated with blood. She ran to him. "Damon!"

"I'm fine," he said, hauling her against his chest with his good arm. "Are you all right?" He drew back and touched her face where Julian had struck her.

"He would have killed you," she whispered thickly.

There was a sharp pounding on the chamber door.

"Who goes there?" Damon said, and for the first time she noticed how pale he'd gone, and how blood was dripping onto the floor. She pulled a towel from the wash table and wrapped it gently over his shoulder. Blood soaked through it.

"Rorke!"

Aurelie ran to the door. Rorke was there with Marigold in his arms. Fayette and the other girls crowded in behind, their faces worried. Kenric and Beldon stood by, their hands touching their sword hilts as they took in the scene, and Damon's bloodied shoulder.

Rorke set Marigold down with Aurelie and stepped aside with Damon, who began to speak to him in a low voice while blocking Julian's unconscious body from his sisters' view. Their faces were already frightened enough, but Marigold pushed between the men.

"Damon!" Marigold cried. The little girl began to sob and Damon grabbed her with his uninjured arm, shock hitting all of them. *Marigold had spoken.*

"I'm all right, sweetling," Damon assured her. "Don't cry."

"She became upset after the games when she realized you were gone and I finally figured out it was you she wanted," Rorke said. "I tried to tell her you were fine, but she had to see you for herself."

"I promised," Marigold half sobbed, half whispered. "I promised Cousin Julian I wouldn't talk, not ever! I promised I wouldn't tell anyone about the cellar, but I did." She looked at Aurelie now. "He said he would kill Damon if I told, and now Damon's hurt. It's all my fault!"

Aurelie's heart wrenched at the full understanding of Marigold's fears. The little girl hadn't spoken for three months, in dread that her brother would die, Julian's threat growing in her child's mind until she was afraid not only to tell about the cellar but to speak at all.

"I'm not dead," Damon said firmly, his eyes fixed on Marigold, then turning to sweep Elayna, Gwyneth, and Lizbet with his gaze. "And I'm not going to be dead—at least not anytime soon. So don't get your hopes up," he managed to joke. "We're going to be fine." Aurelie heard a raspiness in his voice, love for his sisters that ran deep—deeper than Julian's betrayal. "All of us."

They *would* be fine, Aurelie thought, emotion clogging her throat. Without Julian. And without her. Julian had been wrong about Damon's forgiveness.

A sound, a groan, alerted them that Julian was stirring. Damon set Marigold down, flashing a worried glance at Aurelie. She knew there was much he needed to talk to his sisters about. There was still more healing to be done. But tonight, he had to protect them. They didn't need to watch the man they'd grown up honoring as their cousin taken into custody to be deposited in Castle Wulfere's dungeon.

"Come, girls," Aurelie said, nodding to Fayette. She had to get the girls out of here. She looked back at Damon and their gazes clashed briefly, then she looked away. She wanted to stay and cling to him the way Marigold had clung to him, but she couldn't. It was over—and he had to finish the job, round up the rest of Julian's knights, including Santon. He needed his men for that, not her. She'd done her part.

"Go with them," Damon ordered Kenric and Beldon. "I don't want them alone for an instant."

Aurelie could see the young knights would rather have remained behind with Damon, but they followed their duty without question. The two knights, one ahead and one behind, accompanied them through the still-darkened corridors, assuring their safety, and waited outside the door as they went in.

"Belle?" Elayna whispered once they were inside their own chamber. Fayette hustled the younger girls to their beds, where their night shifts were laid out, waiting for them. "It was Cousin Julian, wasn't it? Marigold was right—he hurt Damon. He wanted Castle Wulfere, didn't he?"

"Yes," Aurelie said honestly. "He wanted Castle Wulfere."

"I knew he hated us," Elayna said, a hitch in her voice. "It was in the way he looked at us, especially after Papa died. I knew he wanted to be rid of us— that he thought we should be sent away to be fostered. But I didn't know—"

"It's not your fault," Aurelie told her quickly. "It's not Marigold's fault." She took Elayna by the shoulders and looked her straight in the eyes. "It's not anyone's fault but Julian's. And it's over now. Everything's going to be all right—just like Damon said."

Elayna stared back at her for a long moment, then nodded. "I love you, Belle," she whispered in a thick voice, and Aurelie hugged her again. She kissed the other girls and tucked them in bed.

"Belle?" Marigold said as Aurelie kissed her forehead. "Everything's going to be better now."

She didn't pose it as a question, but Aurelie knew it was.

"Yes," Aurelie promised, drawing back to meet the little girl's serious eyes. She smoothed back the wild, wispy hair from Marigold's forehead. "Everything's going to be better."

Aurelie didn't let herself waste time wishing she

could be part of the bright future of this family that
meant so much to her. No good could come of wishing things were different, and there was nothing she
could *do* about the way things were now.

Was there?

*She could tell Damon that she loved him.*

Aurelie took a deep breath, closing her eyes for a
brief instant as she turned away from the girls. As
wrong as everything had been, she didn't regret that
she'd had the chance to learn to love these girls, and
Damon. Would she regret it if she left without telling
him the truth, the *whole* truth?

In an instant, she made up her mind. She crossed
the room and stepped into the corridor. Kenric remained behind to stand guard over the girls in the
corridor, and Fayette would sleep on her pallet at the
foot of their bed. Beldon accompanied Aurelie. It
was only around the corner and down the tower stairs
to the lord's chamber, to Damon. She could hear the
pounding of men's steps, shouts from the great hall.
The din of celebration had ceased, replaced by a
sounding of the alarm.

The tower stairwell was unlit. She stepped into it
and went down one level. Beldon came alongside her
and took her arm. His hold was uncomfortable, but
before she could say anything about it, she realized
he was pushing her down the next flight of stairs,
which was not where she wanted to go.

She held her ground and suddenly she was fighting
him. "Why—" Her question was swallowed by a hard,
ungiving hand that came out of nowhere and
clamped over her mouth and nose, suffocating her.

Her mind reeled. Beldon stepped back, his round,
youthful face creased in panic—but he wasn't stop-

ping what was happening. *He's one of them,* she realized with a flashing comprehension.

That was the last thing she would remember thinking as the hand that smothered her slammed her head back against the stone wall of the tower.

# Twenty-seven

Rorke stood guard over Julian, the blade of his sword pointed menacingly toward his black heart. The man he'd known as Damon's cousin didn't flinch, didn't even blink.

Blood trickled from Julian's temple, where the stool had cracked his head open. That didn't seem to bother him, either.

Damon spoke to a line of soldiers by the door, aware of what was going on behind him but not focused on his cousin—or brother—now. It hadn't taken long to gather his men, those trusted knights who'd been with him in France. Knights he knew were loyal to him, not Julian; knights who couldn't have been part of the ring of murderers and thieves who had worked out of Castle Wulfere under Julian's direction.

Those men who were part of the ring were who held his thoughts now. Santon, and the others—and how to reveal them. Until they were revealed, no one in Castle Wulfere would be safe.

So far, Julian had refused to cooperate—though he'd been strangely, chillingly, cooperative about everything else. He hadn't exhibited a single sign of resistance since he'd regained consciousness. He'd been stripped of his dagger and sword.

Damon dispatched the company of knights and turned back to advance on his cousin. Rorke flicked him a glance, and in that moment, Julian jumped up, pushing the chair so that it fell backward to the rushes at the same time that his hand moved to pull a blade from a pocket secreted in the back of his tunic. Rorke swore, kicked the chair aside, and pushed the tip of his blade against Julian's throat as Julian leaped, backed against the tapestried wall. He had nowhere to go.

"Drop it," Rorke ordered.

"Take it from me," Julian challenged, but he wasn't looking at Rorke.

His eyes burned into Damon's, sheer hatred pouring forth, hatred Damon now knew sprang from Julian's belief that Damon had usurped his rightful place in Castle Wulfere.

"Come on," Julian sneered. "Will you let your friend fight your battles, or are you man enough to take me for yourself? Prove you are the lord of Wulfere!"

"I don't have to prove anything to you." Damon pulled his dagger from his boot and walked slowly, nonthreateningly, toward Julian, keeping the hand with the dagger lowered to his side. "Stand back," he ordered Rorke.

Rorke hesitated, but obeyed his command.

"You know it's true," Julian said in his quiet, deadly voice. "You know I am your brother. The true, rightful lord of Wulfere."

"Perhaps." Damon didn't want to kill the man he'd grown up loving as a brother—and who might truly *be* his brother. He had to get Julian to drop the dagger. "We'll never know—and it doesn't matter now. My father is dead. You killed him. You're a murderer, Julian. Drop the dagger. This is the end. Don't make me kill you."

"You won't kill me. I'm your brother."

A sudden tension in Julian's body foreshadowed a move. He lunged at Damon, swiping at him with his dagger. Damon sidestepped in time.

"I prayed you would be of a penitent frame of mind," Damon said, warily watching the other man's eyes and his dagger arm. "You're a knight," he ground out. "We were raised as brothers, raised with honor—"

"What honor?" Julian's raw malevolence choked the air between them. "*This* is my honor. I'll die before I watch you rule Castle Wulfere."

Damon remained poised in a defensive stance, his mind suddenly more clear than ever. Julian was never going to give up. He would fight to the death. Julian *wanted* to fight to the death.

Julian's abrupt, mad attack came as no surprise. Damon deflected the stabbing blow with a quick twist of his body, agony ripping into the same shoulder where he'd been wounded before, while wielding his own blade without conscious command. He thrust it into Julian's belly and upward, jerking hard.

"You killed me," Julian gasped, shock and death paling his features as he looked down. His body fell to the ground with a thud, blood spreading out, staining the rushes around him.

Damon dropped his dagger and knelt, his breath coming sharp in his chest, regret and rage slicing together into his heart, heedless of the blood spurting afresh from his shoulder. He turned Julian's body over, hoping he was still alive, hoping for—what? He didn't even know.

"Damn you." He shook Julian's limp shoulders. "It didn't have to be this way," he rasped.

"God's bones," Rorke swore, prying Damon's arms off Julian. "He would have killed you. You can't help him now."

His words broke through Damon's pain. He couldn't help Julian. But he could help his sisters, and Belle. Santon was still out there, and as he looked back at his friend, a prickling realization struck him.

*Beldon was not one of the men who had been with him in France.*

His shoulder throbbed, and he felt blood seeping beneath the cloth Rorke had bound around it in makeshift fashion after Belle had gone. But none of that mattered now.

He had to know Belle was safe. And he couldn't shake the horrible feeling that she wasn't.

"Where's Beldon?" he demanded.


Aurelie woke up to a rocking motion. The air around her was damp and freezing, and her body felt numb except for her head. Her head felt as if someone had split it open from the inside out, and she didn't want to open her eyes. She had the distinct feeling that not only would it be painful, but that she wouldn't like what she saw.

She tried to move her arms, which were uncomfortably positioned behind her back, but her wrists fought against something rough. Rope. *Her hands were tied.*

"Hurry up!" she heard a grating voice. *Santon!*

Her mind spun and she opened her eyes, sharp pain slashing through her temples at even that slight facial movement.

She could see Santon through the thick dark, hauling sacks into the small boat. Beldon was tossing them at him from the dock platform. Both men were so occupied, neither noticed she was conscious. Slowly, carefully, in the pitch black corner of the boat, where she'd been flung, she curled back her leg, tipping up to allow it behind her, reaching desperately with her tied hands for the dagger in her boot. She felt the tip of it, almost had it, but it slipped out of her reach, back inside its sheath. She struggled, grappling uselessly for it, and in the process realized the rope wasn't tight. She rubbed her wrists up and down and almost had her hands free when Santon spun toward her.

He was enormous and his eyes gleamed, reflecting the coursing river. Cautiously, she kept sliding her raw wrists, drawing one hand out of the rope's bond. She lifted her chin at him as he towered over her.

"Leave me here," she tried, fighting for time, understanding without being told what was going on. He was taking the stolen treasure and escaping Castle Wulfere. On the dock platform, she noticed now a man lying in the shadows, dead. One of the guards, she realized. Her eyes followed the rope ladder up the side of the cliff, where the storage basement and cellars of the domestic range were, the portal from here to the castle, and saw a booted foot hanging over the edge.

She didn't know how many men had been part of Julian's plot, but there were two less than there had been this morning. Santon wasn't sharing the loot. She glanced at Beldon, who'd finished tossing sacks into the boat and was working furiously at the moorings.

"You don't want to take me," she said, standing shakily as Santon advanced, the boat swaying with every step he took.

"Oh, I've always wanted to take you, sweet Sister," he said chillingly. "And I will. You're mine now. You and the treasure. I'm not going anywhere without either one of you."

She kept her arms behind her back so he wouldn't know her hands were free, her gaze darting for escape. She didn't know how to swim, but that lack didn't frighten her as much as the prospect of spending another moment in this boat with Santon. She could die if she didn't make it out of the river; but she would wish she were dead if she let Santon take her away from here.

"Damon won't rest till he finds you," she said, trying one more time to avoid the river. "He'll hunt you down like an animal. Leave me here. Take the treasure; you'll be safer without me."

"You're worried about me. I like that. You'll have the rest of your life to worry about me. We'll be together, you and I. Always. Forget about Damon of Wulfere—he will forget about you, sweet Sister. He has already forgotten about you. And if he doesn't, well, he'll simply die."

"No," she whispered, knowing he spoke the truth; he would kill Damon in a heartbeat if he had the chance. Santon didn't possess Julian's patience. It was only Julian who'd held Santon back so long. Santon would kill Damon for the pure pleasure of it, and laugh while he died.

And Santon was never going to let her go. There was no hope she could talk him out of his plan to take her.

Santon glanced behind him now. "Get in the boat!" he shouted at Beldon. "Now!" Beldon threw in the last sack, jumped in, and Santon whirled on him so fast, Aurelie could only stare in shock as she watched a knife appear in Santon's hand and plunge without warning into Beldon's side. The young knight blinked, made an awful choking sound in his throat, and fell backward into the water.

From the cliff above, she heard shouts. Santon jerked his head toward the sound and darted away to push the boat off from the dock. Aurelie seized the chance to dive off the side of the boat. As she hit the water, she heard Damon call out her name.

The river water stung like needles, sharp, icy, and she broke the surface almost immediately, but a hard body slammed her back under. Santon.

He wrapped his huge, meaty fists around her neck and held her there, under the water. Blessed saints, he was going to drown her, and himself, too, if he had to. He'd dragged her under the boat, she realized when her head hit something hard as she fought to rise. Terror washed her mind of any other thought than that soon her lungs would burst and she would have to gasp for the air that wasn't there. She fought him, thrashing uselessly at his merciless body.

Beneath the surface, it was black as pitch. The only light seemed to come from Santon's eyes and the thought flashed through her mind that the last thing she would see was Santon's eyes. *No*, her heart screamed, and even as she continued to fight him, she squeezed her eyes shut and envisioned Damon's eyes.

Bubbles of air escaped her nose and mouth and she could feel her chest spasm. *Don't breathe, don't breathe.* But she knew she had to.

She stopped fighting and reached for her boot. Her knife! Her fingers were almost uncontrollably numb, but a burst of power seized her and she gripped the hilt tightly and opening her eyes she sank it into the side of Santon's neck. His ugly eyes boggled and rolled back and his cruel grip released.

Other hands clutched at her now. She fought those hands, too, wildly, her lungs exploding, then realized it was Damon—not in her imagination but truly there beside her—his desperate gaze searing through the dark water. Damon's eyes. *She'd dreamed of her knight, and he'd come.* Dark spangles blotched her vision and she thought, *This is how it feels to die.*

Time stretched, useless, meaningless, then Damon pushed Santon's lifeless body away and took hold of her urgently, dragging her toward the sound of shouting above.

They burst to the river's surface together, and she felt more hands reaching for her—helping hands. Damon's knights. She was on the dock platform, but she knew she couldn't stand; her quaking legs couldn't possibly support her and it was all she could do to gulp in choking lungfuls of air.

And then the arms around her were Damon's, and he was holding her as if he would never let her go.

"My God, Belle," he whispered shakily into her drenched hair. "My God." He rocked her while she clung weakly to him, to everything that she'd ever wanted and knew would never be hers. "You're all right," he kept saying over and over again as if convincing himself. "You're all right."


She slept through the rest of that night and most of the next day. She was aware of Damon at times, touching her, holding her, whispering wonderful things to her that she knew had to be part of her dreams.

There was a part of her that didn't want to wake up, didn't want to face the reality that it was finished. Candlelight flickered over the room as she finally opened her eyes, and she knew it was night. A full day and night had passed. The nightmare that had occurred only a short time before now seemed as if it had happened years ago. Santon and Julian were distant memories.

But the pain in her heart was fresh.

She turned to see Damon in the chair by the bed, positioned in such a way that he could hold her hand. How long had he been there? she wondered. How long had he held her hand? His face was drawn, haggard. She could see the signs of the thickly padded bandage that he wore under his tunic to protect his shoulder wound. He was the injured one, yet she was the one abed.

Instinctively, she tried to move, and her head fell back, pain crashing through her skull. He must have heard her gasp, because he opened his eyes immediately.

"Belle," he said softly, "you're awake."

She nodded, swallowing tightly. Her throat was dry and parched, but it wasn't that which made it hurt to swallow. It was the thought of leaving this man she loved so much. She would survive, she told herself, but for once in her life, she didn't feel the surge of strength that should have come with that inner command. She only felt regret and misery. She would survive without Damon.

"I was afraid," he said. "Afraid you'd been seized by a fever. I haven't left your side for fear of it. You were in that freezing water for so long—"

"You were in that freezing water, too," she said. "And you were hurt—"

"I'm fine," he cut off her concern. "I'm fine. It's you I'm worried about." He rose and sat on the bed beside her. "How is your head?"

"Terrible," she answered honestly. "But I'll live."

"Thank God," he whispered, and leaned to sweetly, tenderly, brush his mouth against hers. "Because if you died—" He didn't finish and kissed her again.

"What of Santon? Julian? Beldon?" She forced herself to redirect her thoughts, away from his solid heat that she wanted to soak up and hold inside her heart to keep her warm for the rest of her life, alone in the abbey without his light.

She could hear no other sounds. The keep was quiet, calm, and she listened as he told her everything that had happened. Julian was dead; perhaps as he himself had wanted. Whether or not he was his brother, Damon would never know. It was enough to know that he'd killed his father—and that Julian would have had it no other way than that one of them finished in death, either he or Damon. Thank the saints, Aurelie thought with a clutch of both fear and gratitude, it had been Julian.

Santon's body had been dragged out of the river, lifeless, as had been the case of the two soldiers discovered dead on the dock. Beldon had lived long enough to make a confession. Julian had directed Beldon, Philip, Santon, and the two other knights in raids in an ever-widening circle across the countryside, promising a share of the bounty and positions of honor at Castle Wulfere when Julian took his rightful place and built Castle Wulfere into the most powerful castle in the land with the wealth he'd robbed from others. The band of men, only six, had terrorized the area, and Damon's goal now was to see that the stolen goods were returned to their rightful owners or their heirs.

Beldon had known nothing of Aurelie's true identity. That, Damon told her, had been between Julian and Santon. There had been little trust, from what he could see, between the members of the lawless band, and now they were all dead.

Marigold was still talking—in fact, she hadn't stopped talking, Damon told her. And Eudo had come to him privately and begged his forgiveness and forbearance for his own strange behavior. While the steward had known nothing of what had gone on down in the dock and cellars, Eudo had been afraid of Julian, as had many of the castle's people, he'd explained. Julian had been a cruel commander during Damon's absence, and the people of the castle had continued to walk in fear even after Damon's return, afraid he would be like Julian. Only now that Julian was gone was his darkness truly lifted.

There was nothing left to fear at Castle Wulfere.

"I'm sorry that I deceived you," Aurelie whispered when he finished, compelled to clear the air in this final way. "I should have told you who I was as soon as I awoke here. I should have trusted you to help me."

"I didn't trust you," Damon countered, moving to touch her cheek with his hand. "I didn't trust myself. How could you trust me? You were afraid."

"That was no excuse."

"I was afraid, too," he said, "afraid to feel the things you made me feel, so how can I deny you the only excuse that I have for myself?" He shook his head. "You risked your life to save mine, to save my sisters and this castle," he went on, and he was almost angry now, she realized. Angry at her, for risking her life, she understood with a sense of shock. "You could have died."

"So could you!"

"But it was my castle, my home, my sisters. I love them."

"I love them, too!" Tears filled her eyes, and she was shocked to see moisture gleaming from his gaze, too.

"If you had died, it would have been as if I died as well," he said gently, all the anger gone now as quickly as it had appeared. He skimmed his touch down her face, gripping her hands in both of his again, tightly, as if he'd never let go. "When I saw you go into that river, when I swam in to find you and you were so frozen, so pale, I thought you *were* dead, Belle."

"My name isn't Belle," she whispered starkly.

"Belle," he repeated. "You're my Belle, no matter where you came from, or who you were before. It wasn't Lorabelle of Sperling or Aurelie of Brier-meade who healed my sisters. Healed me. It was you,

Belle. Belle of Wulfere. And I'm grateful beyond words."

"Belle of Wulfere doesn't exist," she cried, tearing her hands from him. She couldn't bear his kindness without his forgiveness, and nothing in his words promised that—and she wouldn't ask for it. It was too much to ask of him, she realized—and knew that she couldn't tell him that she loved him, after all. It would only add to the heaviness of his heart. It would be selfish, and she'd been too selfish for too long. She had to think of him first. "Take me to the abbey." She tried to push past him, blocking the pain slicing into her head from so much movement. She was strong enough for travel. There was no reason for delay, for more heartbreak. "It's what I should have done in the beginning."

He wouldn't let her go. He grabbed her shoulders and held on to her. "This isn't the beginning," he said roughly, his eyes so dark and serious and achingly urgent. "Belle of Wulfere didn't exist then—but she does now. She exists here." He touched his chest. "Here in my heart. I love you, Belle."

She felt damp tracks scorching her cheeks. *He loved her?* She was almost afraid to believe what she was hearing.

"You opened my heart, freed my soul." He moved his hand to wipe at her tears, then he was kissing them away. "I can't let you go now," he said huskily. "I can't live without you. I don't *want* to live without you."

He drew back enough to gaze deep into her eyes and search her face. "Forgive me my foolish pride, Belle," he said fiercely, his gaze tortured. "Tell me that you love me, too, and that you'll stay."

"Forgive you?" She blinked. "But—"

Clarity filled his eyes and he shook his head, grasping her face gently in his hands. "Belle, I think I forgave *you* the instant you told me the truth. But I was too proud to admit it. So proud, you might have died without knowing it."

"Damon." She let him draw her against his chest and she felt as if she'd come home, the home she'd never had. The home in his arms she'd wanted all her life, even before she'd ever met him. "I thought you could never forgive me."

"Never forgive you?" He hugged her tight, and she could hear his heartbeat, strong and steady. "How could I not forgive the woman who made me whole when I didn't know I was broken? The woman who showed me the way home when I didn't know I was lost?" He reached down to tip her face up to his. "You were meant to come to me, Belle. I don't know how, or why, but I know it in my heart. I needed you; I just didn't know it. Stay with me, Belle. Live with me. Be my love, my heart, my wife."

He set her down gently, and knelt beside the bed, his hand tenderly gripping hers. "Wilt thou be mine?" he asked formally.

Belle's head didn't hurt anymore; it was her heart that hurt now. Her heart that was bursting about twice as big as there was room for it inside her chest. His agony, his pain, was in the past, and he was asking her to put away her past, too. To meet the future they would build together. It was a miracle, one she'd never expected. But one she realized she'd never truly given up believing in.

"Yes," she whispered. "I love you." Damon smiled

and kissed her again, and she knew she'd finally found her home, her knight, her dream.

And it was sweeter than she'd ever imagined.

## ABOUT THE AUTHOR

Suzanne McMinn writes contemporary and historical romance from her lakeside home in a small Texas town. She has three young children, and she is a middle school English teacher. To learn more about her books, visit **www.SuzanneMcMinn.com** or write to Suzanne at P.O. Box 12, Granbury, TX 76048. Happy reading!

# Merlin's Legacy

## A Series From
## Quinn Taylor Evans

___**Daughter of Fire**                    $5.50US/$7.00CAN
    0-8217-6052-1

___**Daughter of the Mist**              $5.50US/$7.00CAN
    0-8217-6050-5

___**Daughter of Light**                  $5.50US/$7.00CAN
    0-8217-6051-3

___**Dawn of Camelot**                   $5.50US/$7.00CAN
    0-8217-6028-9

___**Shadows of Camelot**             $5.50US/$7.00CAN
    0-8217-5760-1

---

Call toll free **1-888-345-BOOK** to order by phone or use this coupon to order by mail.

Name _____

Address _____

City _____ State _____ Zip _____

Please send me the books I have checked above.

| | |
|---|---|
| I am enclosing | $_____ |
| Plus postage and handling* | $_____ |
| Sales tax (in New York and Tennessee) | $_____ |
| Total amount enclosed | $_____ |

*Add $2.50 for the first book and $.50 for each additional book.

Send check or money order (no cash or CODs) to:

**Kensington Publishing Corp., 850 Third Avenue, New York, NY 10022**

Prices and Numbers subject to change without notice.

All orders subject to availability.

Check out our website at **www.kensingtonbooks.com**